FULFILLING THE PROPHECY

The saddle fit beautifully, as if it had been made for the horse. Steve loaded all of his gear onto the warhorse. He dropped the reins to the floor and turned back to select another mount.

"Hold!" shouted a voice behind him. Steve spun around. Damn—he'd been discovered.

Belevairn's memories supplied the identity of the creature behind the golden mask for him. Lord Daemor, chief among the Twelve. The Dread Lord stood in the entrance to the stables, sword in hand.

"Who are you?" Daemor asked, stepping into the stable. "Dreamer?" Daemor sounded incredulous. "But how . . . ?"

"Lord Belevairn was kind enough to lend me his steed," Steve replied, raising the shotgun to his shoulder.

Daemor charged just as Steve pulled the trigger . . .

Ace Books by Thomas K. Martin

A TWO-EDGED SWORD
A MATTER OF HONOR
A CALL TO ARMS

A CALL TO ARMS

THOMAS K. MARTIN

ACE BOOKS, NEW YORK

This book is dedicated to all of those who contributed to make it all that it could be, but especially to Mary Lewis, who put her own life on hold to be not only critic and test reader, but also housekeeper, cook and grocer. This book could not have been done without her sacrifice. A very special "thank you" to Mary and to all of you.

This book is an Ace original edition,
and has never been previously published.

A CALL TO ARMS

An Ace Book / published by arrangement with
the author

PRINTING HISTORY
Ace edition / September 1995

ISBN: 0-441-00242-0

ACE®
Ace Books are published by The Berkley Publishing Group,
200 Madison Avenue, New York, NY 10016.
ACE and the "A" design are trademarks
belonging to Charter Communications, Inc.

PRINTED IN THE UNITED STATES OF AMERICA

10 9 8 7 6 5 4 3 2 1

Chapter
-------- One ------------

"DESTROY THE NORTHERN bridges!" Erelvar shouted. From his position atop the citadel on the bluff, he watched as one of the towers of the city's northwestern gatehouse crumbled in a shower of collapsing masonry. The last stone had not yet found rest when the sound of a second explosion reached his ears. The remaining tower of the gatehouse was also reduced to rubble. A fortified gatehouse reduced to ruin in a few heart-beats—the twenty men manning it dead, or trapped within the rubble. It was unbelievable. . . .

Even so, Erelvar had recognized this so-called Dragon for what it truly was. Steven had once claimed that the firestaff he had first carried to this world was used for hunting ducks. Erelvar had no difficulty believing that now. *This* was what the Dreamer's people used for war.

Erelvar watched in the early dawn light as the Dragon passed the ruined gate into the city. Why had the catapults not yet fired? Without the bridges there was no way that . . . war engine could cross the river. The thing was fashioned entirely of metal—it would sink like a stone.

As if in answer to his unspoken question, the catapults launched their payloads to the extreme limit of their range. Erelvar watched as the ends of the bridges were demolished. It would be some time before they could be rearmed to destroy the next section. Erelvar wondered whether they would be given the chance.

Another war engine disappeared into the streets of the northwestern quarter. This was not as formidable in appearance as the Dragon. However, even from this distance, Erelvar could see through its open top that it carried men into the city.

1

Somehow, the Morvir had gained access to the weapons of Steven's homeworld.

A stone building within the northwestern quarter of the city crumbled. That located the Dragon for him—apparently its progress had slowed once it entered the city. Excellent. That would give the catapult crews enough time to destroy more of the bridge.

The catapults of the northwestern gate fired again. There was nothing like fear to motivate men to speed. The next section of the bridge to Quarin was destroyed. Erelvar silently gave thanks to Mortos that he had refused the demands of the populace to build bridges directly between the northern and southern quarters of the city. The rivers were now their only effective barrier against the Dragon.

Another building was engulfed in a fiery explosion. As Erelvar watched, the lesser engine departed from the city— empty. It moved faster than horses at full gallop and was soon out of sight over the horizon. No doubt it would return soon, with another cargo of Morvan soldiers.

Movement on the riverbank opposite the northwestern bridge caught Erelvar's attention. The populace thronged about the end of the destroyed bridge. As Erelvar watched, they entered the river, swimming for the undamaged section.

"Tell the catapult crews of the northern gates to continue firing," Erelvar ordered. "We *must* destroy those bridges!"

"Yes, my lord," Morfael replied. The younger *rega*'s face was ashen. He relayed Erelvar's orders to waiting messengers. Before they had left, the catapults fired again, destroying another section of the bridge. Erelvar could hear the horrified cries of the refugees in the river. Their only hope of escape was being destroyed by their own people.

"Prepare to evacuate the castle," Erelvar ordered. If his catapults could reach the end of that bridge there was no doubt that the Dragon's . . . weapon could as well. It could conceivably sit at the end of the bridge and destroy the entire citadel.

"Yes, my lord," Morfael replied again.

"Have the catapult crews on the southern bridges prepare to destroy those as well," Erelvar continued. "They, and I, shall be evacuated last aboard the galley. Go."

"Yes, my lord," Morfael said, turning to leave.

"Be certain the Lady Glorien is among those evacuated," Erelvar added. "Carry her if you must."

"Yes, my lord," Morfael agreed.

After a moment Erelvar glanced away from the battle. From this location, atop the northwest tower, he could barely see the statue that was Steven's tomb. There was something that needed to be done. . . .

Erelvar placed his hand against the stone block that formed the base of the Dreamer's monument. Steven's body was entombed within. This statue had become the destination of the pilgrimages of many of the faithful. There were no visitors this morning.

The two men with Erelvar slipped the heavy chain through the iron ring set into the stone sealing Steven's tomb. Once the chain was secured to the yoke, the team master drove the dray horses forward. With a grating of stone against stone, the three-foot cube of stone slowly slid out of the tomb.

The sound of another distant explosion reached him from the city. How much longer did they have before the Dragon began to attack the citadel?

The stone fell from the opening to the tomb built into the base of Steven's statue. Erelvar held his breath; he was half expecting Steven to crawl out of the tomb on his own. No such thing happened. Erelvar knelt and looked into the tomb.

The stench of decay filled the small chamber. The armored corpse within was simply that—a corpse. Erelvar reached in and lifted the base of the wooden bier that Steven was laid upon, dragging the body out into the light. The sword held in the armored hands seemed to glow in the morning light.

The workmen with Erelvar gagged at the stench, but held their stomachs as they helped lower the body to the ground.

"Have this body placed in a coffin," Erelvar ordered. "Then have it placed on the galley."

"Yes, lord," the workers replied.

Erelvar glanced up at the inscription that had appeared on the base of the statue shortly after Steven had been interred within it.

When the land again has need of it, this Sword shall live again.

"I need you *now,* old friend," Erelvar whispered. "Where *are* you?"

*   *   *

Steve's stomach churned as the *goremka* galloped through the featureless gray fog that surrounded them on all sides. He closed his eyes tightly, hoping that temporarily shutting out the strange perspectives would settle his stomach's unease. How much longer was this trip going to take?

The *goremka* halted its gallop at an equally featureless point in space. How the demon determined its whereabouts was beyond Steve. It apparently knew where they were, however. It began to push forward and Steve could feel the resistance as they began to cross the barrier to the natural world.

A dark rift opened in the mist before them and the *goremka* carried Steve into it. There was a twisting, lurching sensation that threatened to wrest Steve's tenuous control of his stomach from him, and then mount and rider were standing in a room carved from living stone.

"What!?" Steve said in surprise, as he recognized his surroundings. Or, more accurately, as Belevairn's memories recognized them.

"Ragavale!" he said, harshly. "These are the Mistress's stables!" The damned demon had just dumped him in the middle of Delgroth, Daryna's underground mountain fortress.

"As you commanded, Templar," the *goremka* replied, smugly. "This is where Lord Belevairn sent the armored convoy. And now I must depart, as you have also commanded."

"Hold!" Steve commanded. "How am I supposed to get out of this place alive?"

"*That* is your concern, Templar," Ragavale told him. "You ordered me to deliver you to the place where Lord Belevairn transported his forces. I have done so. Good-bye."

Before Steve could object, the *goremka* vanished like so much smoke from beneath him. Steve fell to the floor amid the falling tack and harness of Belevairn's mount.

Steve disentangled himself from the saddle and rose to his feet. He was going to have to get one of these horses saddled up and ready. Damn! It was a four-day ride to Quarin. He would take another horse or two as spares. He could probably trim a day off the trip if he could rotate mounts.

He selected one animal from the stalls as his primary mount. It was a fine horse, deep red with a dark brown, almost black mane. More important, it had roughly the same girth as Belevairn's *goremka*. The tack should fit it nicely.

The saddle fit beautifully, as if it had been made for the horse. Steve loaded all of his gear onto the warhorse. He dropped the reins to the floor and turned back to select another mount.

"Hold!" shouted a voice behind him. Steve spun around. Damn—he'd been discovered.

Belevairn's memories supplied the identity of the creature behind the golden mask for him. Lord Daemor, chief among the Twelve. The Dread Lord stood in the entrance to the stables, sword in hand.

"Who are you?" Daemor asked, stepping into the stable.

"You already know the answer to that question, Daemor," Steve replied, drawing his shotgun from the holster on his mount.

"Dreamer?" Daemor sounded incredulous. "But how . . . ?"

"Lord Belevairn was kind enough to lend me his steed," Steve replied, raising the shotgun to his shoulder.

Daemor charged just as Steve pulled the trigger. The roar of the shotgun echoed through the stables, startling the horses. Daemor flew back as the slug blew a hole in the mail hauberk he wore. Steve pumped the shotgun, loading a magnesium flare into the chamber.

"Say good night, Daemor," he said, firing the flare at the prone *Kaimorda*. The burning magnesium buried itself in Daemor's chest. The Dread Lord began to scream as the fire consumed him.

Steve lost precious time calming his panicked mount as Daemor thrashed in his death throes on the floor of the stables. So much for spare horses—Steve wouldn't have time to get them ready. He had to get out of here *now*.

Steve hoisted himself into the saddle and spurred the horse to a gallop. He wheeled to the right as he entered the central corridor of the stronghold. Fortunately the stables were near the main gates of the fortress.

He reined the horse to a stop in front of those gates. Two massive slabs of stone sealed the entrance to the fortress. There was no mechanism to open the doors that Steve could see.

"Shit," Steve said, in a subdued voice. This was it, the end of the line. He could already hear the sounds of some form of alarm from behind him.

Steve squared his shoulders and glared at the doors. He'd come this far—crossed the barrier between worlds, for Christ's sake! He would be damned if two blocks of stone were going to stop him now.

He pulled one of the rocket launchers from his saddlebags. He was too close—he would have to get a little distance to use this thing without blowing himself to kingdom come. Steve wheeled the horse about and galloped back to the entrance to the stables.

He didn't have time for any mistakes. Pursuit would be organizing quickly. Steve dismounted and tethered the reins to a hook by the stable entrance. It wouldn't do to have his stolen mount panic and run off. . . .

Steve sighted through the scope, aiming for the crack between the stone doors sealing the entrance. That would be the weakest spot in the gates. Hopefully he could blow a hole in the gates large enough to ride through. Hopefully.

Steve squeezed the trigger gently, as a mercenary literally a world away had shown him. The rocket fired, hurling down the corridor toward his target. Steve threw himself prone just as the missile struck the stone doors.

The sound of the explosion was deafening. Small pieces of stone ricocheted down the corridor. Fortunately, most of them were spent by the time they travelled this far. Steve began to rise to his feet. He stopped, on one knee, staring.

The gate was intact. All Steve had accomplished was to blow a man-sized crater about a foot deep into the surface of the stone doors.

"Shit!" Steve cursed. The gates to Delgroth were magically strengthened by Daryna's power. He was going to have to use another one of his remaining three rocket launchers. Damn! He needed those for the tank.

Still, if he didn't get out of here it wouldn't matter how many rocket launchers he had left. He ripped open the saddlebag and drew another launcher out. Hopefully this one would do it.

Daryna had ordered the gates sealed the moment she had felt Daemor's pain. Somehow, someone had felled her chief general within the confines of her own fortress. Now that the alarm had been raised and Morvir dispatched to deal with the intruder, she could tend to Daemor.

She appeared beside him, in the stables. He was still thrashing as something in his chest burned violently at his mummified flesh. She gently reached into his chest, her hand passing through him like smoke. She grasped the burning lump of metal and pulled it from him. Who had done this?

Her answer was found in the form of a small cylinder lying nearby. She reached out and the object flew into her outstretched hand. The memories passed to her from Belevairn identified it—a spent shotgun shell. The Dreamer!

As Daryna rose to her feet she heard the sound of a weapon firing. Steven Wilkinson was within her walls! She must . . .

The impact against the gates struck her before she could act. She collapsed, as if the blow had instead struck her. The stables spun around her as darkness gathered at the edges of her vision.

No! She could *not* let this happen! By force of will, she pushed away the darkness, regathering her Power. The gates still held—barely. She had to stop Wilkinson before . . .

The weapon fired again and the force of the blow against the gates was even more potent than the first. She collapsed, fainting as the stone doors to her fortress were penetrated.

Steve cursed. The second missile had broken through—barely. A faint gleam of light shone through an opening far too small to allow him to pass. Worse, he could hear a force approaching from behind.

He mounted, pulling a third launcher from the saddlebags. That only left him one for the tank. *Oh well,* he thought, *if this third one doesn't do it, it won't matter anyway.* Steve sighted through the scope, aiming just below the opening he'd created.

The horse jumped beneath him at the weapon's discharge. Steve spurred it, using his mount's own fear to urge it forward. The missile struck the weakened gates and the horse shied to halt, rearing beneath him. Stone fragments ricocheted along the walls past them.

Steve fought the animal back under control, urging it forward. If this had been any horse other than one trained by the Morvir, he would have failed. The horse galloped forward through the breach in the stone doors, its eyes wide with fear.

Steve rode out into the moonlit night. Beneath him lay the Burning Hills. From here he would have to pass through the

Poisoned Bog onto the Plains of Blood. How was he going to get through the Bog? Only the Olvir in Erelvar's service had managed to find solid footing through that unnatural swamp. Oh, well, there was plenty of time to worry about that. . . .

The ground shook beneath him. Steve wheeled his mount to a halt, staring in shock. Above him, seven spheres of blue-white light shot down from the sky to pass into Delgroth through the breached gates. One paused, and within it Steve could see a gaunt figure mounted on a pale horse. Mortos saluted Steve with his sword before joining the six that had passed into Delgroth before him.

Steve barely noticed Mortos's salute, however. His attention was captured by the red glow emanating from the top of the mountain that Daryna's fortress was carved into. Delgroth was built into a volcano, and that volcano was erupting! The ground shook again as a cloud of glowing ash belched out from the top of the mountain.

"Oh . . . my . . . God," Steve whispered. He wheeled his terrified mount south, away from the volcano.

"*Hyah!*" he yelled as he spurred his mount away, unnecessarily. It had already decided that it didn't like this neighborhood anymore.

I'm gonna die! Steve thought. *I'm gonna die, I'm gonna die, I'm gonna DIE!*

Jared sat with nine other members of the Twelve in what had once been a barracks in the northwestern quarter of Quarin. This quarter of the city had been secured and the . . . tank . . . was now assaulting the traitor's citadel in the center of the rivers.

Jared was not certain what he thought of these new forces. True, they were performing beyond all expectations. The Morvir had suffered fewer than a dozen casualties taking this quarter of the city and none so far in the assault on the citadel. Still, what would happen when the Morvir realized that they could turn these new weapons on their old masters just as effectively?

"But will a wooden bridge support the weight of the tank?" Lord Phelandor was asking.

Jared was about to answer when the summons struck him. He could tell by the way the other Lords suddenly stiffened in their chairs that they had felt the urgent call as well. Without a word, they all hurried from the makeshift council chamber. Jared was the first to reach his mount and depart for Delgroth.

He did not arrive in the stables as he had planned. Instead, he emerged in midair above the fortress. Some unknown, mystical barrier prevented the *goremka* from entering Delgroth.

Jared stared at the scene below him. Fire and ash billowed from the top of the mountain. The fires of Delgroth were tamed no longer. It was just as well that he had not been able to enter the fortress. Jared trembled in anger—he knew *who* was responsible for this outrage. The prophecy was quite clear— only one person could breach the gates of Delgroth. Somehow, the Dreamer had returned.

The other *Kaimordir* appeared in the air around him. Daryna's call still compelled them all, but they could not obey—dared not obey if they could. For a moment they all simply stared at the events unfolding below them.

"Jared," Heregurth was the first to ask, "what do we do?"

"We return to Quarin," Jared replied, flatly.

"But the Mistress . . . ," Phelandor began.

"Fool!" Jared snapped. "The gods themselves do battle here! This is no place for us. We must hold council immediately!"

All fell silent. Then, one by one, the Dread Lords of Delgroth slowly left reality to return to Quarin. Jared waited until all had left before drawing his sword to salute the fortress.

"Good-bye, my love," he said, softly. "I shall not rest until I have avenged you. I swear it." Then he, too, left for the safety of the Gray Plain.

The galley slowly pulled away from the docks on the south end of the citadel. The Dragon had been attacking the citadel since late afternoon. As Erelvar had surmised, the fortress was well within the range of the Dragon's weapon.

He, Morfael, and the two remaining catapult crews had taken refuge in the underground entrance chamber until nightfall. Now they were slipping away from Quarin without lanterns, hoping that darkness would cover their retreat.

At Erelvar's command the galley was drifting downriver with the current without the luxury of oars. He didn't want to take the slightest chance of any sound giving them away to the

Morvir. One attack from the Dragon could convert this galley into kindling.

Another explosion atop the bluff lit the night. Years of work, destroyed in hours. Erelvar's gaze fell to the coffin that lay in the center of the deck. There were two edges to the prophecy. From the miraculous appearance of the inscription on Steven's statue, Erelvar had concluded that they were victorious—that Steven would return to deal with the Dragon as the prophecy foretold.

Apparently, such was not the case. In killing Steven, Daryna seemed to have defeated that arm of the prophecy. If that was true, the final outcome was also foretold: all that lived would be destroyed at the hands of the Dark One. Erelvar would make certain that she did not succeed without a fight, however.

He whispered an order and the oars were deployed. The galley was nearing the southeastern quarter of the city, on the Umbrian side of the river. Erelvar felt the small ship turn across the current. The bank was a darker blackness in the night before them.

This was the section of the city farthest from the Dragon. Hopefully, it would be far enough that they would not be forced to retreat farther until the Dragon found a means to cross the rivers.

The galley slid neatly into dock without the use of lanterns. The crew leapt onto the dock and lashed the galley loosely to the moorings. Not easily done in the moonless night.

As Erelvar stepped onto the dock, the moonless night suddenly lit—as if the moon had just emerged from behind the clouds. The crew cried out in surprise as they looked up from the moorings. Erelvar's gaze also sought the sky.

In the night sky, almost directly overhead, a star shone, bright as the moon. Against all logic, Erelvar felt a surge of hope rise within him.

. . . *and the light of the Dreamer shone across the land,* the prophecy stated. The Mistress had not won yet. . . .

"What is all the damned commotion about?" Captain Tsadhoq grumbled as he made his way to the front gate of Deldwar. The hundred-ton postern gate had already been winched open. He checked the counterweights on his way out. They were in place, ready to seal the gate in an instant's notice. Good. If they hadn't been he would have had somebody's beard for it—by the roots.

"This had best be good," he continued as he stepped out onto the battlements. "Or someone is going to pay for rousing me from a particularly pleasant dream about . . ." His words trailed off, unspoken.

A star burned in the night sky—as bright as the moon in full. Its silvery light gleamed off the mountain snow.

"He has returned," Tsadhoq whispered into the hush atop the battlements.

"By Vule's beard!" he shouted, throwing his head back exultantly. "He has *returned*!"

"Captain Tsadhoq!" a member of the Guard interrupted, pointing to the northwest. "Look!"

Tsadhoq followed the man's outstretched hand. A column of fire burned on the horizon. Delgroth.

"We had best start sharpening our axes, men," Tsadhoq said, slapping a nearby guardsman on the back. "By this time next week we shall likely be marching on Morvanor!"

The men cheered—a cheer in which Tsadhoq happily joined before turning to leave. This had been a day they had long awaited, and one which Tsadhoq had thought would never come once the Dreamer had been slain outside Quarin. He stopped and turned back to the men.

"Oh," he said, "and someone had best send word to that renegade Morvan down where the rivers meet. Tell him, 'Delgroth burns.'"

Theron Baltasaros waited outside his cousin's bedchamber while the servants woke him. Soon, Solon Baltasaros emerged, eyes still heavy with sleep.

"Theron?" he said. "What is going on?"

"Emperor," Theron replied, ignoring the familiarity in Solon's question, "I have come on a matter of the gravest import."

"I . . . see . . . ," Solon said.

"Kneel," Theron commanded. Solon blinked and then knelt before him. Theron intoned a blessing over his cousin.

"Rise," Theron said, "and walk with me, Emperor."

Solon rose and followed along, slightly behind his priest

cousin. What was this all about? Theron was not prone to this
level of formality often. Not with him, at least. And the
hour . . . something serious was in the wind. . . .

They walked out into the garden. The moonlight stole the
color from all the flowers, rendering them in varying shades
of black, silver or white. Moonlight? There was no moon
tonight. . . .

Solon looked up into the sky, following the direction
indicated by Theron's upraised arm. A star burned in the sky,
eclipsing all those around it with its brilliance.

"What . . . does it mean?" he asked, quietly.

"It can mean only one thing," Theron replied. "The Dreamer
has returned, and the Dragon is loose upon the world."

"Lindra protect us," Solon said, signing himself.

King Arven stood on the battlements of Mencar. The rich,
summer forest was beautiful in the light of the new star. It was
a pity the news from Quarin was so dark. He felt a presence
appear behind him.

"What means this star, Nolrod?" he asked. "Why has it
appeared, the night after the Dragon has attacked Quarin?"

"It heralds the arrival of he who will defeat the Dragon,
Majesty," the lore-master replied. "And it marks the passing of
Delgroth."

"Praise the *Kanir*," Arven said, breathlessly.

"Indeed, Majesty."

Arthwyr ap Madawc stared into the night sky from the walls
of his manor. No matter how long he stared at it, the new star
refused to disappear.

"What is it?" asked one of his clansmen.

"How in Daryna's Hell should I know?" Arthwyr replied.
"Get a priest."

"No . . . wait," Arthwyr said as Alhric turned to leave.
"Get a priest of Uldon." Unless Arthwyr was mistaken, this star
had something to do with the prophecy of the Dreamer. . . .

Chapter
-------- Two ------------

DELGROTH CONTINUED TO belch fire and ash into the sky behind him. Fortunately the feared eruption had never materialized—so far. Like Earth's Vesuvius, two thousand years ago, Delgroth did nothing more than hurl volcanic ash into the atmosphere.

Steve had ridden hard all night, driving the horse beneath him unmercifully. He had probably made between twenty and thirty miles. Now, however, the horse was failing. For that matter, Steve wasn't doing too well himself. It had been over seven months since he'd ridden any distance. Correction—this body had *never* ridden. Steve's backside was probably one solid blister.

He reined the horse to a stop and gingerly dismounted to look back at the glowing tower of ash behind them that was Delgroth. Perhaps the horse could make it a little farther without Steve's weight. Steve glanced up at the sky.

What he had thought to be a moonlit night had turned out to be nothing of the sort. Instead, a brilliant star burned in the heavens where Steve remembered no such star being.

Nova, perhaps, he thought. *Wonder when it blew.* It was turning into quite a night—volcanoes erupting, stars exploding. Steve couldn't help but wonder what was going to happen next as he led the horse south.

"Please, God," he said aloud to the night, "no earthquakes."

"Silence!" Jared shouted above the din in the makeshift council room. "Silence!" he shouted again, slamming his open palm down on the heavy, oak table.

"Are we a gathering of old women?" he asked once the

13

assembled *Kaimordir* fell silent. "Or are we the rulers of Morvanor?"

As Jared had expected, that statement set off another round of babbling.

"What of the Mistress?" asked Phelandor.

"Where is Daemor?" Heregurth asked. "We cannot proceed without Daemor."

"The Mistress is *gone!*" Jared shouted, bringing silence to the council chamber again. "And Daemor is dead," he continued. "As is Belevairn."

"How can you be certain?" Hilarin asked.

"Did they join us in the air above Delgroth?" Jared asked in reply. "Would *anything* have prevented Daemor from answering that summons other than death?"

One by one, the Dread Lords acknowledged the truth of Jared's words.

"Daemor was in Delgroth, at last report," Jared continued. "He would have perished when the fires of the mountain were released."

"What of Belevairn?" someone asked.

"Belevairn was killed on Earth by the Dreamer," Jared replied.

"What?!"

"How can you know . . . ?"

"Preposterous!"

"Silence!" Jared shouted again. "You all know the prophecy," he continued. "Only the Dreamer could have breached the gates of Delgroth."

"But the Dreamer is dead," Phelandor insisted.

"No, he is *not,*" Jared replied. "Belevairn found him alive on Earth. Daemor and I both had knowledge of this."

"All of this is irrelevant," Lord Hilarin said. "The Mistress *is* gone. Daemor and Belevairn *are* dead, else they would have joined us above Delgroth. Lord Jared, where do we go from here?"

"Like it or not, this council of the Ten now rules Morvanor," Jared replied. "We must choose one from among us to lead it."

Master Kerandon trembled slightly as he released the Power he had gathered for the failed sending. The other *kaivir* in the circle similarly dismissed the Power they had gathered to assist him.

All in all, it had not been a pleasant evening. Ever since his servant had awakened him with the news of the sudden appearance of a new star in the heavens the news had gone from bad to worse.

Kerandon was well versed in the prophecies. The star could herald only the return of the Dreamer. An event that had supposedly been made impossible six years ago. Kerandon knew that Belevairn had encountered the Dreamer alive on Earth during his travels there.

Somehow the Dreamer had returned. Any doubt of that had been destroyed when Kerandon's sending to Delgroth had failed. The Rite of Far Visions had quickly shown him the reason for that failure.

Delgroth burned. The Dreamer had returned and shattered the gates in accordance with prophecy. The Mistress was no more.

And now he found that he could not reach Lord Belevairn, either. The lord of the *kaivir* must still be on Earth. It was conceivable that he was not even aware of the Mistress's passing.

This left Kerandon in a predicament. Even a fool could see that there was about to be a major restructuring of the balance of power in Morvanor, and Kerandon was no fool. If Lord Belevairn were here, his Power would make him the strongest among the Twelve. With the aid of the *kaivir* it would not be difficult for him to take command.

Since he was away, however, Kerandon was certain that Daemor would act to remove Lord Belevairn's base of power—namely, the *kaivir*. The commander of the Twelve would not be able to tolerate losing his position. His cgo would never allow it.

Jared, on the other hand, would do what he felt was best for Morvanor. That annoying selfless streak of his could possibly be put to use, provided Kerandon was able to reason with the *Kaimorda* before Daemor got to him.

"Issue a sending to all of the *kaivir*," Kerandon ordered. "Everyone is to gather at the Academy. We will erect our defenses and await Lord Belevairn's return there."

"Yes, Master Kerandon," his assistants responded.

"And have the slaves ready the carriage and the horses. We leave for the Academy at dawn."

"As you command."

Kerandon took a step back and sat in the chair that waited behind him. He did not like hiding in a closet like a frightened youngling but for now it was necessary. For now . . .

"Six votes for Jared," Hilarin announced. "Three for Phelandor and one for Kephas. Jared is High Lord of the Council of the Ten."

"First," Jared began, "we need to discuss what we are going to do with these Special Forces."

"What do you mean?" Phelandor asked. "We proceed with the invasion, of course."

"Why?"

"What?"

"I said, 'why,'" Jared repeated. "We cannot conquer either Olvanor or Umbria. More accurately, we cannot hold them— we do not have the resources. Our first priority is to establish our rule in Morvanor."

"Our rule is already established," Kephas objected.

"Is it?" Jared asked. "Now that the Mistress is gone, how long will it be before the Morvir think to overthrow us? Especially now that they have weapons capable of destroying us?"

A long period of silence followed as the other members of the Council considered Jared's words. Phelandor was the first to speak.

"We must destroy the Special Forces," he said.

"Precisely," Jared agreed. "The only question now is how?"

"I suspect that you have already determined that, Lord Jared," Lord Fanchon replied. "What is your plan?"

"We need time," Jared replied. "Time for us to consolidate our position in Morvanor. With the Mistress eliminated, the Northern Kingdoms are going to become bold. I would expect them to invade *us* within a year.

"I suggest," Jared continued, "that we allow our two problems to solve themselves for us. We form the Special Forces into two units. One unit will be sent into Umbria. They will take all of our available explosives and rocket launchers. Their goal is not to conquer but to destroy. Every castle, every manor they pass they are to raze to the ground.

"The second unit will proceed through Olvanor with the tank. They are to destroy Mencar and then attack the Regency. Their goal is also to wreak as much destruction as possible before they expend their weapons or are destroyed."

"No more Special Forces," Phelandor observed, "and it will be years before the Northern Kingdoms can recover enough to attack us."

"What is to prevent the Special Forces from turning on us before we can implement this plan?" Kephas asked. "With the Mistress gone they have no reason to obey us."

"We simply fail to inform them of that," Jared replied. "We ten are the only ones with that knowledge."

"What of the recruits in the Northern Camp?" Fanchon asked. "Surely they have seen the eruption?"

"The Mistress has released the Fires of Delgroth," Jared replied. "That is all the explanation they should need."

"Then what is to be done now?" Phelandor asked.

"You shall command the Special Forces in Olvanor," Jared replied. "Kephas will campaign in Umbria. Heregurth shall return to the training camp in the Burning Hills and march all of the recruits and all of the equipment to Quarin. The rest of us will return to Morvanor. For now, carry on with the bridge—nothing has happened."

"As you command, High Lord," Phelandor replied. There was a pause before the others echoed Phelandor's words.

Jared watched as the other Lords departed. It was not impossible that the Mistress might return someday. If she did, he was going to make certain that Morvanor was waiting for her.

Now he just had to decide what needed to be done about the *kaivir*.

Morfael opened the door to the council chamber without knocking. Erelvar looked up from the maps and papers.

"Yes?" Erelvar asked.

"The northeastern quarter has fallen," Morfael informed him. "The Dragon is now attacking the Olvan quarter."

"From across the river?"

Morfael nodded in reply.

Erelvar shook his head. Even stopped at the river, the Dragon was destroying his city. Once the Morvir finished their bridges, there would be no stopping them.

"Have the messages been sent to the kings?" he asked.

"Yes, my lord," Morfael replied. "Magus Felinor assures me that the kings shall receive them ere nightfall."

"Excellent. And Steven's armor?"

"It . . . has been removed. The armorers are cleaning it and mending the straps as we speak."

"Thank you, Morfael," Erelvar said, returning to the reports that lay before him.

"My lord?" Morfael sounded troubled. Erelvar again looked up from the table. His friend had been quiet, reserved for the last few days. But then the events of the last few days had been . . . draining.

"What troubles you, my friend?" he asked.

"What . . . should I do with Steven's . . . with Steven, my lord? It does not seem meet to leave him . . . unburied in his casket."

Erelvar nodded solemnly in agreement.

"Take him to the crematorium," he replied. "Have Steven's ashes sealed in a golden urn and bring them to me."

"At once, my lord!" Morfael replied, obviously pleased by the solution. He departed quickly, closing the door behind him.

Erelvar returned once again to the latest reports from the survivors of the northwestern quarter. The Morvan infantry carried weapons of unspeakable destruction. A single warrior was capable of killing an entire patrol. If they encountered severe resistance from a fortified position, the Dragon would reduce that building to rubble and the infantry would then root out the defenders.

There were no reports of the Morvir having suffered any casualties whatsoever. They had apparently destroyed the city and his fortress without losing a single man. Without Steven's knowledge it was impossible to fight these weapons. Erelvar slammed his hand on the desk in frustration.

Where *was* he? The star that had appeared in the sky last night could have only one meaning. According to the prophecy, the "light of the Dreamer" would shine across the land once he had returned and destroyed the gates of Delgroth. Somehow, Steven *must* have returned and must even now be on his way to Quarin.

Erelvar blinked as an unexpected thought occurred to him. Prophesied hero or not, his friend was not superhuman. If Steven had returned and if he were afoot, it would take him several days to reach Quarin from Delgroth. Assuming that he did not run afoul of the Mistress's armies between here and there.

Erelvar rose from his chair. He must speak with Magus Felinor immediately. If Steven were yet alive, the sorcerer could find him.

Thirst burned in Steve's throat. He had taken shelter in a shallow cave—an overhang, really. In his flight from Delgroth he had not had time to take any provisions—no food, no water. Now the midday heat of the Burning Hills wrung the water from his body.

He pressed back farther into the cooler shadow of the overhang. The stone felt cool against his hot, dry skin. Steve glanced at his watch—the sun would set in another eight hours. Once he was south of the Poisoned Bog, he could drink from the first stream he found that was fed from the Iron Hills. Until then he would just have to travel at night.

That would slow him down considerably. He would have to travel harder—lead the horse to keep from laming it. It wouldn't be a good idea to ride the horse through the Bog, in any case.

Steve shuddered at the thought of the Poisoned Bog. How was he going to cross that? Ten miles of swamp filled with toxic waste—no way to determine where he could find firm footing.

Steve shook his head. Worrying about the Bog wasn't going to do him any good. He would find a way to cross it when he got there. For now he needed to rest.

The *goremka* brought Jared back into reality just outside the city of Morvanor. For a moment he simply sat and examined the walls and the gatehouse of the capital city.

All seemed normal. The walls were manned—no panic or alarm seemed to be spreading throughout the city. All was as it should be.

Jared shook his head. This would not last. The news of the Mistress's . . . absence could not be contained forever. Soon the newly formed Council of Ten would face the task of maintaining order once the fall of Delgroth became public knowledge.

Jared frowned. The *kaivir* would have that knowledge already—he was certain of it. Convincing the others that it was imperative to destroy the Special Forces had been simple. Convincing them to purge the Mistress's elite cadre of sorcerers would be nothing of the sort. The Special Forces were new and untrusted—the *kaivir* had been with them for centuries.

Without Daryna and Belevairn to keep them under control, however, they were the more dangerous of the two. The Morvir, at least, were bred and trained to loyalty. The *kaivir* were trained to Power, in all of its forms. They would be quick to attempt to seize control of the kingdom, as would their master if he still lived.

But then, it occurred to him, it was possible that the *kaivir* were not aware of Belevairn's demise. Their master had been out of touch for long periods of time during his operations on Earth. Jared smiled. If that were indeed the case, they might delay their bid for power to await his return. That could possibly give Jared the time he needed to convince the others to act against them.

He urged his mount forward, toward the gates. It was time to rejoin the others at the compound.

The image of the council chamber wavered in the pool of quicksilver and vanished, like a candle flame snuffed out by the wind. Kerandon cursed. Even with the Mistress gone, the *Kaimordir* were still afforded some protection from his magics by her Power in the golden masks they wore.

There was no doubt, though. The Twelve were returning to Morvanor. The only questions were, what would they do upon arriving and when would Lord Belevairn arrive? Kerandon was certain that Belevairn would seek him out before meeting with the others.

He was also relatively certain that the Dread Lords would not attack the *kaivir* immediately. Especially not now that the sorcerers had gathered their strength at the Academy.

Kerandon turned from the bowl and crossed the room to his worktable. A space had been cleared large enough for the map of the Academy and the surrounding lands that now laid upon it.

He had ordered wards erected around the entire Academy. The wards were not strong enough to refuse entrance to a member of the Twelve. After all, it would not do to bar Lord Belevairn. The wards *would* ensure that none of the other Dread Lords could come upon them completely by surprise.

Kerandon studied the map. If Daemor decided to attack before Belevairn returned, how would the attack come? *Galdir* would be little more than a nuisance. It was unlikely that they would be used. The *regir* would not be effective on horseback against the fortified academy.

Thank Daryna . . . Kerandon smiled. He would have to make an effort to stop using that idiom.

It was fortunate that the alien war-engine was engaged at Quarin. Otherwise the Dread Lords could breach the walls of the Academy before the *kaivir* were aware that an attack was in the offing.

Siege tactics would be next to useless against them. Kerandon could launch attacks at leisure against the besiegers and the *kaivir* could bring supplies in by portal. An almost frivolous use of the Power, but certainly justifiable.

No, the attack would have to be swift to be successful and Daemor would know that. The best strategy seemed to Kerandon to be a simultaneous attack by the Morvir while all of the *Kaimordir* forced their way into the Academy. The Dread Lords could conceivably create enough of a distraction to allow the Morvir to gain entry.

That should be simple enough to stop. If Kerandon doubled the number of *kaivir* empowering the wards, he could then instruct them to render the wards impenetrable at the first sign of trouble. That should give him enough time to rally the rest of his sorcerers to the defense.

Kerandon smiled. The *kaivir* should be able to hold out long enough to ensure that Lord Belevairn took his rightful place as the ruler of Morvanor with ease.

"The *kaivir* have fled the city," Lord Fanchon said angrily as Jared walked into the council chamber. Jared paused in mid-stride before continuing on to the the council table.

"I am not overly surprised," he replied, taking his seat at the head of the table. "I was expecting something of the sort. In fact, I would guess that you will find they have evacuated *all* of the cities and are gathering at the Academy."

"What?" Fanchon exclaimed. "But why?"

"*Who* are the *kaivir* loyal to?" Jared asked.

"Themselves," Hilarin answered, quietly. "And to Lord Belevairn."

"Precisely," Jared agreed. "With the Mistress . . . gone, there is nothing they fear more than Belevairn. Hilarin, what do you think Lord Belevairn would do in this situation, if he were still alive?"

Hilarin laughed, sharply.

"Seize power, of course," he replied. "And probably eliminate both you and Daemor and whoever among us didn't immediately bow down before him."

"We are *very* fortunate that Lord Belevairn is already eliminated," Jared agreed. "In that, and that alone, the Dreamer has done us a service."

"Never did trust the damned sorcerers," Lord Hhayim observed, irritation bringing out the distant remnants of his Delvan speech. "A man can trust the men under him, but a sorcerer's always lookin' to put a knife in your back."

"The question," Hilarin said, "is what will the *kaivir* do, now that their master is dead?"

"That may be our advantage," Jared replied.

"Yes," Fanchon agreed. "They will not dare attack us without Lord Belevairn's assistance."

"Oh yes they would," Jared disagreed. "The *kaivir* are every bit as dangerous to us as the Special Forces. More so, I believe, as Lord Hhayim observed."

"Then how is Belevairn's death an advantage?" Hilarin asked.

"Because the *kaivir* may not know that he is dead yet." Jared waited while the import of his words was weighed.

"They'll *wait* for him!" Hilarin chuckled almost under his breath.

"We cannot assume that, however," Jared replied quickly. "Hilarin, you and Lord Hhayim must travel to Southcliff and Southport. Verify that the *kaivir* have indeed abandoned those cities. Fanchon, find out if they have left Northguard."

"As you command, High Lord," Hhayim replied. Jared watched while he and Fanchon departed. Hilarin waited behind.

"Was there something else, Lord Hilarin?" Jared asked.

"Yes, High Lord," Hilarin replied.

"Well . . . ?"

"I wished to apologize. In the past I have mistaken a distaste for politics on your part as an inability in that arena. I stand corrected."

"'Tis war, Hilarin," Jared replied. "The battlefield is different, but 'tis still war, nonetheless."

"Indeed, High Lord," Hilarin agreed. "For now, the others follow, but in the future . . . well, pick your allies carefully."

Jared leaned back in his chair, studying the other Dread Lord carefully.

"Are you making a bid for such standing early?" he asked, suspiciously.

"Frankly, yes," Hilarin confessed, spreading his hands, palm up. "There is no other Lord I would be more willing to follow in the Mistress's . . . absence."

"Other than yourself."

Hilarin shook his head resolutely.

"No, High Lord," he replied. "I do not envy your position. *I* would not care to wear the target on my back."

"I shall remember that, Hilarin. Go now—we must learn what the *kaivir* are about."

"At once, High Lord," Hilarin replied. He actually bowed before he left the room. Jared watched the door after he left. Whatever his motives, Hilarin spoke truthfully about one thing. Jared would have to pick his allies very carefully, indeed, once the current business was over.

Jared's eyes narrowed. Once the kingdom was secured,

however, he had someone to find. Politics would have to await his revenge on the Dreamer—wherever he might be.

Steve inspected the Morvan camp through his night glasses. No one moved, no sentries patrolled the barbed-wire fence surrounding the camp. It looked abandoned.

The Morvir had built a road through the Poisoned Bog. It certainly made sense; it would have been impossible to move the tank through the Bog otherwise. At the mouth of that road they had built an army base, complete with Quonset huts and sandbagged gun emplacements.

Steve examined one of those emplacements carefully. He could find no sign of life. For that matter, he wasn't certain there was even a gun in the emplacement.

Caution said to skirt the camp, move through the Bog, and try to make it onto the road farther down. The parched skin of his throat said to search the camp for supplies—for water. Surely the Morvir hadn't drained the water tower that stood in the center of the camp.

Steve's throat won. He wouldn't make it much farther without water. The horse wouldn't make it back into the road, much less to Quarin. Steve might be able to make it a few miles farther but his fate would be the same in the end.

He rose and gathered up the reins. Steve approached the camp cautiously, half expecting to be hailed or gunned down at each step. In the light of the nova, or whatever it was, he would be easy to spot. No challenge came, however, either spoken or fired.

The gate stood closed and locked. Steve eyed the padlock and glanced around the camp one last time. There was no doubt at this point—the camp was abandoned. Steve pulled the shotgun from the saddle holster and aimed it at the padlock.

The twelve-gauge slug blew the lock in one shot as the report echoed through the empty camp. Steve reholstered the shotgun and unwrapped the chain locking the gate. He led his horse into the abandoned camp. Where had everybody gone?

Heregurth rode at the head of the company of recruits. They were making good time—they would pass the southern edge of the Bog well before morning. The trucks that would have

ansported the company to the other world for their training
ur were, instead, laden with the munitions from the camp.

They had been sent ahead, with a full platoon divided among
e trucks for protection. They should be halfway to Quarin by
ow. The remainder of the company was travelling afoot. It
ould still be a few days before the bridges were repaired. The
ew company should arrive just in time to cross into the
orthern Kingdoms.

Heregurth glanced to the North. The column of fire still
arked the location of Delgroth. It was hard to believe that the
Mistress was gone—destroyed by a mortal man. Jared was
ght; these new weapons were far too powerful. . . .

Heregurth smiled. Not powerful enough to have saved the
an who felled those gates, however. No man could have
urvived once the fires of the mountain had been released.

"Burn, Dreamer," Heregurth whispered. "Burn in the Hell of
our own making."

Steve gasped as the icy water of the shower hit him. The
ater warmed quickly. God, it felt wonderful to let the water
ill over him and wash the grime of the last two nights' travel
f him.

Steve lathered up the brush and turned to scrub his mount's
oat. The warhorse didn't quite know what to make of the
Morvan latrines, but Steve got the impression the animal was
njoying the attention.

"What's the matter, girl?" he asked, laughing. "No one ever
ive you a hot shower before?"

The animal snorted and shook her head as if in response,
ending a spray of water from her mane. Steve ducked as the
eluge hit him in the face.

"Hey!" he objected, laughing again. "Watch it there!"

He finished lathering up the left side of the animal's coat and
urned her around to get the other side. A knight did not rest
ntil his steed had been cared for. Steve had not wanted to wait
n getting into the shower, so bringing the horse in with him
ad seemed a good compromise.

Once Steve had finished scrubbing the horse's coat he turned
o his own shower. It felt good to soap away the sweat and grit
hat had worked its way into his skin.

Soon he was clean. He led the horse from the showers and towelled her dry. He dressed before combing out her mane and tail.

"There you go," he said, patting her flank. "Now you're probably the cleanest horse on the planet. Let's go find you a nice, warm stall or something."

Steve led her from the barracks out into the cold night. To the north he could still barely see the red glow from Delgroth over the horizon. The volcano continued to spew ash and cinder into the air. How much longer would it be before that airborne tower of ash collapsed and came racing down the Burning Hill like an avalanche? Was the camp far enough away? Or would it be turned into another Pompeii, buried in volcanic ash for centuries?

"Wouldn't *this* place surprise archaeologists a few thousand years from now?" Steve chuckled.

There was a small stable near the northern gate. Steve bedded his mount down in one of the stalls, then hayed and watered her before leaving. She would be safe there while he searched the camp for supplies.

The Morvir had cleaned out the camp pretty thoroughly before they left. No weapons or ammunition had been left behind. All the day-to-day supplies were still in place: food, clothing, dishes and such. Steve packed up enough food to last for the trip to Quarin. Hopefully he would find something to hold water elsewhere in the camp.

One item of note *had* been left behind, it turned out. In the motor pool sat a canvas-backed army truck. Steve stared in surprise. Why had *this* truck been left behind? All of the other vehicles had been taken.

Steve opened the door and climbed into the driver's seat. This could take days off his travel time to Quarin. Steve looked around for the ignition. There was no keyhole, so he decided that the large button on the dash must be the starter.

Nothing happened when he pressed it—nothing. That explained why it had been left behind. The Morvir had not been able to get the damned thing to start.

Steve pounded the steering wheel. Damn! And there was no way *he* was going to get this thing running. What little he knew

bout cars would fit in a thimble and he knew *nothing* about
iesels. Damn!

Steve got out and opened the hood, refusing to accept that
ate would play such a terrible jest on him. Maybe the battery
as dead. If he could find a charger or another battery he might
till be able to get this thing started.

He found the battery and possibly the cause of the trouble.
he positive post and clamp were severely corroded. Steve
ooked around the motor pool for some tools. He worked the
lamp loose and scraped the post with a discarded screwdriver.
ome steel wool left lying on a worktable finished up the post
nd got most of the corrosion off of the clamp.

Steve climbed back into the truck and took a deep breath
efore pressing the starter. The engine roared to life.

"Yes!" Steve shouted. He inspected the truck's controls.
here was a clutch, a brake and a gas pedal. Where was the
earshift?

It was on the steering wheel. Steve pushed in the clutch and
orked the lever, selecting a likely gear. Cautiously, he let up
n the clutch and the truck began to roll backward.

"Well, I found reverse," he mumbled, stopping the truck
nd choosing another gear. He pulled out of the motor pool and
rove the truck around the camp once. Satisfied that he could
rive the truck, he returned to the motor pool and parked the
ehicle. He still wasn't comfortable with the thought of driving
own a makeshift road at night. Besides, it would be dawn soon
nd those beds in the Morvan barracks had looked real
omfortable. . . .

Chapter
-------- Three -----------

DAWN BROKE ON the third day of the Morvan attack. Erelva
stood on the battlements of the Umbrian quarter, watching the
sun rise. Magus Felinor's attempt to locate Steven had produced mixed results. According to his old friend, Steven was
indeed alive—somewhere. Exactly where was not clear.

The magus was fairly certain that Steven was in this world
and not back in his own. For some reason, however, Felinor
had not been able to summon Steven's image to determine his
exact location. Some Power prevented the Rite of Far Vision
from finding him.

Hopefully, that was not because he had been captured by
the Morvir. Delgroth was destroyed—that word came from the
Delvir in their mountain cities to the north. The fires of the
mountain raged unchecked by Daryna's power. If Steven had
been captured, he would be in Morvanor, not in Delgroth.

"My lord," Morfael said as he climbed the stairs to the
battlements.

"The bridge?" Erelvar asked.

"They will have completed it by tomorrow morning,"
Morfael replied.

Erelvar nodded. Once the Morvir completed the bridge to the
bluff, this quarter would fall under attack. The northeastern
quarter and the Olvan quarter had already been taken by the
Morvir. The Dragon had destroyed all resistance in those
quarters long before the Morvir had crossed the river on rafts to
secure them. Once the Dragon could reach the bluff, it would
be able to attack the Umbrian quarter as well.

Somehow they would have to delay that. Erelvar had to buy
as much time as possible in the hope of Steven's arrival.

"We must burn that bridge," Erelvar said.

"That would be suicide, my lord," Morfael objected. "The crews labor throughout the night. There is no way to approach it undetected."

"Then we shall not do so. Have the Morvir taken the bluff?"

"Not to my knowledge," Morfael replied.

"As soon as night falls have a catapult loaded onto the galley along with enough barrels of oil for one volley."

"Only one?"

"One shot is all that the Morvir will allow us, my friend," Erelvar replied.

Tsadhoq was not in high spirits. The last time he had led the Royal Guard to find the Dreamer, he had returned after losing two-thirds of his men. Now, as he led his men once again toward Quarin, the prospects of their return were even slimmer.

The messages from Quarin bore grave news. The city and the fortress had been all but destroyed by the Dragon. Lord Erelvar had taken refuge in the Umbrian quarter and was attempting to keep the Dragon from crossing the rivers into the Northern Kingdoms.

A brave man, that one, Tsadhoq was forced to admit. Although Tsadhoq had never quite trusted the renegade Morvan, the events of the last few days were proof that Erelvar had forever severed his ties with his homeland.

And now, according to prophecy, the Dragon had arrived and Lord Erelvar was the first to feel its wrath. Bravery alone would not avail against such a monster—it would take a miracle to stop it.

Their only hope lay in the Dreamer. Tsadhoq and his men, and all men everywhere, would have to buy time for him to arrive and slay the Dragon. And if the price of that time was their lives, well, then such was their duty. . . .

King Arven stood on the balcony looking down at the crowd assembled before him. The tribal chieftains waited quietly for their king to speak.

"Chieftains of Olvanor," Arven began. "I bear glad tidings and dark tidings.

"As many of you already know, the Dragon of prophecy has attacked Quarin. This is a grave matter and one that weighs heavily on the hearts of all Olvir—indeed of all men everywhere.

"What many of you do not know, however, is that our victory has already been sealed."

A murmur of surprise rose from the crowd. King Arven paused and the crowd quickly fell quiet again.

"A brilliant star has appeared in the heavens. This star marks the coming of the Dreamer—he who will slay the Dragon. This star also marks the passing of Delgroth and the end of the Daryna."

A collective gasp heralded his open mention of the Dark One's name.

"Yes," Arven agreed, "men need no longer fear to speak the name of the Dark One. Delgroth burns—our friends to the north, the Delvir, have seen this for themselves. Daryna is no more."

Arven fell silent as a great cheer rose from the throng below. He waited patiently while his subjects voiced their joy. Once it passed, he began again.

"The Morvir are still with us, however," he said. "The Dragon does their bidding as surely as it did the bidding of their dark mistress before them. The days ahead will be difficult and full of death.

"Take your people to the winter lodges—but be prepared to flee. Give not one inch of the Land that is not bought with Morvan blood. We must slow these invaders lest the Dragon overwhelm us before the Dreamer arrives to slay it.

"I shall ride toward Quarin with the *daegir*. The armies of Mencar shall not sit idly by. Let any of your men who wish it join with us at Bralmendel. We shall face the Dragon there."

Theron Baltasaros stood in the prow of the lead galley. The three banks of oars bit the water in perfect rhythm behind him. Six full crews were on constant rotation on each of the twelve galleys that carried the Veran Guard. The oars had not missed a stroke since they had set off this morning.

At this rate they should be at the mouth of the Bitterwine by nightfall. From there it would be at least another full day before they reached Quarin. Before today Theron would not have

believed it possible to make the journey to Quarin this quickly.
Today he wondered if it would be quickly enough.

Would they arrive in time to be of help to Lord Erelvar? Or
would they arrive only to find Quarin reduced to rubble, or
burned to ash? Theron would have to consult with the magi
once they reached the Bitterwine. At least that way, he would
not be walking into a surprise.

Even if the legion arrived in time, however, the men would
be fatigued from manning the oars for such an extended period
of time. Fatigued or not, what could even a legion, even the
Veran Guard, do against the Dragon?

Theron signed himself and bowed his head in prayer.

Arthwyr ap Madawc stormed from Lord Madawc's hall.
Alhric quickly fell into step beside him, hurrying to keep up.

"What happened?" he asked.

"The old fool will do nothing!" Arthwyr replied. "He says
that the Dragon is too far away to be of concern to clan
Madawc. Let the Aldwyns deal with it."

"What are you going to do?"

"Me?" Arthwyr asked. "I am forbidden to do anything. After
all, I am third in line to inherit the clan. Never mind that, if the
Dragon makes it this far, there will be nothing to inherit."

"Surely the Dreamer will stop it before then," Alhric said.
"The prophecy . . ."

"I *know* the Dreamer, Alhric," Arthwyr said, stopping to face
his clansman. "He is a good man, a brave man. But he cannot
move mountains with his bare hands."

Arthwyr's hand brushed the knife that Steven had given him
at their parting during the war six years ago. Steven had died at
the end of that war, but now, somehow, he lived again,
according to the priests. Arthwyr was not going to abandon him
to die *this* time.

"Furthermore, he is my friend," Arthwyr continued. "I left
him once to follow bad orders. I shall not abandon him again."

"But you are forbidden—"

"To Daryna's Hell with that!" Arthwyr replied. He turned
and began walking toward the stables.

"Alhric, you can marshall the defenses of the manor as well

as I. I am taking the horsemen to clan Aldwyn; they will not be very useful in a siege."

"Yes, lord," Alhric replied.

Arthwyr nodded in acknowledgment. His old friend Cai Aldwyn had become clan chief two years ago, when his father had died of fever. If Arthwyr knew Cai, he was already preparing to ride to Quarin. . . .

Morfael watched as the workers loaded the catapult onto the galley. The netting and the barrels of lamp oil had already been loaded aboard. Once the sun had set, the dray horses would be loaded aboard and they would depart for what was left of the fortress.

His gaze drifted across to the Olvan quarter. Smoke billowed up from the fires that burned out of control, amid the ruins. Two days; in two days Quarin, and the city around it, had been reduced to rubble.

Morfael was surprised at how little he felt. No fear, no sorrow. A great . . . emptiness seemed to have engulfed him. Morfael had seen men in that state before, in battle. When all concern and feeling seemed to drain out of them—when there was no hope left.

Erelvar sought only to delay the Dragon. Even he knew there was no defeating such a thing. But still, he strove with every effort to hold it at bay. Morfael should find strength in that.

Instead, he found only more emptiness. Morfael's gaze sought the sky. The new star was visible, even in the day, as a dim companion to the sun.

The priests claimed that its presence marked the return of the Dreamer and the fall of Delgroth. Word from the North claimed that Delgroth was, indeed, destroyed. Now the priests claimed that the Dreamer would come and destroy the Dragon.

But that hope did not live in Morfael. He himself had taken Steven's body to the crematorium. There had been no life, no hope there—only death and decay.

He *had* hoped. Once the inscription had appeared on Steven's tomb, Morfael had hoped for the return of his friend. He could still remember finding Steven's lifeless body in the forest, staked naked to the ground with a gaping wound in his chest.

Morfael sat as the memory struck him. He still remembered the feelings of helplessness that had struck him. The anger— and the guilt. He had allowed Steven to ride out alone that day. Had all but delivered his friend to the Morvir, who lay in wait for him in the forest.

Tears of anger welled in his eyes. The anger rose up like a wave inside him. The Morvir had taken so much from him. Steven, Aerilynn—so much. He looked at the ruins of the Olvan quarter again, through new eyes.

How many of his friends had died these last two days? Morfael trembled in rage. How many of his cousins in the Olvan quarter were now food for the Land?

The anger lifted him to his feet, burned away the fog that had clouded his mind these last two days. The pain that now burned in his heart was a welcome relief from the numbness that had swallowed him.

"Remove the arm, you fools!" Morfael ordered the workers. "You'll never get it loaded otherwise and Lord Erelvar wants this bucket ready to sail by nightfall."

Morfael watched as the workers obeyed. Lord Erelvar wanted to delay the Dragon as long as possible in the hope that Steven would return in time to destroy it. Morfael didn't know if Steven was alive or not, but he would be damned before he handed the battle to the Morvir. . . .

Steve looked through the field glasses at the cloud of dust ahead of him. As he had guessed—the Morvan army was on the march. That certainly explained the deserted base. Why leave the men there once Delgroth was destroyed? Far better to march them out where they could be put to use. . . .

Steve wondered who was in charge now that the Mistress was out of commission. Somehow, he just couldn't see the remaining Dread Lords sitting down to tea and discussing it calmly. With any luck, they were fighting among themselves and would do Steve's job for him.

The prophecy didn't say anything about that, though. Once Delgroth had fallen, Steve was supposed to give his "sword" to the "Arm of Death" so that he could defeat the "Dragon."

Steve lowered the binoculars. He wasn't *about* to hand the single remaining rocket launcher over to Erelvar. Prophecy or not, his friend would kill himself with it and that wouldn't do anybody any good.

For the moment, however, he simply had to decide what to do about this infantry column. The only solution seemed to be to circle around it far enough out to avoid being seen. He would have to backtrack about a mile and then circle around to the west.

He should probably wait until dark—the truck would kick up more dust than those men. Steve shook his head. God only knew where that tank was by now. He could probably make it to Quarin by nightfall if he could get around the Morvir without being spotted. He was just going to have to risk it. . . .

Jared guided his mount back into reality. The burning hooves sizzled on the damp leaves in the forest surrounding the Academy. The semi-fortified Academy looked somewhat picturesque in the early-morning light.

The reports had come to him all during the night: none of the *kaivir* were to be found anywhere. They were either all here, or en route.

This was a problem. Had the Academy been manned solely by force of arms, it would have been an easy target. Jared did *not* relish the prospect of having to face this much concentrated Power, however. No force of arms would be sufficient to unseat the sorcerers from this place.

Jared nudged his mount in the ribs and it began to walk toward the front gate. For the first time in many centuries Jared felt something akin to fear. If the *kaivir* decided to attack, he would be ashes before he realized he was in danger.

No attack came, however, and Jared stopped just short of the drawbridge. Like all of the Dread Lords, once his mortal life had passed, Jared had acquired a small scent for the Power. A wall of it stood before him.

A ward, more than likely. Jared urged his mount forward again, until the *goremka* could feel the resistance of the ward. It was weak enough that he could have pushed through, but Jared retreated. That would let the *kaivir* know that he was here and that he was not attempting to force entrance.

Soon, but not as soon as he was accustomed to being

acknowledged, an image appeared before him. Belevairn's aid, Master Kerandon.

"Greetings, Dread Lord," Kerandon said.

"Greetings, Master Kerandon," Jared replied.

"What brings you to the Academy this early, Lord Jared?" Kerandon asked.

"You know as well as I why I am here," Jared replied. "We have much to discuss. May I enter?"

Jared fumed internally but did his best to show none of it. To be forced to ask permission to enter *any* building in Morvanor was unheard of among the Twelve.

The image of Kerandon turned to glance behind him. After a moment, he turned back and nodded to Jared.

"Of course, Dread Lord," he replied. "The ward is opened. You may enter freely."

"Thank you," Jared replied, biting back the acidity in his response. He nudged his mount in the ribs and rode forward as the image of Kerandon vanished.

So, he thought, *the dance begins.*

Kerandon smiled as he released the surrogate image. Excellent. Jared had come to him. Between Jared and Daemor, Jared was the most likely to listen to reason. Furthermore, he had come alone and his manner was . . . respectful. This looked promising.

Kerandon waved a hand and one of the *kaivir* hurried to meet Lord Jared.

After a few moments, Lord Jared was admitted into Kerandon's chambers.

"Greetings, Lord Jared," he said, smiling pleasantly. "Welcome to the Academy." He did not bow to the Dread Lord.

"Thank you," Jared replied, apparently ignoring the slight. He looked about the room, suspiciously.

"We are quite alone, I assure you, Dread Lord," Kerandon said.

"Good," Jared replied, relaxing a little. He turned to look out over the Academy's courtyard. It was filled with tents housing the lesser-ranking *kaivir*.

"This is not a good time for Morvanor to be without the *kaivir*, Master Kerandon," Jared began.

"This is not a good time for Morvanor, in any event," Kerandon agreed.

"True. Why have the *kaivir* been gathered here, Kerandon? What do you fear?"

Kerandon thought for a moment. As always, Jared was not one to dance about or mince words. How much could Kerandon trust him?

"May . . . I speak frankly, Dread Lord?" he asked.

"Of course," Jared replied. "I no longer carry the authority of the Mistress, after all."

Kerandon blinked in surprise. *That* was an admission he had not expected to hear.

"Ah, yes," Kerandon replied. "To be honest, Dread Lord, we fear you."

"Me?"

"Not you specifically, Lord Jared. We fear that others among the Twelve may attempt to seize power and might very well attempt to eliminate us before Lord Belevairn can return."

"I have no interest in power," Jared said.

"Of all the *Kaimordir*, I would believe that of you, Lord Jared," Kerandon agreed. "The others . . ." Kerandon spread his hands in emphasis.

"Yes, that is the problem," Jared agreed.

"Yes, Dread Lord," Kerandon replied. "I am glad that you understand."

"Have you heard from Lord Belevairn?"

Kerandon paused. Exactly how far should he trust Lord Jared?

"I'll take that as a no," Jared said, before Kerandon could reply.

"You are indeed astute, Lord Jared," Kerandon said. Damn! He had not intended to be so obvious!

"What is the situation in Morvanor?" Kerandon asked.

"Quiet," Jared replied, "for now. But the storm is brewing."

"I imagine so. How many follow Daemor?"

"Daemor is dead," Jared replied.

"Dead!" Kerandon could not conceal his astonishment. Had Lord Jared . . .

"Yes," Jared replied. "He was in Delgroth when . . . it fell."

"I . . . see," Kerandon replied. This could change things—drastically.

"I hope so," Jared continued. "This places me in command of Morvanor, technically."

"Technically?"

"Come, Kerandon. The Mistress is gone, Daemor is dead—who will the Lords follow?"

"Themselves," Kerandon concluded.

"Indeed. The lines are forming and alliances are being forged. Soon their attention will turn to the *kaivir,* as you have foreseen."

"Of course, Lord Jared. But . . . what is your point?"

"I need Belevairn's aid to hold Morvanor together—I need the *kaivir,* Kerandon."

"Am I to understand that you seek an alliance with Lord Belevairn against the others?"

"I do not know how to say it any more plainly."

"Indeed not." Kerandon's head swam. If this was true, it was better than he could have hoped for.

"I shall inform you the moment that Lord Belevairn has returned, Dread Lord," Kerandon assured him. "I am certain he will want to meet with you."

"Excellent," Jared replied. "Let us hope that he returns soon."

"Yes, Dread Lord."

"In the meantime, may I suggest that you find a safe place to store copies of all your tomes and books," Jared added. "Just a suggestion, mind you. You know your work far better than I . . . but it might be a sensible precaution."

"Indeed, Dread Lord," Kerandon replied. "I had not thought of that."

"A good general plans for all contingencies. If you decide to do so, find someplace safe. Farewell, Master Kerandon."

"Farewell, Lord Jared," Kerandon said. "And good fortune."

"Thank you." Jared turned and left his chambers. Kerandon sat in the ornate sitting-room chair as soon as the door closed behind him.

This was far better than he could have hoped for. Lord Daemor was dead. Kerandon could count on restraint from Lord Jared—he was always cautious and considered in his actions. Besides, with the other members of the Twelve vying for power, Jared felt that he needed Lord Belevairn and the *kaivir* to preserve Morvanor.

Jared's last comment still puzzled him. Still, it would not be unwise to heed such advice. If an attack did come here, valuable knowledge could be lost. Kerandon rang for his attendants.

Lord Jared guided his mount onto the Gray Plain as soon as he crossed the drawbridge out of the Academy. He brought it back into reality almost immediately, arriving in the clearing about a mile away, where he had left Lord Hilarin.

"Well?" Hilarin asked when Jared emerged.

"The trap has been baited and the rabbit is sniffing at the carrots," Jared replied. "They are indeed awaiting Belevairn's return."

"What do you wish of me, High Lord?"

"Watch the Academy," Jared commanded. "It is likely that one or more wagons will be leaving shortly."

"Wagons?"

"Yes, I suggested to Kerandon that, in these troubled times, he might want to find a safe place to store copies of the *kaivir*'s library. Follow them and find where they choose to place them."

"And then we can train our own loyal *kaivir*," Hilarin observed, smiling.

"Yes . . . precisely," Jared replied, looking aside at Lord Hilarin. Hilarin had always been possessed of an acid wit, to be sure, but this type of intuitive leap was not in keeping with his character.

"Well played, Lord Jared," Hilarin said. "*Very* well played."

Jared merely nodded in response before returning to the Gray Plain. He was going to have to keep a closer watch on Hilarin. There were depths there he had not suspected. Probably because Hilarin had not *wanted* anyone to suspect them, Jared was beginning to realize. Although a skill in games of court and intrigue *would* be in keeping with Hilarin's Nymran heritage. . . .

Yes, Lord Hilarin, he thought, *as you said, I shall have to choose my allies very carefully. Very carefully, indeed.*

* * *

"What transpires at the Academy?" Lord Selwyn asked as Jared entered the council room.

"As I had hoped, they indeed await the return of Lord Belevairn," Jared replied. "Master Kerandon has assured me that I will be informed 'the moment he returns.'"

"You'll never get *that* message," Hhayim grumbled. "Even if Belevairn *were* still alive."

"Actually, I believe I would," Jared replied. "Kerandon believes that the Lords are in chaos—fighting among ourselves. He thinks that I am seeking an alliance with Lord Belevairn against the rest of you."

"I take it you aren't?" Lord Fanchon said.

"There would be little point in that," Jared replied. "With the Mistress gone, our only security lies in our unity. Belevairn was the greatest threat to that unity. But it doesn't hurt to allow Kerandon to continue in his delusion."

"That should buy us a few days," Fanchon observed.

"Yes," Selwyn agreed. "We need the time to formulate an attack and gather our forces."

"No, we can gather no armies," Jared countered. "That would give the *kaivir* too much warning. And there is a simpler way to eliminate them. One which leaves us with no witnesses of the attack."

"How?"

"Before I elaborate I want all of you to return to Quarin," Jared said, handing a list to Lord Fanchon. "Return with the items I have listed and with Phelandor and Kephas. Selwyn, you will proceed north from Quarin and collect Lord Heregurth. This attack will require all of us."

A moment passed while the assembled *Kaimordir* perused the list Jared had given them.

"As you command, High Lord," they finally acknowledged.

Hilarin watched as three wagons pulled away from the Academy. Lord Jared—correction, High Lord Jared—had certainly surprised him. Not only had he immediately identified all of the large potential threats to his newfound power, Jared had also, with the *kaivir*, proven to be adept at disinformation and manipulation.

Furthermore, he had apparently divined a way to keep a few of the *kaivir* in existence, but loyal to the new council. Why else would he have the sorcerers so carefully preserve their knowledge for him?

Hilarin had chosen better than he knew. It was doubtful that Jared would even know how many of the other's votes Hilarin had swayed to support the new High Lord. Of course, it hadn't been too difficult. The others were accustomed to following Jared. And he was certainly a better choice than Phelandor or Kephas. They *wanted* the power—Jared tolerated it.

Hilarin nudged the *goremka* forward. It wouldn't do to lose the wagons, after all. High Lord Jared would not be pleased with him if that happened. . . .

Lord Selwyn left the Gray Plain once again to emerge in the air above the Plains of Blood. A cloud of dust on the horizon rewarded him—he had finally located Heregurth.

When he reemerged over the dust cloud, however, Selwyn saw that it was not Heregurth he had found. A single truck sped across the Plains, toward Quarin. Curious, Selwyn glanced toward the north.

Another cloud of dust sat on the horizon. *That* must be Heregurth and the Morvir. Selwyn spared another glance downward at the lone vehicle. Why had this one tarried behind the others?

Ah well, there was no time to worry about it now. Selwyn had to collect Heregurth and return to Morvanor. He would ask Heregurth about it. . . .

The truck bounced dangerously on the uneven track that Steve followed. It was obvious that a large number of vehicles had passed this way earlier. It was equally obvious, however, that there had not been enough of them to level the ground out.

Steve was going to have to slow down below thirty or he was going to wreck the truck. He had just begun dropping his speed when he felt something . . . odd. It was similar to the feeling of being watched, but not quite the same.

Steve glanced in the mirror. There was nothing behind him. The sensation persisted, however. Something to the left . . .

Steve glanced out the window. Nothing. He shook his head,

irritated. This was no time to be getting spooked. He had successfully skirted the Morvan infantry and was well on his way to Quarin and his date with the "Dragon." There would be plenty of time, and reason, to get spooked at that point.

After a moment the uncomfortable feeling passed. Steve sighed, unconsciously, in relief.

The *goremka* stamped impatiently beneath Jared. It knew, through some demonic sense, that a battle was in the offing. Jared could feel that it was eager for the taste of blood.

If all went well, there would be no blood for his mount in this battle. The *kaivir* must be eliminated quickly or the Council of the Ten might become the shortest-lived ruling body in history.

"We ride," Jared commanded, kicking his steed in the ribs. The others followed him onto the Gray Plain. Jared's mount stopped once they had reached that point which lay outside the Academy.

"Is everyone clear on their role?" Jared asked. "We will not get a second opportunity. . . ."

"We are not raw recruits, Jared," Hhayim snarled. "Let's get on with it."

"Very well," Jared agreed. "Then we attack now."

Jared once again spurred his mount forward and emerged into reality just outside the ward protecting the Academy. The others, presumably, emerged at their prearranged attack points.

They would have only seconds before the *kaivir* responded to their arrival. Jared lifted the rocket launcher to his shoulder and sighted through the narrow window that was his target.

"Farewell, Master Kerandon," he said as he pressed the trigger.

The front gatehouse tower erupted into flame and flying masonry as other rockets were fired. As Jared watched, most of the Academy was engulfed in fiery explosions. Jared felt the ward around the sorcerer's stronghold vanish.

That was the signal to penetrate the Academy. Jared unslung the AK-47 he carried and slipped onto the Gray Plain.

He emerged inside the ruins of the Academy. Fires burned everywhere. He would have to be very careful—the Mistress was no longer available to heal him if he were burned. Any injury he sustained would be with him through eternity.

Jared fired at a fleeing figure illuminated by the flickering flames. The sorcerer's arms flung outward as he fell. So, there *were* survivors. Jared had half hoped that would not be the case.

The *goremka* advanced into the burning ruin. A body, dressed in what had moments before been rich robes, caught Jared's eye. Kerandon.

Jared felt Power behind him. He turned and fired, killing a sorcerer who had been hidden behind an overturned bookcase. Jared turned and pressed on into the Academy.

The sounds of more explosions reached him from the courtyard. Hilarin and Hhayim were assaulting the junior *kaivir* bivouacked in the courtyard. The rifle-mounted grenade launchers should make short work of that task.

Jared shook his head as he advanced into the Academy. This was not a battle, it was a massacre. The most powerful force of sorcerers in the world had been all but eliminated in a matter of moments. These weapons were *far* too powerful.

The sound of heavy gunfire reached him. Jared turned toward the sound. A loud explosion rocked the building. Someone had just fired a grenade *inside* the Academy. The sounds of the battle faded.

Jared found them. Three of the Lords picked their way through the scattered corpses. They turned quickly at the sound of Jared's approach. The firelight flickered wickedly off their masks. Jared wondered if he himself looked as intimidating. . . .

"So much for the *kaivir*," Lord Selwyn observed.

"Have you encountered any other survivors?" Jared asked.

"A few—three, in fact."

Jared nodded.

"Our work here is almost done," he said. "Search the rest of the Academy and then gather the others and return to Morvanor. I shall join you there after Hilarin and I visit a nearby cave."

"Cave?"

"I shall explain when I return to Morvanor."

"Yes, High Lord," Selwyn replied.

Jared found Hilarin in the courtyard. The mutilated bodies of the junior *kaivir* littered the flagstones.

"How nice of the *kaivir*," Hilarin said, "to gather in one place so that we could kill them."

"Remember that, Hilarin," Jared replied. "Against these weapons, there is no safety in numbers. The Morvir could do the same to us."

Hilarin looked about the courtyard. For once, his humor seemed to desert him.

"A sobering thought," he agreed.

"Come," Jared said, "lead me to the cave the *kaivir* secured their treasures in."

"As you command, High Lord," Hilarin said, bowing extravagantly. Apparently nothing could silence his wit for long. . . .

Chapter
-------- Four -----------

STEVE'S HEART SANK at the sight that greeted him through the binoculars. Quarin had grown during his absence. From here, Steve could see that a walled city surrounded the fortress both on the Plains of Blood and on the Olvan side of the river. He could only assume that the city extended onto the Umbrian shore as well.

However, that city was in ruins—as was Quarin itself. Only this quarter looked relatively intact. The Morvir must have used the tank to blow the gate and then taken this quarter with infantry. Steve scanned the top of the bluff again.

Nothing could have survived that assault. From what Steve could see, no two stones had been left standing on top of one another. The Morvir must have used a considerable amount of the tank's ammunition for that attack.

The question now, however, was where was the tank now? Was it still in Quarin? That seemed likely. The Morvir guarded the wall and the breach where the gate must have once stood.

Somehow, Steve was going to have to get into the city and see if he could learn more. That would *not* be easy. There was no way he was going to climb the wall, and the breach was too heavily guarded for him to sneak in.

Steve scanned the far side of the river. The wall on the far quarter had apparently extended along the riverbank as well. Good old Erelvar, as paranoid as ever. So gaining access along the riverbank was out as well.

He studied the wall. The mound of rubble near the breach could offer some concealment. What were his chances of climbing up that and then down into the city at night?

Not good, apparently. The Morvir had guards posted on the

44

wall near the top of that mound. Damn! There had to be a way in.

Steve would have to wait until nightfall and try approaching along the riverbank. That would be the place for postern gates, where heavy equipment could not be brought to bear on them. Hopefully, he would be able to find *some* way of getting into the city.

"The galley is ready, my lord," Morfael said when Erelvar opened the door.

"Excellent," Erelvar replied. The sun had set just a few minutes before. "Let us be off."

"Yes, my lord," Morfael agreed. "Although I have not loaded it exactly as you ordered."

"What . . . do you mean?"

"There is enough oil on board for *two* shots, my lord," Morfael explained, smiling. "Just in case we get the opportunity."

Erelvar smiled. It was good to see Morfael more like himself again.

"Just in case," he agreed.

Steve cautiously approached the city wall, crawling on his belly through the tall grass. The rocket launcher was strapped to his back, on one side of his pack. The only other weapons he carried were his .44, a couple of grenades in his pack, and the sword that had been blessed by the monks of St. Michael's.

He did not like leaving his shotgun behind, but he was carrying enough as it was. It and the .30-30 were safely stored in the truck. Steve reached the cleared ground surrounding the wall.

This was the tricky part—especially in the light from the nova. He pulled the night glasses from their compartment on his pack. The Morvan guards paced atop the wall. Steve counted; he would have to reach the wall during the small amount of time the guard was walking away from him.

Twenty seconds, from the time the guard turned away to the time he turned back. Piece of cake—he only had to cross a hundred feet or so of open ground. Plenty of time—he could almost stroll.

Don't get cocky, Steve, he warned himself. *One stumble would eat up a lot of precious time.*

He waited impatiently for the guard to turn away again. Now!

Steve jumped to his feet and raced across the open ground, counting off the seconds in his head. The ground was rough and uneven, slowing him more than he had thought. Still, his count had reached only twelve by the time he made it to the wall.

Steve huddled at the base of the wall. His dark clothing would stand out if he stood against the wall. Far better to huddle on the ground and think like a dirt clod. He tried to quiet his breathing. Dirt clods did not gasp for breath after doing the fifty-yard dash. Sound would give him away faster than sight, at this point.

Another twenty seconds passed with no alarm being raised. So far, so good. Now to make it to the river and around the end of the wall.

He started crawling slowly along the base of the wall. He felt painfully exposed. At any moment, he half expected to take a bullet in the back.

He made it to the riverbank safely, despite his concerns. Cautiously, he peered around the edge. There was some activity on the bridge to Quarin. Steve fumbled the binoculars from his pack.

Umbrian and Olvan workers carried timbers out onto the bridge. Steve scanned to where the work was being done and smiled.

The bridge ended about two-thirds of the way across the river. Good old Erelvar—he had managed to destroy the bridges before Quarin had fallen. Now Steve knew where the tank was. It must still be in this quarter of the city.

Unfortunately, this did not give him a way into the city. There was far too much traffic in and out of the gate for him to sneak in. Still, he had better get a closer look. For all he knew, the tank was sitting just inside the gate waiting to be blown up.

Erelvar breathed a sigh of relief when the galley touched up against the side of the dock away from the Morvir. Two men jumped out to secure the craft to the dock.

"Quietly," Erelvar whispered. "If one sound reaches the Morvir, we will *all* be dead men."

"Get the catapult on the dock," Morfael ordered. He was leery of working on the open dock in the bright starlight. However, the workers and guards on the bridge would be blinded by the light of the torches they worked under.

The catapult was fairly small—for a catapult. Eight strong oarsmen were able to lift the base over the lip of the galley and up onto the dock with only a little difficulty. The two men on the dock stepped in to help once the catapult had been lifted up to them.

"Careful," Erelvar admonished. "If it drops, they shall hear us for certain."

The arm was slightly easier. Once it had been laid across the base, the men began unloading the oil onto the base, as well. They would use the catapult base as a wagon to carry everything up the ramps to the top of the bluff. They would reassemble the catapult in the entrance chamber, where they could use light without being seen.

"Hitch up, men," Erelvar ordered. The catapult was small enough that they had not brought horses to pull it. Twenty men ought to be able to haul it just fine, and much more quietly.

"Come on," Morfael urged. "We do not have all night. . . ."

Steve watched the gate from behind the meager cover of a pilaster supporting the river wall. Not good. He couldn't tell if the tank was behind the gate or not.

However, he could tell that this was not going to be his way into the city. There were definitely too many guards and too much traffic. He would have to work his way back and look for another. . . .

A light atop the bluff caught his eye. As Steve watched, it grew from a faint light to a ball of fire. The ball of fire suddenly arced up and away from the bluff.

The barrels of oil shattered on impact with the bridge, covering the last hundred feet or so in flames. Burning workers plunged, screaming, into the river.

Yes! Steve thought, as the guards rushed onto the bridge. This was *just* what he needed. He stepped from behind the pilaster and ran toward the gate. He was less than a hundred feet away. He should be inside the city before anyone could recover from this attack.

He ducked into a narrow alley as soon as he passed through the gate. Steve pressed back into the shadows and waited, making no effort to cover his breathing. With all the shouting that was going on, no one would hear him.

Well, he thought, *I'm inside. Now what?*

Now he had to find that damned tank, that was what. After a moment, a second ball of fire flew from the bluff, drenching the next two hundred feet of the bridge in flames.

"Thanks for the diversion, Lord Erelvar," Steve whispered, hoarsely. "Now get the *hell* out of there!"

Erelvar did not even watch to see if the second volley struck the bridge. No sooner had he pulled the firing lever than he turned and ran toward the ramp to the dock. It was a good thing that Morfael had brought that second volley's worth of oil. They had indeed gotten the opportunity to use it.

He had just made it to the ramp when an explosion erupted where the catapult had been. It was much smaller than the blasts the Dragon's weapon had produced. This must be yet another weapon.

Erelvar ran down the ramp as fast as he could. The Morvir would be mobilizing the Dragon soon. The galley had to get away before that happened or they would all die.

Steve crossed the street quickly, ducking into another alley. The Morvir were patrolling the streets heavily—probably in response to Erelvar's attack on the bridge.

He was never going to find the tank this way. It was time to take the high ground so that he could see something besides twisty little streets.

Steve climbed a set of rickety stairs leading to the second floor of a two-story building. An inn or tavern of some type, he guessed. He climbed up onto the railing around the small landing. It was none too stable.

He couldn't quite reach the lip of the roof. He was straining, standing on his toes in a vain attempt to gain a finger hold when a hoarse whisper to his right almost made him fall.

"Need a boost, m'lord?"

Steve gasped and collapsed against the wall for support. He ought to avoid falling into the filthy alley. Who in the hell . . . ?

An occupant of the building had opened the door at the top of the landing. An Umbrian. Judging from his portly appearance and apron, Steve guessed that he must be the innkeeper.

"Careful, m'lord," he said, offering Steve a much-needed hand down. "That railin' is none tae strong."

"I . . . noticed," Steve agreed once he regained the landing. "Why are you helping me?"

"Well," the man said, "I can tell ya don' do this fer a livin', m'lord. Were ya a thief, ya would ha' been on the roof ere I could open the door."

"That still doesn't answer my question."

"I figure ya must be plannin' some deviltry fer them stinkin' Morvir, m'lord," the innkeeper explained. "'Specially since ya've stolen one o' their fire staves."

"That's true," Steve agreed. "Do you know where they are keeping the tank?"

"Tank, m'lord?"

"I mean the Dragon," Steve corrected. "Do you know where the Dragon is?"

"Aye, that I do," the innkeeper said. "But surely ye're not thinking about—"

"I most certainly am."

"But, lad, 'tis suicide! Only the Dreamer can . . ." The innkeeper paused and looked at Steve carefully and then signed himself.

"Ye're him, aren't ya?" the innkeeper said, eyes wide. "Ye're the Dreamer."

Oh, well, Steve thought, *in for a penny, in for a pound.* He was going to have to trust the innkeeper at this point.

"Yes," he admitted. "I am."

"Quickly, m'lord," the innkeeper urged, "get inside ere we're seen. I'll tell ya all ye need ta know."

"Thank you," Steve said.

Lord Jared walked into the council chamber with Hilarin. The other eight Lords fell silent as they entered.

"So," Selwyn asked, "what was in this cave you had to visit?"

Jared took his seat at the head of the council table. The other Lords waited quietly for him to answer. Jared looked around the room. Now he was going to have to convince them to undo what they had just done.

"Everything we need to rebuild the *kaivir*," he replied.

"What!" Hhayim shouted.

"But how . . . ?" Phelandor asked.

"Why?" Selwyn objected.

Jared slammed his hand on the table. He was going to have to get a hammer or a bell or something. . . .

"Morvanor cannot afford to be without the *kaivir*," Jared continued once the outburst had died down. "Without sorcerers, the Nymrans of both the Empire and the Regency would be able to overrun us. Contrary to the propaganda, their sorcerers are every bit as skilled as the *kaivir*."

"But they are too dangerous to us," Selwyn objected. "That was why you claimed they had to be destroyed."

"No," Jared said. "They had to be destroyed because they were not loyal to *us*. Also, their power was too centralized."

"I believe," Hilarin explained, "that the High Lord is proposing that we each train a handful of *kaivir* to serve under us. That way, they will not be able to band together against us."

"That is almost correct," Jared agreed.

"Almost?" Kephas asked.

"Yes," Jared confirmed. "There is something that must be done before that plan will work."

"What?"

"Tell me, Kephas, what is the requirement that the *kaivir* use, pardon me, used, to select the youths they apprenticed from the barracks?"

"An ability to sense the presence and use of the Power," Kephas replied. "So?"

"All of us were warriors, soldiers before we joined the ranks of the Twelve," Jared explained. "As such we had no use for the Power, no sense of it. Once we accepted the Mistress's masks, however, we became creatures of the Power. Once our mortal lives passed we became even more so. Is there one of you now who *cannot* sense the presence and use of the Power?"

"Are you suggesting," Hhayim asked, "that we become . . . *kaivir*?"

"The only way that we can control the sorcerers we train is to become them," Jared replied.

"But that will take years," Phelandor observed.

"Yes, it will," Jared agreed. "That is why it is so imperative that we throw the Northern Kingdoms into disarray. To give us the time we need."

"I see no need . . . ," Hhayim began.

"The Mistress is *gone!*" Jared shouted. "What will you do, Hhayim, when your mount is slain one day? Do you want some *kaiva,* whose loyalty is not secured by Her Power, to know the name of your *goremka*?"

Hhayim thought for a long time. Eventually, his innate distrust of the sorcerers won out.

"I most certainly do not," he agreed.

"Then you had best be able to fashion your own," Jared said. "And what if one of us is injured? Do we want our new *kaivir* to hold *that* power over us as well?"

The Lords mumbled a general agreement that they did not.

"Then we had best start learning the Art ourselves," Jared finished. "And we had best start soon."

"So," Selwyn said, "that still does not tell us what was in that cave that Hilarin took you to."

"I suggested to Kerandon that it might be wise to protect the *kaivir's* library by securing copies of all their books in a safe place," Jared explained. "Then I left Hilarin behind to watch and to follow them."

"The *kaivir* took three wagons to a nearby cave soon after that and left them there," Hilarin continued. "Then they used the Power to make the cave appear to be part of the hillside. And to ward it."

"Once they were killed the illusion, and the ward, faded."

"Three wagons full of books?" Phelandor asked. The number obviously impressed him.

"No," Jared replied. "Apparently only one wagon carried their library. The other two were filled with gold."

"Gold!" Kephas said. "Where did the *kaivir* get that much gold!"

"A good question," Jared replied. "And one I do not have an

answer for. Only one wagon was necessary to carry the library."

"One . . . wagon," Selwyn muttered.

"Your pardon, Lord Selwyn?" Jared asked.

"That reminds me of something that has nothing to do with what we are discussing," Selwyn explained.

"Heregurth," he said, "why was one of the trucks travelling to Quarin alone?"

"Alone?" Heregurth asked.

"Yes. On my way to collect you, I saw a lone truck headed toward Quarin."

"I do not know," Heregurth said. "Unless one of the trucks broke down and they left the driver behind to get it running again. We had to leave one truck behind in the camp because it was not running."

"Phelandor," Jared asked, "did either you or Lord Kephas receive word that one of the trucks would be delayed?"

"No, High Lord," Phelandor replied. "All of the trucks arrived together, except the one that was left behind."

Kephas nodded in agreement. Jared abruptly stood up from his chair. He urgently summoned the *goremka* to him.

"Then *that* is the truck Lord Selwyn saw," he said. "The one that was left behind!"

"Impossible," Heregurth objected. "We left no one behind with it. Who could have both fixed it and then driven it to Quarin?"

"The Dreamer, you fools!" Jared shouted. "He is probably already in Quarin. If the Dragon is not already destroyed, it soon will be!"

The *goremka* appeared in the council chamber. Without a word, Jared mounted and disappeared onto the Gray Plain.

"The Dreamer?" Phelandor asked once Jared had left.

"Obviously," Hilarin replied, hurrying from the room. "And we had best join the High Lord in Quarin."

Steve looked out of the alley at the makeshift motor pool the Morvir had set up inside the city. Plow a couple of buildings over, conscript the locals to clear away the rubble and, *voilà*! Instant motor pool.

The tank was here, all right. Along with an armored

personnel carrier and two other armored vehicles. Apparently the trucks were being stored elsewhere.

The motor pool was heavily guarded, and there was currently a lot of activity here. Fortunately, the rocket launcher had enough range to reach it from here. Steve unslung it from his pack. This was his only rocket, so he was going to have to make it count. It would have been nice if he had a few more. Then he could take out the APC and the other vehicles as well.

Steve sighted on the tank. The engine was supposedly in the back, according to the briefing Williams had given him back on Earth. Steve sighted carefully on the back of the tank.

He took a deep breath, released half of it and held the rest. Slowly, he pressed the trigger. The rocket launcher fired just as the tank began to move.

Steve cursed and looked up from the sight in time to see the rocket narrowly miss the back of the tank. The Morvir were shouting as the missile struck one of the unidentified vehicles broadside.

The explosion was incredible. Steve turned to run down the alley as multiple explosions rocked the compound. That damned thing must have been *full* of ammunition. With any luck, it would still take out the tank.

Steve hit a main street and turned toward the gate to the bridge. That gate would be his only chance of getting out of the city. An explosion destroyed one of the buildings flanking the alley. So much for taking out the tank—it was after him.

A few seconds later the other building was also engulfed in a fireball. Screams and shouts echoed through the night. Steve ran faster than he had ever run in his life. Thank God, he had been running for exercise for months, now. He pulled one of the grenades from his pack; the gate would be an angry beehive by now.

His lungs burned from lack of air. The uneven cobblestones bruised his feet. Steve ignored all of that. He could hear the tank grinding its way over the rubble of the ruined buildings. Another round of explosions came from the area of the motor pool. Steve turned down a cross street to the street that led to the bridge gate.

He had been right. Morvan guards filled the gate. He pulled the pin and hurled the grenade into their midst before they had spotted him. Steve kept running—he could still hear the tank somewhere behind him.

The Morvir abandoned the gate when the grenade bounced among them. A ball of fire and flying shrapnel cleared out the stragglers. Steve poured on the speed, ignoring the fiery pain in his air-starved lungs.

I've probably set a record for the mile, he thought.

Steve flew out through the gate and onto the bridge. Bad idea—automatic gunfire nipped at his heels as he ran out onto the bridge. Steve ran a few more paces before diving off the bridge into the water. Pure, burning agony flared up his right calf as he jumped. He'd been hit!

The cold water of the river helped him stay conscious. Down! He had to swim down. Let the current carry him where he wanted to go, but he needed depth to protect him from the bullets. Slowly Steve descended into the murky depths of the river, his lungs begging for air.

"My lord!" Morfael shouted excitedly as he entered Erelvar's chambers.

"What is it, Morfael?" Erelvar asked, looking up from the maps.

"Something is happening in the northwest quarter!" Morfael explained. "There was an enormous explosion, and now there are sounds of battle."

"He is here!" Erelvar shouted, standing up from the desk. "Come, Morfael, we must get men along the river searching for him. That is his only way to us."

"At once, my lord!"

Jared looked upon the remains of the motor pool. Only random chance had saved the Dragon from destruction. If the Morvir had not been preparing to respond to the attack from the bluff, it would now be a twisted hulk, like the ammunition transport and the armored personnel carrier.

The second ammunition transport was also heavily damaged, but still mobile. The tank had suffered minor damage to its rear quarter.

"We are very fortunate that the fuel truck was with the other vehicles," Hilarin observed.

Before Jared could agree, Phelandor and Kephas appeared beside him. Their mounts snorted and pawed the ground.

"The Dreamer?" Jared asked.

"Whoever it was escaped the city from the bridge gate," Phelandor replied. "He cleared the gate with a hand grenade and ran out, supposedly right through the explosion."

"I highly doubt that," Hilarin objected.

"As do I," Phelandor agreed. "The guards atop the wall opened fire on him. He may have been hit."

"May have?" Jared asked.

"According to them, he fell into the river in an uncontrolled manner."

"Search the opposite bank," Jared ordered. "And get men on that bluff. I do *not* want another attack coming from there."

"Yes, High Lord," Phelandor replied.

"What do we tell the Morvir?" Hilarin asked. "We do not want the Special Forces to know the Dreamer is about."

"That is simple," Jared replied. "We obviously have a traitor."

"Obviously," Phelandor agreed.

"What of the bridge?" Jared asked.

"It is still burning," Phelandor replied. "The attack has delayed us by approximately a day, I would guess."

Jared shook his head. He had been so concerned with matters in Morvanor that he had completely neglected this front. He would not make that mistake again—not with the Dreamer about.

Steve clung to the pilings of the dock on the bluff. His lungs and his right calf burned like fire. From here he could see that the Umbrian quarter of the city was completely undamaged. That was where he would find Erelvar.

The question was, could he make it that far? The answer was probably no, but he had to try. If he remained here the Morvir would undoubtedly find him or he would bleed to death. Once the fire in his lungs had subsided a little, Steve swam away from the dock, letting the current help carry him to his destination.

*   *   *

Morfael patrolled the western shore with five men. Was it possible? Had Steven somehow returned from the dead to destroy the Dragon? And if he had, how likely was it that he would survive long enough to make it here?

They had already come across half a dozen bodies washed up on the shore from the attack on the bridge. Morfael's keen Olvan eyes spied another corpse half in the water. He cautiously made his way down the steep bank to the water. The man was dressed in clothing similar to the Morvan uniforms, with the green and brown mottled patterns.

Morfael gasped in surprise when he turned the man over. In the bright starlight, Steven's features stared back at him. Before Morfael could check Steven's pulse, his friend's eyes fluttered open.

"M-Morfael . . . ?" Steven croaked.

"Yes, my friend," Morfael replied, tears coming to his eyes. "It is I. I cannot believe you are alive."

"I . . . I have . . . returned," Steven said before passing out of consciousness once again.

Chapter
-------- Five ------------

THE BRIGHT MORNING sunlight woke Steve early. He buried himself deeper into the cover and rolled onto his side, away from the light. His right leg throbbed—must have overdone his run at the track.

Steve blinked as memory returned. No—he had been running from a tank. And his right leg hurt because he'd taken a bullet in it. He sat up in the bed.

Back on Earth the room would have been described as Tudor. Stained wooden beams framed white wattle-and-daub-constructed walls. A large fireplace ordained the room's outside wall and was framed by open windows.

In Quarin, the style was called Umbrian. Steve must have made it to the Umbrian quarter of the city. Judging by how much his leg *didn't* hurt, he must have also been visited by a healer.

Throwing back the covers and examining his leg confirmed that. Only a faint scar marked where the bullet had passed through the meat of his calf. He was lucky it hadn't struck the bone—he probably wouldn't be here now.

Steve stood up, looking for his clothes. He found them, along with local attire about his size, in the room's armoire. The camouflage fatigues had been cleaned and pressed. His Templar mantle had also been removed from his pack and cleaned.

Steve selected clothing more suited to his current environment than the fatigues and dressed. There was actually a pair of white linen trousers and tunic. He put those on and draped the mantle over his shoulders after buckling the sword belt around his waist.

A glass mirror was set into the armoire door—an expensive

touch here. Steve studied his image. Dressed in these clothes, he *looked* like a Templar.

The door to his room opened onto a hallway. One side of the hallway was open to the large common room below. He was in an inn of some type.

"Steven!" a familiar voice called from downstairs. Steve looked down and saw Morfael's fair Olvan features looking up at him from a table in the common room. Steve smiled and waved back before heading down the stairs.

The din from the common room ceased when Steven started down the stairs. All of the men seated below were armored in one fashion or another. Most wore bronze breastplates over leather in the Umbrian fashion. A few Olvir were visible in mail. Morfael was the only unarmored man in the room besides Steve.

The common room was absolutely quiet by the time Steve reached the bottom of the stairs. He looked around the room at the people staring back at him. Steve smiled.

"What's the matter?" he said in Umbrian. "Is sleeping late that great a crime around here?"

A few hearty laughs and a great many more nervous chuckles greeted his comment. Soon the room was drowned in conversation again. Steve made his way to Morfael's table.

"You handled that well," Morfael observed as Steve sat down.

"Thanks," Steve replied. "Can a guy get some breakfast around here?"

"Already on its way," Morfael assured him. For a long time, the Olvan warrior simply stared at him. Steve was starting to feel a bit self-conscious before Morfael spoke again.

"By the *Kanir*," Morfael finally said, "it is good to see you again, my friend. I thought you dead and gone six years ago."

"Has it been six *years*?" Steve exclaimed.

"Aye, that it has," Morfael replied. "I must say, you don't look as if you've aged a day."

"It has only been seven months back in my world," Steve explained. "Less than a year."

"Your world? So you have not spent the last six years in the Halls of Mortos?"

"No, I'm afraid not," Steve said. "After Belevairn killed me here, I awoke in a hospital back home. Apparently my other body had been in a coma the whole time."

"For a year?"

"No, for a month," Steve replied. "Don't forget time moves more slowly on my world."

"I . . . do not quite understand, but it is not important," Morfael said. "How did you get . . . back to our . . . world?"

"Belevairn was kind enough to lend me his steed."

"Belevairn *helped* you?"

"Not exactly. I killed him and rode his *goremka* back to Delgroth."

"You shall have to tell this story to Lord Erelvar," Morfael said, shaking his head.

"He's still alive, then?" Steve asked.

"Yes, very much so. We evacuated the fortress long before the Dragon attacked it."

"Good," Steve observed. "Very good."

The barmaid brought a plate heaped with sausages, eggs and biscuits. Steve thought she pressed against him a little too long as she put the plates down, but then they did that here. He watched as she walked away. Nice . . .

"They've got prettier barmaids than when I was here last," he noted.

"One of the benefits of civilization," Morfael replied. "Eat quickly. Lord Erelvar wants to meet with you as soon as possible."

"And I him," Steve agreed as he attacked the plate of food. Was he supposed to *eat* all of this?

Tsadhoq studied the horizon. From this distance, he should have been able to make out Erelvar's fortress against the sky atop the bluff. Instead, the top of the bluff looked like the top of a bluff—as if the castle had never stood there.

The Delvir marched on the southern bank of the river, the Umbrian side. The men were tired. They had marched without rest for more than two days. Few of them showed it, however.

"We'll rest here for a few hours," Tsadhoq announced. "Avram, Hebhel, scout ahead. See what awaits us at Quarin."

"Yes, Captain," the two men replied. They actually sounded

eager, despite how tired Tsadhoq knew they must be. As they departed, Tsadhoq found a convenient rock to sit on. He was getting too old for this.

Morfael led Steve back up the stairs of the inn. He knocked and then opened a door and motioned for Steve to follow him in.

Erelvar stood up from behind the conference table he was seated at. Just as Morfael was typical of the Olvir, Erelvar was the stereotypic Morvan. Broad shouldered and a full head taller than Steve. His dark features split into a broad smile.

"Steven!" he said, coming around the table to grasp Steve's forearm firmly in greeting. "By Mortos, it is good to see you again."

"And you, too," Steve replied. "I have thought of you often, Lord Erelvar."

"Steven, I would like you to meet Lord Aldwyn of Umbria," Erelvar said, indicating the other man who stood by the table.

"A pleasure, Lord Aldwyn," Steve replied, bowing slightly. God, he had *forgotten* how rigid the formality was! Aldwyn smiled.

"We have met before, Dreamer," he said, smiling and stepping forward to grasp Steven's forearm as Erelvar had. "But you may not remember me."

"I remember you quite well, Cai Aldwyn," Steve replied, also smiling. "Have you heard from Arthwyr ap Madawc recently?"

"Not recently," Cai replied. "The last I heard, which was a few months ago, he was holding a manor for his clan. He has done well for himself."

"Cai and I are almost finished, Steven," Erelvar told him. "If you will give us a few moments I will be able to talk with you at length."

"Of course, Your Grace," Steve replied.

"In the meantime you may wait in the other room," Erelvar said. "There is someone else who wants to see you again."

Steve nodded and bowed before leaving the room. The other room was a bedchamber, but was also being used as an office.

Lady Glorien turned from the window and a smile lit her face. Steven had forgotten how beautiful Erelvar's wife was.

Her golden hair and green eyes were typical of her royal Olvan heritage.

"Steven!" she exclaimed, coming forward to meet him. She held out her arms. They exchanged a brief embrace before she stepped back to look at him.

"'Tis a miracle," she said, "to have you back with us."

"It is good to be back," Steve replied. Glorien led him to a pair of chairs by the window. Morfael brought over the small chair behind the desk to join them.

"I must say," Glorien began, "you haven't aged a day since . . ." Glorien paused, uncomfortably.

"Since I died?" Steve finished for her.

"Yes," Glorien agreed. There was a long pause. Finally, Glorien broke the silence.

"What . . . happened that day, Steven?" she asked.

"There's not much to tell," Steven said, shrugging. "The Morvir were waiting in the forest for me. I tried to make it back to Quarin, but they cut me off. I managed to kill two of them, but they overwhelmed me."

Morfael had gotten up to stand by the window as Steve spoke.

"That's not all there was to it," the Olvan warrior said when Steve did not go on. He turned to face Steve. "We found you—*I* found you—staked to the forest floor. The whole clearing stank of sorcery."

"Yes," Steve agreed. "Belevairn was with them. He performed the Rite of Transference upon me."

"The Rite of Transference?" Glorien asked.

"Yes. He killed me, and as my soul left my body, it passed through him. He learned everything I knew. Everything about my home, my world, our science—everything. And I . . . learned everything he knew. I was forced to become one with that monster."

Morfael turned away, back toward the window. Steve could tell he wasn't looking out of it.

"What's wrong, Morfael?" he asked.

"Can you forgive me, Steven?" Morfael asked in reply.

"Forgive you?" The question confused him. Steve stood and stepped behind Morfael. "For what?"

"I should not have let you ride out alone that day," Morfael replied. "I should have gone with you."

"As I recall," Steve began, "you asked to come with me and I told you to go jump in the lake."

"I should have gone with you!" Morfael insisted.

"Are you my mother or something?" Steve asked. "I wanted to be alone that day and I would have been very upset with you if you had not allowed me to be. The blame for what happened that day lies with Belevairn—and I have settled that debt. No, Morfael, I will not forgive you because you have done nothing to be forgiven for."

Morfael turned from the window to face him. For a moment they just looked at one another.

"Have you carried that guilt for the last six years?" Steve asked. Morfael simply nodded.

"Well, get rid of it," Steve replied. "I am speaking to you as a friend—and as a priest. That guilt does not belong to you. Let it go."

"Priest?" Morfael asked.

"I was invested into a holy order of knights back home," Steve explained. "I am, for all intents and purposes, a priest as well as a knight."

"That's wonderful," Glorien inserted. "You must be proud."

Steve turned to her, smiling. He and Morfael had almost completely forgotten her presence.

"Yes, I am," he replied. "I was told that I am the first to be ordained into the Templars in the last seven centuries."

Just then Lord Erelvar opened the door.

"Cai has left for Castle Aldwyn," he said. "We can talk now, Steven."

"What is the situation?" Tsadhoq asked when Avram and Hebhel returned. Avram shook his head.

"Not good, Captain," he said. "The fortress is gone. The northeastern quarter and the Olvan quarter are all but destroyed. The Umbrian quarter is intact, however. If anyone from the fortress is still alive, they will be there."

"I see," Tsadhoq replied. Well, at least they hadn't arrived to find Quarin *completely* destroyed.

"Lieutenants," he said, "form up the men. We are marching on to Quarin."

Theron watched the bowl of mercury as Magus Philos worked his craft. An image of Quarin slowly formed on the naturally mirrored surface of the quicksilver. Theron gasped once the image became clear.

The destruction of the fortress was absolute. Not one stone stood upon another. When the Regency had first rebelled against the Empire, one city, south of the river, had been reduced like this. It had taken the Imperial legions over a month to wreak this much destruction. *This* had transpired in less than four days.

"Show me the city," Theron commanded.

The image floated from its position over the ruined fortress to the Olvan quarter of Quarin. The destruction there was not quite as absolute as that at the fortress had been. Still, it was more severe than Theron would have thought possible.

The quarter north of the Olvan quarter was largely undamaged. Still, the gatehouse was gone and several large stone buildings were collapsed.

"What is that?" Theron asked, indicating a location near the bridge. The image in the bowl descended toward that location. In the center of a burned and levelled area sat two large armored wagons. They were burned and twisted—destroyed by some great force.

In another cleared area, across the street, sat two other armored wagons. One had a round tower with a long cylinder protruding from it. Somehow Theron knew he was looking on the Dragon.

He remembered the firestaff the Dreamer had first brought with him from his world. It, too, had possessed a long tube through which it spat smoke and fire. This was a weapon from Steven's world—and it was a hundred times larger. Theron felt his heart sink. How could they fight something like this, which could destroy an entire city in a matter of days?

"Show me the bridge from this quarter," Theron said. There had been some activity there.

Conscripted workers carried timber out onto the bridge. Half of the original stone causeway was gone. The Morvir were rebuilding the rest with timber. Theron's heart sank further. Erelvar had destroyed the bridges. The Olvan quarter had been destroyed from across the river!

"Show me the rest of the city," Theron said. The northeastern quarter was as heavily damaged as the Olvan quarter. When they got to the Umbrian quarter, Theron smiled. It was intact. Erelvar had bought time by destroying the bridges. The Umbrian quarter was where they would find him.

"We will debark about five miles south of Quarin," Theron told tribune Kupris. "From there I shall march north to the Umbrian quarter of the city with a maniple of the *triarii*."

"Yes, Imperator," Kupris agreed.

"The remainder of the legion will wait with the galleys," Theron told him. "They are *not* to set foot on Umbrian land."

"Yes, Imperator," Kupris agreed again.

". . . and then Morfael found me on the shore," Steve finished. "Or so I've been told."

"That is correct," Erelvar confirmed. For a moment he sat there, digesting what he'd been told. It had taken several hours for Steven to tell him his tale. It had been a fantastic one.

Steven had tracked Belevairn on his own world only to be captured himself. Then he had escaped to kill the Dread Lord and use the knowledge from Belevairn's memories to force the *goremka* to bring him here. On his arrival, he had killed Lord Daemor before felling the gates of Delgroth. Then he managed to escape the eruption of that mountain to finally make it here. All just to fail in his attempt to destroy the Dragon. Erelvar shook his head.

". . . *and the Dreamer fled from the face of the Dragon*," Erelvar quoted.

"You can say that again," Steve replied. "I thought I was a dead man."

"So," Erelvar said, "how do we destroy this . . . tank?"

"We don't," Steve replied. "There isn't a single weapon on this world capable of destroying it. Actually, the Morvir have some that would do the job, but we'd never be able to get our hands on them."

"Can we make something?"

Steve shook his head.

"No," he said. "If we had gasoline or something like it, we might be able to make Molotov cocktails."

"Cocktails?" Erelvar was thoroughly confused. How could drinks destroy the Dragon?

"Fire bombs," Steve replied. "Gasoline is a flammable liquid. You fill a bottle with it, stuff a rag in it and light it. If you hit a tank with *enough* of those you can fry it. At least, you can with antiques like the one the Morvir have."

Erelvar turned and met Morfael's eyes. He wondered if his own expression was as horrified as that of his *felga*.

"Antiques?" he asked, turning back to look at Steven.

"Oh, yeah," Steven confirmed. "The tank the Morvir have wouldn't last a minute against a modern tank."

"We can be glad they did not bring a . . . modern tank, then," Erelvar concluded.

"Yes, you can," Steve agreed. "A modern M-1 would have gone *under* the damn river."

Erelvar and Morfael exchanged another glance. Erelvar shook his head in astonishment.

"Just when I think that I have seen the worst your world has to offer, you tell me that I am facing outdated weaponry," he said.

"Tanks are nothing," Steven replied. "Erelvar, my people have weapons that can destroy entire cities in the wink of an eye and leave nothing behind except a hole in the ground. Fortunately, everyone is too afraid to actually *use* those. My people have the power to destroys the entire world down to the last living thing, if *that* ever happens."

"Good gods," Morfael breathed. Erelvar was forced to agree with him. How had Steven's people survived such terrible weapons?

"You can be *damn* glad that Belevairn couldn't get his hands on any of those," Steven asserted.

"Indeed," Erelvar agreed. If Belevairn had, then he and Steven would not now be having this conversation. As it was, they still had to deal with what he *had* managed to obtain. . . .

"We have oil . . . ," Erelvar began, returning to the previous conversation. Steven shook his head.

"It doesn't burn hot enough," Steve replied. "We would need something *much* hotter and much more volatile."

"Delvan Fire," Morfael said. Erelvar snorted derisively.

"Then we are all dead men," he said. "The only manner in which the Delvir relinquish that is by catapult."

"If the Dreamer asked them for it, they would," Morfael replied. Erelvar looked at him in surprise. Morfael might be correct at that.

"What is Delvan Fire?" Steven interrupted.

"Death," Erelvar replied. "I have seen engines that would slough away burning oil for hours reduced to burning wreckage in moments after a dousing with Delvan Fire. They keep it in metal drums because it will soak through wood and explode with the slightest spark."

Steven nodded his head, deep in thought. Erelvar glanced up as the guard opened the door to the makeshift council chamber.

"Sounds like just what the doctor ordered," Steven said, nodding. "How do we find the Delvir to ask them about it?"

"How do ye find us to ask us about *what*?" a gruff voice replied. Erelvar smiled. He recognized the short, muscular man who elbowed his way past the guard into the room.

"Captain Tsadhoq," he said. "We were just discussing how you could help us against the Dragon."

"Nice of ye to wait for us, Morvan," Tsadhoq replied, lifting his beard-case indignantly. "Mind letting us in on your plans for us?"

Steven rose and turned to face the Delvan captain.

"We need all the Delvan Fire you can bring us," he replied. "And we need it yesterday."

"Vule's beard!" Tsadhoq exclaimed. "Dreamer!"

"Hello, Tsadhoq," Steven said, smiling. "It's good to see you again."

"Not half as good as it is to see ye, lad!" Tsadhoq replied, stepping forward to clap Steven on the back. "Ah, ye should see the glow on the horizon from Delgroth. A pretty sight it is."

"I saw it a lot closer than that," Steven replied. "And it didn't look that pretty when I was standing on the slope below it."

Tsadhoq laughed.

"I imagine not," he said. "I imagine not. Delvan Fire, eh?"

"Yes," Steven replied. "It sounds like the only thing I know of that will stop the Dragon."

"How soon do ye *really* need it?" Tsadhoq asked.

"Ask Erelvar," Steven replied.

"The Morvir will finish the bridge to the bluff tomorrow," Erelvar replied. "They can start repairing the bridge to the Olvan quarter immediately. That should take them two days, since they have already begun from the Olvan side. It would be four days before they could complete a bridge to the Umbrian quarter. We need the Delvan Fire before the Dragon starts to move."

"Four days," Tsadhoq noted. "Hmm. Nae, we cannot get word to Deldwar and then get supplies back here that quickly."

"We've *got* to," Steven objected. Before Erelvar could reply, Tsadhoq winked at him, smiling.

"It cannot be done, lad," he said. "So I guess ye'll have to settle for the hundred gallons we brought with us."

"Lord Aldwyn left for Quarin yesterday morning, m'lord," the castellan informed Arthwyr. "He went to discuss the resettlement of the refugees from Quarin."

Arthwyr sighed. Adlai had been castellan when Cai's father was Lord Aldwyn. If he hadn't arrived when he had, Arthwyr would still be arguing with the guards at the gate about being allowed to see a man who wasn't even here.

"Has Quarin fallen, then?" Arthwyr asked.

"All but, m'lord," the castellan replied. "The Umbrian quarter is apparently still intact, but only because Lord Erelvar destroyed the bridges."

This was not good news. Arthwyr could either wait here for the gods knew how long, or he could journey to Quarin and hope to run into Cai along the way. Of course, he could also run into the Morvir if they managed to cross the river.

Still, Arthwyr would rather be on the field than trapped in the castle. The Dragon could not kill what it could not find.

"Thank you, Adlai ap Aldwyn," Arthwyr said. "I will ride to Quarin to meet Cai."

"You are more than welcome to wait here, Master Arthwyr," Adlai told him. "I would be wary of travelling abroad with things as they are."

"From what you have told me," Arthwyr replied, "I would be *more* wary of staying in the castle."

                              *   *   *

Steve stood atop the battlements of the Umbrian quarter. It was impossible to see the northwestern quarter from here. The bluff that Quarin once sat upon blocked all view of the Morvan activity. Their only reports came from Olvanor, and those reports said that the bridge would be finished by morning.

Erelvar had been evacuating the Umbrian quarter all day. The refugees were taking shelter in the ruins of Bath and Aberstwythe, which were razed in the war six years ago. Now, only a few hundred men manned the walls. All others had been evacuated. The Delvir had joined the main body of Erelvar's force to the east.

Now it was Steve's job to remember every old war movie he'd ever watched. What does the infantry man do against the big bad tank when he doesn't have a bazooka? Dropping a hand grenade in the hatch was out of the question. Not only would it be next to impossible, but it would do little more than kill the crew. Do a few minor repairs, drop another crew in it and the Dragon would roll again.

The Delvan Fire was their best bet. It was fortunate that the Delvir had brought so much of it with them. Tsadhoq had a thousand men under his command and every one of them had carried a one-pint can of the stuff—over a hundred and twenty gallons in all. Steve had gotten a whiff of it at one point. Just enough to identify it as the substance his mother kept in her laundry room for those *really* tough stains—naphtha.

The question was, what to use as a delivery system? They wouldn't be able to use a catapult—the tank would blow anything like that to kindling before they could aim it. Coke bottles weren't exactly easy to find around here and the Morvir would shoot anyone long before they got close enough with any type of Molotov.

There only seemed to be one solution. If you can't get Mohammed to the mountain, you bring the mountain to Mohammed. They would have to get ahead of the tank once it started moving, no mean feat in itself, and prepare a trap for it.

The problem was, if the tank went into Olvanor, they had no way to move across the river. Erelvar had sent the galley downriver as part of the evacuation, but it was too small to move that many men and supplies across the river. They would need a small fleet for that.

Morfael climbed up the battlements behind Steve. Steve smiled at his friend and went back to staring across the river. It was getting near sunset.

"A sovereign for your thoughts," Morfael said.

"Thoughts are getting expensive these days," Steve noted.

"No, 'tis just that the sovereigns are worth less now that there is nowhere in town to spend them," Morfael replied. Steve laughed.

"Can't you guess?" Steve asked.

"The Dragon?"

"That *is* the topic of the day," Steve agreed.

"Indeed it is," Morfael agreed. Then, after a pause, he said, "Someone has arrived to see you. Erelvar sent me to bring you."

"Who?"

"Prince Theron," Morfael replied.

"Theron?" Steve asked, turning. "Did he bring ships?" Even one Nymran trireme could solve the crossing problem.

"I . . . do not know," Morfael said. "It *would* be the fastest way here. . . ."

"Let's go find out," Steve replied, heading down the steps from the battlements. If Theron had brought ships, that solved *one* problem. . . .

Chapter
-------- Six ------------

PHELANDOR WATCHED AS the drawbridge lowered to complete the last twenty feet of the causeway. The tank waited to cross into the tunnels that formed the entrance to the bluff. Now they would be able to sack the last remaining quarter of the city. With any luck they would kill the Dreamer *and* the traitor in the process.

However, Phelandor did not believe in luck. He had learned long ago—long, long ago—not to trust that fickle lady. Phelandor nudged his mount and crossed the causeway into the gatehouse. The convoy followed behind him.

The Special Forces had occupied this bluff since the night before, when the traitor had launched his attack against the bridge from it. As such, they had already determined that there was ample room for the tank to maneuver in these corridors.

Phelandor reached the large underground chamber near the south end of the bluff. Even he could not help but be impressed by the workmanship in this place. The traitor may have betrayed the Mistress and Morvanor but Moruth—or Erelvar, as he called himself now—was a man of vision. Were it not for the Dragon, this fortress would *never* have fallen.

The convoy proceeded up the ramp to the top of the bluff. Dawn was just beginning to lighten the eastern horizon when they emerged atop the bluff. The predawn light and the light from the Dreamer's star cast odd shadows amid the ruins of the fortress.

The damage Phelandor had witnessed in the northwest quarter and the other quarters of the city was nothing compared to the absolute devastation of the fortress. And this had been done in only half a day of constant bombardment. Phelandor shook his head. He was glad the route to the other world was lost with Belevairn. Nothing could stand against such weapons. He turned to watch dawn lighten the rooftops of the Umbrian quarter.

"We are in place, Dread Lord," one of the Morvir reported.

"Let the attack begin," Phelandor ordered.

Steve ran through the corridors of the ancient Aztec pyramid, searching for Belevairn. The sounds of explosions from the battle outside vibrated through the structure. He knew the sorcerer was in here somewhere—Steve *had* to find him.

He backed up against the wall by an intersection. Just as he began to turn and step into the corridor someone grabbed him by the shoulder. Steve spun to attack his unseen assailant. . . .

"Steven, awaken!" Morfael shouted, catching Steve's wrist as he swung at his friend.

Steve blinked. He was sitting in bed. Morfael was shaking his shoulder and had just caught the roundhouse punch Steve had thrown in his sleep.

"What's . . . ?" Steve began. An explosion shook the inn.

"The Dragon!" Morfael shouted. "The Dragon is attacking! Hurry!"

"Shit!" Steve shouted, jumping from the bed. He heard the whistle of an incoming shell just before another explosion shook the inn. Steve ripped his nightgown off, throwing open the armoire. Morfael left the room, presumably to round up other stragglers.

Steve hastily tied his few possessions up in a tunic. He cursed as the box of ammunition for his pistol fell from its pocket on the pack. He quickly scooped the bullets back into the box and placed it in the pack.

Shrugging into the pack, and gathering up his bundle, Steve hurried down the stairs to the common area. The inn was empty. Steve hurried toward the front door.

Dawn was just breaking to the east as Steve stepped out into the street. Another explosion lit the sky to the west. The Morvir were probably already crossing on rafts, if they were using the tactics Erelvar had told him they used on the Olvan quarter.

Morfael handed Steve the reins to a horse. He mounted, holding his makeshift bundle on the saddle in front of him.

"*Hyah!*" he shouted, kicking the horse in the ribs.

Hell of a way to wake a guy up in the morning, Steve thought as another explosion shook the town.

Arthwyr gathered his men at dawn. They had camped for the night at the ruins of Aberstwyth with the refugees from Quarin. There Cai had told him that Steven had, indeed, arrived in Quarin. Cai had also mentioned an encounter with Delvan scouts. Apparently the Delvan Royal Guard had returned for the party as well.

"Erelvar was expecting the Morvir to attack sometime today," Cai said as Arthwyr was preparing to ride out. "Be careful, old friend."

"You as well, Lord Aldwyn," Arthwyr replied. "Your castle will be the first to feel the Morvir's wrath."

"They have tried to sack Castle Aldwyn before," Cai replied, smiling. "As you well know, Arthwyr."

"Yea," Arthwyr agreed. "But now they have the Dragon. I think that, in your place, I would abandon the castle and take to the hills. Fight them from there. Crossbows and knives in the dark, Lord Aldwyn."

"It is a thought worth considering," Cai said. "Quarin was certainly no protection for Erelvar."

"No, 'twas not. According to the priests, our only hope lies in the Dreamer."

"Well, I hope the gods do not mind if mortal men do what ought they can as well," Cai replied. Arthwyr snorted in amusement.

"If it goes as usual, the gods shall leave us to do all the work while they take all the credit," he said.

"Safe journey to you, Arthwyr ap Madawc," Cai replied. "May the gods you jest about watch over your worthless hide, anyway."

"They have to," Arthwyr replied. "Who would they have to laugh at if I were gone? Farewell, Cai."

Cai nodded and stepped back. Arthwyr rode out, waving briefly to the Aldwyn lord. It was half a day's ride to Quarin. He would probably run into the survivors on the way. Hopefully, Steven would be among them.

*   *   *

Lord Jared arrived atop the bluff shortly after dawn. All was quiet. The tank sat near the edge of the bluff, facing the one remaining quarter of the city. As far as Jared could tell, the war machine was unmanned.

"Why has the attack ceased?" Jared asked one of the Special Forces.

"The enemy has evacuated the city, Dread Lord," the man replied. "Lord Phelandor wanted to leave it as intact as possible for our occupation."

Jared nodded. So, Erelvar had evacuated. Not surprising. He had already seen firsthand what the Dragon was capable of.

"Where are Lords Phelandor and Kephas now?" Jared asked. The soldier nodded in the direction of the Umbrian quarter.

"Overseeing the occupation, Dread Lord."

"Very good," Jared replied. Jared rode off the edge of the bluff and over the river toward the Umbrian quarter, surveying the damage as he did so. With surprise, he noted that there had been no damage to the wall. Apparently Phelandor and Kephas had directed all of the shelling to the interior of the city, seeking to drive out the inhabitants without damaging the defenses. *Very* good.

The streets of the quarter were deserted, save for a few Morvan patrols which Jared encountered. These directed him to an inn from which Phelandor and Kephas were directing the occupation of the city. The two lords had fashioned the common room into a makeshift council room. They looked up from the largest table in the common room as Jared walked in.

"High Lord," Phelandor said, standing. "The occupation proceeds well."

"Very well, Lord Phelandor," Jared agreed. "I must commend you and Lord Kephas for taking the quarter without damaging its defenses."

"Thank you, High Lord," Kephas responded.

"Let us be careful of using that . . . title in the presence of the Morvir," Jared cautioned, joining the two lords at the table.

"Can you be spared from here for a few hours?" Jared asked. Phelandor and Kephas exchanged a glance.

"Not easily, Lord Jared," Phelandor replied. "Is something amiss?"

Jared shook his head.

"No," he replied. "I am about to bring a vote to the council and wanted you to be present for it."

"One of us could attend," Phelandor told him. "But I do not think it would be wise for both of us to leave here at this time. What . . . is the subject?"

"Alliance with the Coasts," Jared replied. "I wish to be granted the authority to negotiate an alliance with the North Coast and the South Coast and to appoint one of the Ten as an ambassador to each."

"Have we come to this?" Phelandor asked, shaking his head.

"Neither the pirate king nor the prince will honor *any* agreement with us," Kephas objected. "Not for very long, at any rate."

"That is why I want one of the Ten sitting there to keep an eye on them," Jared agreed.

"You have my vote on this, High Lord," Phelandor told him. "Cast it as you see fit. Kephas can return with you to witness that I have given you my support."

"Thank you, Phelandor," Jared replied. "Then Kephas and I shall depart—"

"A moment, Lord Jared," Phelandor interrupted.

"Yes?"

"We have something you should see before you leave," Phelandor told him. "You may wish to take them back with you to show the others."

"What?" Jared asked, his eyes narrowing suspiciously.

"These," Kephas replied, bringing out a very small wooden box. He opened it to reveal three bullets.

"These were found, loose, in the bottom of an armoire upstairs," Phelandor explained. Jared reached out to take one of the bullets. Phelandor pulled the box away.

"Take care, Lord Jared," he warned. "Do you not feel the Power?"

Jared drew his hand back and looked more closely at the bullets. Indeed, each of them glowed with the inner light of the Power—deadly Power. The bullets themselves were fashioned of silver.

"Consecrated bullets?" he asked.

"Yes," Phelandor confirmed. "There is only one person we can think of who would have such things."

"The Dreamer," Jared said, still staring at the bullets.

Theron watched from the forest as the Morvir continued across the river to occupy the Umbrian quarter of Quarin. Erelvar had been wise to evacuate the city. Had he attempted to stand and fight, they would all be dead.

"We must rejoin the legion, Imperator," Kupris told him. "The Morvir will be canvassing the area soon."

"Yes, Kupris," Theron agreed. With only one maniple of the *triarii*, they dared not risk an encounter with the Morvir. From what Theron had seen, however, he suspected it would make little difference if the entire legion were with them.

Fortunately, Steven's plan for destroying the Dragon did not involve a direct confrontation. The plan, as it stood now, was to entice the Dragon into a pit filled with barrels of Delvan Fire. Apparently the substance that moved the Dragon was highly flammable, as were its weapons. Steven believed that the Delvan Fire could destroy it.

Theron spared a last backward glance toward Quarin. However, it was not Quarin that he saw. If Steven were wrong, if the Dragon could not be stopped, that would soon be Validus the Morvir were taking—not Quarin.

"Where will they take the Dragon?" Erelvar asked. They were several hours east of Quarin, camped in the forest. The refugees had gone on to Aberstwyth.

"My guess is Olvanor," Steven replied. "The terrain farther east of here gets pretty rugged. That tank will have a hard time navigating some of the passes. I'm not even sure it could make it to Castle Aldwyn."

"Good news for Umbria," Morfael noted.

"So," Erelvar speculated, "that means the entire force will probably proceed into Olvanor." Steven did not seem convinced.

"They have to bottle up Umbria, as well," he pointed out. "If the Morvir attack Umbria, the Olvir will probably stay in their forests. If they attack the Olvir, however, the Umbrians are likely to venture into Olvanor to get a shot at them."

"So you think they'll split their force?" Erelvar asked.

"If it weren't for the terrain," Steven replied, "I think they'd take the whole force into Umbria. But they almost have no choice but to send that tank into Olvanor. That means splitting their force, because they can't ignore the Umbrians. So they'll either attack both, or they'll hit Umbria with everything they have."

Erelvar nodded. Steven's assessment seemed sound to him.

"This is all well and good, lad," Captain Tsadhoq observed, "but it still does nae tell us where to set our dragon trap."

"Perhaps we should set *two* traps," Morfael suggested. "Would half of the Delvan Fire destroy the Dragon?"

"That's it, Morfael!" Steven agreed. "Yes, half of the Delvan Fire should do just fine. That way, we can be prepared for them, whichever direction the tank goes!"

"King Arven has gathered his army atop Bralmendel," Erelvar said. "We can place one trap along that route. Theron's legion can act as bait for a similar setting in Umbria."

"Can Theron's sorcerers help ensure that the tank crew drives into the pit?" Steven asked. All eyes turned to Felinor, Erelvar's magus.

"Yes," the young sorcerer replied. "Provided the Dragon is not warded against such things. If the Morvir have one of the *kaivir* aboard, then it will only serve to warn them of the trap."

"I certainly would, were I commanding that force," Erelvar observed. The Dragon was simply too valuable not to be afforded that type of protection.

"So Theron's magi should only do so if the tank looks like it's going to miss the pit," Steven concluded.

"Correct," Felinor agreed.

"Get word to Arven," Erelvar ordered his magus. "I shall pen the missive for you to send. We can inform Theron of the plans when he arrives here tonight."

"If the legion is going to be on this side of the river," Morfael said, "our force should move into Olvanor to assist them."

"No," Erelvar disagreed. "Without the Dragon, the Olvir can defend their own land against the Morvir. The Morvan weapons work only if their bearers have a target to use them on."

"Umbria has a lot more viable targets than Olvanor," Steven agreed.

"And the Morvir in Umbria will probably be prepared to operate without the support of the Dragon," Erelvar added. "Not to mention, if the entire force moves into Umbria we do not want to be stranded in Olvanor."

"So now we hurry up and wait for Theron," Steven stated.

"Indeed."

Arthwyr approached the forest outside Quarin cautiously. The refugees he had encountered on the road had told him that Erelvar was camped within the forest. Arthwyr did not want to be mistaken for an attacking force, although he doubted that the fifty knights with him would be seen as much of a threat.

They had barely penetrated the forest when they were hailed by sentries. Olvan sentries, apparently. At least Arthwyr could see no one.

"Who goes there?" the unseen voice demanded. Arthwyr imagined that he could almost hear the bows being drawn.

"Arthwyr ap Madawc!" he shouted in reply. "I have come to meet with Lord Erelvar and the Dreamer." For a moment there was no reply.

"You alone may pass," the voice finally announced. "Your men will wait here."

Arthwyr nodded in response to the questioning looks from his men. They dismounted and took their ease beside the trail while Arthwyr rode on. Soon Arthwyr was hailed by another ring of sentries. Erelvar had his camp well protected.

The final ring of sentries was the most impressive. Delvir, in heavy Delvan scale armor, barred the road with their double-bitted axes.

"Who are ye and what business do ye have here?" one of them asked.

"I am Arthwyr ap Madawc," Arthwyr replied. "I have come to meet with Lord Erelvar and the Dreamer."

"Wait here," ordered the same one that had challenged him. He turned and disappeared into the camp.

Arthwyr waited for what seemed to be forever. Soon a figure dressed all in white, save for a mantle trimmed in red with a red, crossed symbol in the center of it, hurried toward him. When the figure got closer, Arthwyr recognized it as Steven.

"Steven!" he shouted, dismounting. The Delvir let him pass.

"Arthwyr, you scoundrel!" Steven exclaimed, smiling. "It's good to see you!" Steven held out his hand in greeting.

"Is that the best ya' can do?" Arthwyr demanded, pulling Steven in by the wrist for a bear hug.

"Watch . . . the . . . ribs . . . ," Steven gasped, laughing. Arthwyr released him and held him out at arm's length, looking him over.

"You have not aged a *day!*" Arthwyr said. The Umbrian sounded thoroughly disgusted.

"That's what everyone says," Steve replied.

"Well, 'tis true," Arthwyr asserted.

"What are you doing here, Arthwyr?" Steven asked. "Cai told me that you were the lord of a manor now."

"Aye, I am," Arthwyr agreed. "But when the priests told me that the Dreamer had returned, I knew that my place was here."

Arthwyr flipped the edge of Steven's mantle.

"Speaking of priests," he said, "ya look like one yourself in this thing. What is it?"

"Well, I actually *am* a priest now, sort of," Steven replied.

Arthwyr raised an eyebrow.

"'Sort of'?" he asked. "That sounds like a maid telling her lover that she is a little pregnant."

"I was ordained into a holy order of knights back home," Steven explained.

"Ah!" Arthwyr exclaimed. "A priest *and* a warrior. Now that's my idea of what a priest *should* be!"

"I thought you would approve," Steve said, smiling.

"Of course," Arthwyr replied, placing his arm around Steven's shoulder as they walked into the camp. One of Erelvar's squires had arrived to take the horse.

"So, are you a healer as well?" Arthwyr asked. Steven blinked. Apparently Arthwyr's question had caught him off guard.

"I . . . I don't know," Steven replied. "I hadn't thought about it. . . ."

"I've heard that not all have the gift," Arthwyr added quickly. He had not meant to embarrass his friend. "You have done well for yourself, Steven."

"Thank you."

"Arthwyr ap Madawc," another voice said. Arthwyr looked to see Lord Erelvar standing before him.

"It has been a long time," Erelvar continued, holding out his hand.

"Yes, it has, my lord," Arthwyr replied, grasping Erelvar's forearm in greeting. "I have fifty knights waiting back at your first sentry post. May they enter the camp?"

"Of course," Erelvar replied. "Morfael?"

"I shall see to it, my lord," Morfael replied. "Greetings, Arthwyr. How are you?"

"As well as one can be in these times," Arthwyr replied. "I hear that Quarin has fallen. Is the Lady Glorien well?" Erelvar nodded in response.

"She is in the camp," he replied. "We evacuated well before the Dragon could attack. Come, Arthwyr, we would welcome your voice in our council."

"Thank you, Lord Erelvar," Arthwyr relied. Arthwyr followed as Erelvar led them back to the camp's central tent.

"You want the Veran Guard to bait a trap for the Dragon?" tribune Kupris shouted. "Are you mad?"

"That will be enough, tribune," Theron interrupted.

"But, Imperator . . . ," Kupris began.

"Silence!" Theron commanded. Kupris fell silent.

"I have reservations about this plan as well," Theron continued. "But we must learn more, and accusing Master Wilkinson of madness is not productive."

"Forgive me, Imperator," Kupris said. Theron nodded in response.

"I know it sounds crazy," Steve said, "but it's the only way we have to destroy the Dragon."

"At the cost of the Veran Guard," Theron added.

"Maybe not," Steve assured him. "We have to make certain the tank can't get a clear shot without rolling over the pit. Once the naphtha . . . that is, once the Delvan Fire goes up, the legion should have enough time to retreat."

"You mean enough time to run for our very lives," Kupris corrected. Tsadhoq spat contemptuously.

"If the Nymrans do nae have the stones for it," he said, "the

Royal Guard will bait the trap. And we do nae mind running for our lives, either. Nae from what the Morvir are carrying. . . ."

"Thank you, Tsadhoq," Steve replied. "But I don't think bravery is the question. The Veran Guard is the only standing legion in the Regency. Without it, Validus is defenseless."

"And that also makes it more tempting bait than the Royal Guard," Erelvar added.

"I think that both forces will have to act as the bait," Steve said.

"Both?"

"Yes," Steve continued. "Either one alone, the Morvir might be willing to take with small arms. If both forces are in an entrenched position together, they would be much more likely to bring up the tank."

"Aye, and with three days, we can entrench it well," Tsadhoq said, nodding to Theron. "Especially with the legion's help."

"I must admit," Theron said reluctantly, "that it sounds like the only option we have."

"I knew it," Kupris muttered.

"Do you have something to say, tribune?" Theron asked.

"No, Imperator," Kupris replied.

"Good."

"Now the only question," Erelvar said, "is where to lay that trap. Arthwyr?"

"Before Aberstwyth," Arthwyr replied. "I suggest that we march east until Steven finds what *he* thinks is the best place for it."

"Excellent idea," Erelvar agreed. "We head east in the morning."

Steve found Theron in the Nymran camp, of course. Out of respect for the forest, and the elaborate sentry net Erelvar had established, they had forgone their usual fortifications. The layout was roughly the same, however. Steve was able to walk straight to the command tent.

"Good evening, Master Wilkinson," Theron greeted him once the guard had announced Steve's presence. "How may I help you?"

"I have some questions that I wanted to ask you," Steve told him. "That I wanted to ask a priest."

Theron blinked in surprise.

"Please, come in," he said, holding the flap aside for Steve o enter.

"I must confess," Theron continued, "I am surprised, and leased, that you came to me. I would have expected you to onsult with Erelvar."

"Tonight I need the voice of Wisdom," Steve replied.

"Not the power of Death," Theron concluded. "I understand. Vould that more, even among the priesthood, saw how lependent the *Kanir* are upon one another."

"Theron?"

"Yes, my friend?"

"This is . . . not one of the questions I was going to ask ut . . . where is Artemas? I would have thought he would ead your magi." Steve watched as Theron's head dropped lightly.

"Artemas is . . . dead," Theron replied.

"Oh," Steve said. "Theron, I'm sorry—I did not know. . . ."

"I know," Theron said. "He died experimenting with . . . ew magics."

"Magics he learned from me," Steve said quietly.

"He knew they were dangerous," Theron added. "It was ertainly not *your* fault. We all warned him, or tried to."

"His notes . . . ?" Steve asked.

". . . were sealed," Theron finished. "The emperor banned urther research in those areas."

"Good," Steve said. "I'm sorry, Theron."

"As I said, it was not your fault," Theron replied. "Now, vhat were the questions you came to ask?"

"Well, back on Earth I was ordained," Steve began.

"Truly?" Theron asked. "To which calling?"

"I was ordained into a holy order of knights," Steve replied.

"I ask again, to which god are you a priest?"

"To God," Steve replied.

"I . . . do not understand," Theron said.

"Mortos appeared to me," Steve explained. "Only he did not ppear as Mortos. Instead, in my world, he is known as the rchangel Apollyon—a servant of the God I serve."

"A . . . servant?"

"Yes," Steve said. "He said that God is the same in all

worlds, but that he is known by different names in differen
lands."

"You are a priest of Kanomen!" Theron exclaimed. "A pries
to the *father* of the *Kanir*! None such have walked the worl
in . . . centuries."

"There have been priests of . . . Kanomen before?"

"Yes, but only in times of great need," Theron explained.

"Well, I suppose this qualifies," Steve noted.

"Indeed," Theron explained. "So tell me, holy father—hov
may I serve you?"

"Can we dispense with the formality?" Steve asked. "I
makes me a little . . . uncomfortable."

"Certainly. Does . . . Erelvar know of this?"

"No," Steve replied. "How could he? I just found out myself
from you. He knows that I took holy orders, but he didn'
question with whom."

"I see," Theron said. "If you like, I will help you present i
to him."

"That sounds like a good idea," Steve agreed.

"Is there anything else you need to ask, Father Wilkinson?"

"Yes," Steve said. "Arthwyr asked me a disturbing questio
today."

"And that was . . . ?"

"When I told him of my ordination, he wanted to know if
was a healer," Steve explained. "I had to tell him that I didn'
know."

"*That* we can test," Theron replied.

It was near sunset when Steve left Theron's tent and walke
through the camp toward his own tent. Theron's test ha
been nothing more than performing mass together, essentially
Theron had been required to step Steve through most of th
ceremony, but when it was done, he had been able to give Stev
at least a partial answer.

Whether or not Steve was a healer still remained to be seen
What *had* been determined was that Steve was able to summo
the Power in ritual. According to Theron, if Steve were capabl
of that, then he could definitely be taught to be a healer. As i
was, he might be a natural healer, one who did not nee
teaching but whose faith was sufficient.

With your faith, if you can find it, Mortos had said to him, back on Earth once. Steve had found a great deal of it—enough to protect him from Belevairn's sorcery. He suspected that he would need to find a great deal more of it before this was over. . . .

"Greetings, Dreamer," a soft voice said from behind him. Steve spun toward the sound of the voice, his hand flying to the hilt of his sword.

"Forgive me for interrupting your soul walk, Dreamer," the man said. He was ageless, ancient and young, as were most of the older Olvir.

"You are a lore-master," Steve noted. The man nodded.

"I am Nolrod, advisor to His Majesty, Arven of Olvanor," the man said.

"Does Erelvar know you are here?" Steve asked.

"I did not come to see Erelvar, Dreamer," Nolrod replied. "I came to see you. His Majesty wishes to speak with you regarding this trap you wish us to lay for the Dragon. I am to bring you to him."

"We are marching east in the morning," Steve said. "Once we have begun a similar trap here in Umbria, I am planning to journey to Olvanor." Nolrod shook his head.

"Tonight, Dreamer," he said. "You shall be returned here long before morning, I promise."

"But . . . how?"

"Walk with me, Dreamer," Nolrod replied. "And follow closely." With that, he simply turned and walked away.

Steve hesitated for a moment. Then, with a shrug, he followed behind the lore-master.

Chapter
-------- Seven ------------

JARED BROUGHT HIS mount to a halt on the Gray Plain. Hilarin and Heregurth reined to a halt beside him.

"We do not know what type of reception we will encounter," Jared warned them. "Be prepared to flee back here at the first sign of trouble."

"I do not like having to deal with these vermin," Heregurth said, "let alone having to face the prospect of fleeing from them."

"That attitude will likely get you killed without the Mistress to back you up, Heregurth," Hilarin replied. "These people are about to become our loyal and trusted allies — at least that's how we shall have to treat them."

"If we are prepared, then . . . ?" Jared suggested.

"Yes, High Lord," Hilarin replied.

Jared guided his mount forward, passing from the ethereal realm of the Gray Plain into the bright daylight of a sparse forest. He looked around, trying to determine the direction to the nearest road.

"This way," he said, once he had determined the direction from which the sounds of traffic were emanating. He had attempted to emerge just off the northern road to El-Adrid, the capital city of the Southern Coast. Judging from the sounds, he had been at least partially successful.

If the heavy traffic on the pitiful road were any indication, they had arrived very close to the city. Travellers stopped and stared at the unexpected sight of three of the *Kaimordir* emerging from the forest. Jared ignored them as he turned south, toward the city of El-Adrid.

The road was such only by virtue of the fact that everyone followed it to the city. It was deeply rutted and consisted mostly of mud mixed with animal excrement. Jared guided his mount to ride about half a foot above the actual road itself. Hilarin and Heregurth followed suit. Jared did not want to make too flashy a display on his arrival, but there *were* limits.

After a short ride, about a mile or so, they entered the outskirts of the city. The stench intensified as the smell of human waste mingled with the salt smell from the ocean. The inhabitants of El-Adrid stopped to stare as Jared's entourage passed. Although the Coasts were home to the castoffs of all the kingdoms as well as the Empire, the sight of three of the Dread Lords was a new thing to these people.

Soon, the walls of the city came into view. Jared sneered beneath his mask. Buildings leaned against the outer wall, some almost as tall as the battlements. If the buildings hugged the wall this tightly *outside* the city, they must be even more dense inside the city. The wall might as well not be there for all the protection it gave.

An armed body of men, similar enough in appearance to barely be recognized as organized troops, left the gate to meet them. Jared reined his mount to a halt and Hilarin and Heregurth stopped just behind him.

"G'day, m'lords," one of them, presumably the commander, said in the polyglot that passed for language in the Coasts. "What is your business in El-Adrid?"

"We seek audience with the king," Jared replied, in Umbrian.

"Whoever he may be, this week," Heregurth muttered sotto voce.

"You may pass," the guard captain told them, "on foot. Dismount and leave your . . . steeds outside the city."

Jared glanced down at the road. Though his natural senses were long dead, the magic of his golden mask conveyed the stench from the vile ooze of the road. That in itself was enough to dissuade Jared from dismounting. The fact that he did not wish to be inside the city without a quick escape was almost a secondary consideration.

"I think not," Jared replied. The captain smiled, wickedly.

"This ain't Morvanor, *Dread* Lord . . . ," the guard captain began.

In response to his mental command, Jared's *goremka* stepped forward. Jared reached down before the guardsman could react and lifted him to eye level by the front of his mail tunic.

"You may play your power games with any other traveller you wish," Jared told him coldly, his eyes burning red behind the golden mask. The captain's eyes were wide with fear.

"But you shall *not* play them with *me*," Jared continued. "We request passage into the city to seek audience with your king. If you allow us past the gate, we shall be about our way. If you do not, we shall leave, *after* I have hung you from the gate with your own entrails. Do you understand me?"

"Y-yes, Dread Lord," the guard captain replied. There was no trace of sarcasm in his voice.

"May . . . we . . . pass?" Jared asked.

"Y-yes, Dread Lord," the man repeated. Jared's mask passed another odor to him. The guard captain was adding his own scent to the road below.

"Excellent decision, *Captain*," Jared said, his voice thick with contempt. "You were *obviously* born to command." Jared released his hold on the guardsman's mail tunic, dumping him into the muck below. Then he spurred his mount forward, passing through the gate into El-Adrid.

Master Levas hurried in response to the summons from King Morgaine. The palace staff quickly stepped aside to allow him to pass. Levas was the most powerful man in the castle, next to what passed for the royalty.

However, that was only natural. Sorcerers were rare in the Coasts and a *kaiva* of the third order was almost unheard of. Levas had already survived two transitions of rule and one failed coup due to that rarity. He would likely survive any other that occurred simply because he was too valuable to whomever held power to be disposed of. He was not an easy man to dispose of, in any event. Master Kerandon himself had learned that many years ago.

Levas found Morgaine awaiting him in the throne room.

"You sent for me, Your Majesty?" he asked, bowing as he approached the throne.

"Aye, Master Levas," Morgaine replied. "Your former masters have come to call."

Levas blinked. The Morvir? Levas had been spying on

Morvanor recently, with the sudden appearance of the Dreamer's star. For the first time in his twenty-three years of exile, he had been able to summon the image of the Academy with the Rite of Far Visions. Or more accurately, what was left of the Academy.

Likewise, he had been able to summon an image of Delgroth. It, too, had not fared the return of the Dreamer well. And now the Morvir were here? Had they sent the Dragon against the Southern Coast?

"An invasion, Your Majesty?" Levas asked, knowing that was highly unlikely. If the Morvir *were* to attack, they would attack the Northern Coast, which bordered Morvanor on the south.

"Hardly," Morgaine replied, picking at his filthy beard. "Three of the Twelve are here to seek audience with me."

"Audience!" Levas exclaimed. Why would even *one* of the *Kaimordir* seek audience with the louse-infested king of the Coasts, let alone three?

"Aye," Morgaine agreed. "That was my reaction, too. They are on their way to the palace even now. I want ye to perform a truth spell for my audience with them."

"I . . . cannot do that, Your Majesty," Levas replied.

"What?" Morgaine asked, his voice dropping dangerously low. "Why is that, *kaiva*? Are ye yet loyal to your old masters?"

"It is the masks, Your Majesty," Levas explained. "The masks are imbued with the Power of the Mistress. My art cannot penetrate their protection."'

"What *can* ye do?"

"I would suggest a ward, Majesty," Levas replied. "To protect you from any use of the Power on *their* behalf."

"Then do so," Morgaine said.

"Yes, Majesty." Of course the ward would protect Levas as well.

The palace was little more than a well-fortified manor house. Unlike the outer wall, however, no buildings encroached on either side of the wall surrounding the palace. Jared eyed the structure critically. The Morvir could take something like this in a day, even without the new weapons.

Still, he was not here to conquer, but to negotiate. Jared

hoped that the palace did not smell as bad as the city. Perhaps that was the city's best defense. No one could put up with the stench long enough to conquer it.

The guards at the gate were expecting them. Apparently, word travelled quickly in El-Adrid. Grooms met them inside the wall to take the *goremkir*. Jared dismounted and handed the reins to one of the grooms while mentally ordering his *goremka* to cooperate. The demon steed grudgingly accepted the commonplace handling it was about to receive.

"King Morgaine awaits ye, Dread Lords," a filthy valet told them. Maybe Jared could have Hilarin introduce the habit of bathing down here once he assumed his post as ambassador.

The smell of the city *did* abate somewhat once they entered the palace grounds. Jared was beginning to have second thoughts about this alliance. What could this filthy, undisciplined rabble of pirates offer Morvanor?

He knew better than that. Filthy and undisciplined as they might be, they were still the fiercest naval raiders in the world. No ships dared pass the Gates of Uldon from the Inner Sea and, during high tide, no ship on the Inner Sea was completely safe from them. The Coastal pirates had sacked several Umbrian coastal cities and even a few Imperial holdings.

Although small and indefensible, the palace was opulent beyond belief, inside. Jared had never seen so many golden furnishings in one building as he saw in the manor's entry hall. Not only would the palace be easy to take, it would be profitable as well. . . .

"Wait 'ere, lords," the valet informed them, "whilst I announce ye." Jared doubted that the palace had seen this much formality in years. The valet returned and motioned for them to enter the audience chamber. He held the door for them as the three *Kaimordir* passed.

Jared stopped in surprise as he entered the audience chamber. The king was a huge black-bearded man. The item of surprise was behind his throne. Standing to the king's left was an ancient man dressed in the formal attire of a *kaiva* of the third order. Jared could sense the barrier of Power that surrounded the raised dais.

Hilarin nudged Jared in the back, prodding him back into motion.

"Is not this a surprise?" Hilarin whispered.

"Indeed," Jared agreed. The entourage stopped at the foot of the dais. Jared nodded to the king while Hilarin, and then Heregurth, bowed deeply.

"And why do ye not bow, Dread Lord?" the king asked.

Hilarin spoke before Jared could reply.

"High Lord Jared has been elected to head the Council of Lords that now rules Morvanor, Your Majesty," he replied. "As such, he is our ruler with the standing of a king in his own right."

"I see," the pirate king replied. "Welcome to the Southern Coast, High Lord. I am Morgaine, king of the North and South Coasts. I had heard that changes were . . . taking place in Morvanor."

Jared glanced to the *kaiva*. He had a good idea where that information was coming from. Morgaine followed his glance to the sorcerer.

"Ah, ye have noticed my advisor," Morgaine said. "Perhaps you know Master Levas?"

Jared did indeed recognize the name, if not the man. Levas had been killed by Kerandon in a battle for control of the *kaivir* over twenty years ago—or so they had believed. Instead, he had apparently been hiding here since that time.

"Indeed, I do, Majesty," Jared replied. "Although we had thought him dead many years ago."

"Lord Jared," Master Levas said, nodding to his former master. "Or should I simply address you as 'High Lord' now, Dread Lord?"

"Either of the three will do," Jared replied. Levas nodded again in acknowledgment.

"Ye have journeyed far to seek an audience with me," Morgaine said. "What does Morvanor wish with the Coasts?"

"We come seeking an alliance between our two kingdoms, Majesty," Jared replied.

"Alliance?" Morgaine asked. His surprise temporarily broke his composure, but he recovered quickly.

"Yes, Majesty," Jared said. "I have brought with me Lords Hilarin and Heregurth to serve as ambassadors to you and His Highness to the north, respectively."

"Ambassadors," Morgaine observed. "Ye *are* serious about this, then."

"Very serious, King Morgaine," Jared replied. Morgaine thought for a moment, picking something from his beard that scuttled away when he flung it to the floor. Jared made a mental note to have his clothing deloused when they returned to Morvanor.

"I fail to see what advantage there would be in our two kingdoms forging such an alliance," Morgaine finally said.

"There would be many advantages to such an alliance, Your Majesty," Hilarin replied. "It is no secret that Morvanor has the most powerful army in the world. It is also a well-known fact that the Coasts have the most feared navy in the world. Together, we would be immune to attack."

"Aye," Morgaine agreed, "I suppose the idea has *some* merit. I must confer with my advisors. Can ye return tomorrow afternoon?"

"Certainly, Majesty," Jared replied. It had been too much to hope that the alliance could be forged in a day.

"Good, good. We will discuss this in more detail then."

"Until tomorrow, Your Majesty," Jared said, nodding before turning to depart the throne room. Hilarin and Heregurth bowed before turning to follow him.

The three Dread Lords walked in silence out of the palace. They mounted the *goremkir* as the grooms brought them out and Jared immediately left reality for the Gray Plain.

"Do you think they shall accept the offer?" Heregurth asked once they had achieved the safety of the Plain.

"I believe so," Jared replied. "Morgaine just needs time to get over his astonishment so that he can negotiate effectively."

"The more pressing question," Hilarin said, "is will they agree to increase their raids on Umbria and the Regency during our campaign?"

"I do not intend to ask them to," Jared replied.

"But," Heregurth said, "I thought that was the entire point of this alliance. . . ."

"For the short term, yes," Jared agreed. "However, I am not going to request it. I am simply going to pass on the information that those targets are less defended than normal. Once the pirates know that the Umbrian armies and the Veran

Guard are engaged against us, their own greed will drive them to attack our enemies. That way, it will not become an item of negotiation with which they can wrest concessions from us."

"Ah," Hilarin said. "Nicely planned, High Lord."

Morgaine turned to Levas once the Dread Lords had left the throne room.

"Well?" he asked. "Is this some trap, Levas?"

"I . . . do not know, Majesty," Levas replied. "As I said before, I can work no truth magic on the *Kaimordir*."

"No, but ye know them better than any here," Morgaine said. "Can they be trusted?"

"Trusted?" Levas laughed. "Never, Your Majesty. However, Lord Jared *can* be trusted to act with caution and discretion to further his own goals. The other Lords have chosen their new master well."

"What is their purpose?"

"It may be exactly as they have stated, Majesty," Levas replied. "They may wish the use of our navy. That is something they cannot take from us by force of arms. It must be freely given to them."

"So we can use that to gain concessions from them, as well," Morgaine observed.

"Yes, Majesty," Levas agreed. "However, one had best negotiate with a knife in his boot when dealing with the Dread Lords. . . ."

The others were waiting in the council room when Jared returned, except Lord Kephas. Lord Phelandor had apparently arrived to take his place.

"What news from Quarin?" Jared asked, taking his seat at the head of the council table. Hilarin had dug up an ornate, almost thronelike chair from someplace to place at the head of the table.

"We have taken the Umbrian quarter," Phelandor reported. "Even as we speak, the bridges to the Umbrian and Olvan quarters are being repaired."

"How long?"

"Two days for the bridge to Olvanor," Phelandor replied. "Four for the bridge to Umbria."

"Lord Hhayim," Jared asked, "when will the regular troops arrive in Quarin?"

"The morning after tomorrow," Hhayim replied.

"So, our Olvan operation begins in two days," Jared observed.

"Lord Selwyn," Jared said, "you will take command of our Quarin garrisons once Phelandor passes into Olvanor."

"Yes, High Lord," Selwyn replied.

"One question, High Lord," Phelandor said.

"Yes?"

"Supplies," Phelandor said. "If I am taking the Dragon and the remaining ammunition transport into Olvanor, I will need the fuel truck."

"That is correct. . . ."

"What of the trucks going into Umbria? They shall need fuel as well."

"The trucks have a range of over two hundred miles," Jared stated. "That should be sufficient to exhaust the Special Forces in Umbria."

"Yes," Phelandor agreed, "but the men will become suspicious if we do not have enough fuel to get the trucks *out* of Umbria."

"Good point," Jared observed. "How many trucks are you taking into Olvanor?"

"Eight," Phelandor replied. "The other sixteen are being sent into Umbria."

"Take the fuel cans from the eight going into Olvanor and place them on the trucks being sent into Umbria," Jared ordered. "As trucks are emptied, send each one back to Quarin with just enough fuel to make it back. That should extend our range convincingly enough."

"Yes, High Lord."

"What of the alliance?" Hhayim interrupted. "Am I the only one who is curious of the outcome?"

"Morgaine wishes to 'consult with his advisors,'" Jared replied. "He wants us to return tomorrow afternoon for further talks. At this point, I believe only the details remain."

"Do you truly think they will be of any help against the Northern Kingdoms?" Lord Fanchon asked.

"I do," Jared asserted. "Any additional damage that can be

done either to Umbria or the Regency will mean that much longer before the Northern Kingdoms can pose a serious threat to us."

There were general murmurs of assent from the gathered Lords.

"What of the army?" Hilarin asked. "How goes the plan to inform the officers of the Mistress's . . . absence?"

"It goes well," Selwyn replied. "The officers wish to keep their privileges. By slowly informing them and making them responsible for those beneath them, we are suffering a minimum of dissension."

"How minimal?" Jared asked.

"We have been required to kill only a few dozen officers," Selwyn replied. "And only a few hundred of the Morvir. As our base of loyal, and informed, troops grows, these numbers are diminishing."

"Excellent," Jared said. "How much of the army has been . . . converted?"

"Almost half," Selwyn replied. "We should have the army firmly under our control long before word of the Mistress's fate reaches the general populace."

"And then it shall be business as usual," Hilarin observed.

"Indeed," Jared agreed. "Then that leaves us with only one loose end left to tie off."

"What is that?" Hilarin asked.

"The man responsible for all of this," Jared replied, his voice lowering in anger. "I *want* the Dreamer, Dread Lords. I want him found and then I want to be informed of his location so that I may go and kill him."

Silence fell across the council room as the *Kaimordir* exchanged glances.

"Yes, High Lord," they quietly acknowledged.

Chapter
-------- Eight -----------

STEVE FOLLOWED NOLROD through the darkening forest. How on Earth did the lore-master think he was going to get Steve to Olvanor and back before dawn? Not to mention back in time to get any sleep at all.

The trails that Nolrod followed twisted through the thick underbrush. Something was wrong—the two of them should have encountered the innermost ring of Erelvar's sentries by now. This was not right. . . .

The sound of a rapid creek reached Steve's ears. There weren't any creeks inside the camp! Steve hurried to catch up to the ancient lore-master. He had a feeling that if he lost Nolrod now, he wouldn't be anywhere he knew how to get back from.

Soon they emerged into a clearing. A massive, stony hill towered above them, lit from behind by the setting sun. Huge slabs of rock littered its sides, like standing stones kicked over by an angry giant.

"Bralmendel," Nolrod announced.

"But . . . ," Steve began, "that is, we . . . how?"

"It is simple," Nolrod replied, "when one knows the ways of the forests as I do."

"Yeah . . . right," Steve replied.

"King Arven awaits us at the summit."

"Well," Steve said, "I guess we'd better not keep him waiting."

"What do you *mean* he is not in the camp!" Erelvar shouted.

"Just that, my lord," Morfael replied. "Steven cannot be found anywhere. I did, however, find an Olvan *rega* who claims to have seen him speaking with a lore-master."

94

"A lore-master?" Erelvar asked. "Here?"

"Yes, my lord," Morfael replied. "My guess is that Steven left with him."

"Well, he is probably halfway to Bralmendel by now, then," Erelvar concluded.

"No, my lord," Morfael corrected, "he is probably already there."

"Greetings, holy father," Arven said, rising and bowing as Steve approached.

"G-greetings, Your Majesty," Steve replied nervously.

"It is a shame that we did not have the chance to meet when last you visited our world," Arven said. "I am glad that we have the opportunity, now."

"As am I, Your Majesty," Steve replied.

"Please, simply call me Arven, holy father," the king requested.

"Only if you agree to call me Steven, instead of 'holy father,'" Steve agreed, smiling.

"So be it," Arven replied, also smiling.

"Nolrod told me that you wished to speak of our plans to trap the Dragon," Steve began.

"Yes, but there is time for that," Arven said. "Please, sit. Have some wine and let us talk."

"But with all due respect, I have to be back by dawn. . . ."

"You shall be, I assure you, Steven. Sit for a moment and listen, feel the land about you."

Steve sighed and sat on a stone facing the Olvan king. The Olvir, as always, marched to the beat of a different drum.

"What do you feel?" Arven asked.

Steve blinked. Arven actually wanted him to feel the land—he hadn't meant to just relax. Steve closed his eyes and listened, felt. After a moment, he opened them.

"It is very . . . *peaceful* is not the right word," Steve replied.

"Quiet, perhaps?" Arven suggested.

"Yes," Steve agreed. "Quiet."

"We are atop Bralmendel," Arven said. "A place that is not a place, and where time is not time as we know it."

"Majesty?"

"Bralmendel is not of this world alone," Arven explained. "Atop this hill, we are closer to the afterworld than any other place on this world. Many wondrous things have occurred in this vicinity."

"Such as?"

"Days may pass here," Arven said, "but only hours will pass without. Or hours may pass here, while years pass without."

"Is that all?" Steve asked.

"Is that not enough?"

"Uh, no—I meant, is there anything else strange about this place?"

"Once, there was an Olva named Rishar," Arven began. "This was many centuries ago, when the Plains of Blood were filled with the *galdir*. Rishar was a mighty hunter, a great warrior and King Lindril's closest friend.

"One day Rishar was struck down in battle by a *galdan* spear," Arven continued. "His comrades carried him from the field while King Lindril's forces turned the hordes away. Later that night, Rishar died from his wound, for the spear had been tainted with a vile poison that not even the king's healers could remove.

"King Lindril buried his lifelong friend on that battlefield. On his way back to Mencar, he stopped at Bralmendel to pray for solace and for the soul of his friend. At the base of the hill, a she-wolf approached him, carrying a cub in her mouth. She dropped the cub at Lindril's feet and fled into the underbrush.

"Lindril was puzzled by this and, taking pity on the small creature, he lifted it in his hands and gazed into its eyes. In that cub's eyes he saw the gaze of his old friend, Rishar. He took it and raised it and it grew into a huge, mighty wolf that served and loved its master well. Some even said after that that they had seen King Lindril sitting and speaking with his old friend Rishar by the fire at night."

Arven took a sip of his wine while Steve rubbed at the goose bumps that had risen on the back of his neck.

"There have been other Spirit Animals since then," Arven continued. "All close friends who were lost before their time. All loved ones whose duty was not yet dispatched. They may always be recognized through their eyes."

"And they can change back into the people they once were?" Steve asked.

"Some can," Arven said. "All Spirit Animals have some special Power, bestowed upon them so that they may best serve the one for which they have returned."

"That's quite a story," Steve said.

"There are many such tales in Olvan lore," Arven said. "We have a rich history."

"Yes," Steve agreed. "It's too bad I don't have time to hear more of it."

"Perhaps during happier times," Arven suggested. "But now, there is someone here who wishes to see you."

"What . . . ?" Steve said. "Who . . . ?" Arven nodded to indicate someone behind him. Steve turned.

The mare was beautiful. Slender, graceful and white as snow. Steve rose to his feet as his gaze was drawn into the mare's turquoise eyes.

"Oh, dear God," he said, stepping forward. He reached out and wrapped his arms around the mare's neck, tears running down his face. The horse nuzzled his cheek.

"Aerilynn," he said. "Oh my God, Aerilynn."

"We found her exactly one year before your star appeared in the sky, Dreamer," Arven said behind him. "She came to Mencar and made it known that we were to keep her for you. It seemed appropriate to bring you together here.

"She will allow no one to ride her, save for one time when she carried me," Arven continued. "She will not tire, and neither will you so long as you ride her. And she knows the ways of the forests better even than Nolrod. You may return to Erelvar's camp anytime you desire."

"Thank you, Arven," Steve said, wiping the tears from his eyes. "Thank you."

"It pleases me to have pleased you," Arven replied. "I shall leave you now. We shall talk in the morning."

"But . . . ," Steve began to object.

"Remember where you are, Steven," Arven interrupted. "Days on Bralmendel are not what they seem to be."

"Oh . . . right."

"Good night." Arven turned and walked away. Steve turned

back to . . . Aerilynn. The tears returned and he buried his face in the horse's neck, weeping bitterly.

Then he felt her arms circle around him. He pulled his face away and looked into Aerilynn's eyes. Her silver hair flowed down past her waist, unbraided. Her hair was the only covering she wore.

"Aerilynn!" Steve exclaimed. "You . . ."

"Yes," Aerilynn replied. "But I may only appear such at night when we are alone."

"Oh, thank God," Steve said. "Thank God you've come back to me."

"I could not stay away, my love."

Steve pulled her to him for a long, slow kiss. When they parted, she grabbed his wrists and pulled.

"Come," she said. "They have a tent for you. . . ."

The dawn light awoke Steve. He rolled over onto his side. The place that had been occupied by Aerilynn was empty. He rose and pulled on his trousers. He was going to have to get these washed.

She was outside, grazing on the grass near the tent. Steve shook his head—this was going to take some getting used to. The mare tossed her head and trotted over to him.

"Good morning," he said, laughing. "I see you've had breakfast."

Oats? whispered in his mind. Steve blinked in surprise. That had been Aerilynn's voice. She could communicate with him?

"Sure," Steve replied. "I'll get you some oats. I love you, Aerilynn."

Love master, too, the whisper replied in his mind.

"I'm not your master!" Steve objected. The mare backed away a pace, dropping her head.

Bad?

"What? No, you're not bad," Steve assured her, petting her nose. "Aerilynn, what's wrong?"

"Her mind is less complex in the beast form," Arven's voice said from behind him. "When she is a horse, you *are* her master. However, that does not mean it is not love that she feels for you. That is the way with animals, after all."

"Arven," Steve replied, "did you know . . . ?"

"That she could assume her Olvan form? No, I did not, but we all hoped that she could."

"She wants breakfast," Steve told the king.

"I'll see that the grooms bring her a bag of oats," Arven replied. "And some apples. After she has eaten, we must ride out to survey where you would have us place this trap."

Carry master? Aerilynn's voice whispered eagerly to him.

"Not right now," Steve said, turning to the mare. "You can have your oats, first." This was not going to be easy to get accustomed to.

Master nice to me. Love master. Not easy at all.

"Shall we also have breakfast?" Arven asked. "The grooms can tend to her. They know who she is."

"That sounds like a good idea," Steve agreed. "I *really* need to ask you some questions."

"Has he returned yet?" Erelvar asked, lifting the tent flap.

"No, my lord," Morfael replied. "He has not returned in the five minutes since you last asked."

"Five . . ."

". . . minutes," Morfael finished. "Yes, my lord. According to the glass, he has been gone from the camp for only a little over two hours. May I suggest that you get some sleep? I promise, I will have you awakened the *moment* he returns."

"Perhaps . . . I should . . . get some sleep."

"An excellent idea, my lord," Morfael concurred. "Good night."

"This should be the ideal location," Steve said. "The tank cannot fire on Bralmendel without coming past this ridge."

"It could climb the ridge . . . ," Arven began.

"I don't think so, Majesty," Steve replied. "It is too steep. They would come around."

"They could circle the other direction," Arven pointed out.

"Yes, they could," Steve agreed. "Although this is the best way for the tank to come. Still, you will have to be prepared to lure them this way."

"Perhaps the lore-masters could use their art to draw the Dragon this way," Arven suggested.

"I would use that only as a last resort, Arven," Steve replied.

"If there is a *kaiva* aboard, that will only serve to alert them that there is, in fact, a trap laid for them."

"True," Arven agreed.

"The main thing that is going to draw them to Bralmendel is your presence here," Steve said. "Your presence here should be too great a temptation for them to pass up."

"So," Arven said, smiling, "I have gone from being king to being the bait for a Dragon trap."

"That's no joking matter, Your Majesty," Steve said. "I hope you have a means of escape if things go badly here."

"I also know the ways of the forests, my friend," Arven replied. "But I shall not leave my men unless I have absolutely no other choice."

"I never thought you would, Majesty."

"Is there anything else about this pit you need to tell us?" Arven asked.

"No, I think we've covered all the details," Steve said. "I will have the Delvan Fire sent over first thing upon my return."

"There will be men and horses waiting to transport it," Arven assured him.

"Good," Steve replied. "Then I suppose I shall take my leave of you. Thank you, Arven. Thank you for everything." He was not simply referring to his reunion with Aerilynn. Arven's Olvan subjects had recovered Steve's belongings from the truck he'd abandoned on the plains. It felt good to have his shotgun back.

"My pleasure, Steven," Arven said. "When this is finished, you shall have to visit me in Mencar."

"I shall," Steve promised.

"And take good care of Aerilynn," Arven charged him. "She is a rare prize, indeed."

"She certainly is," Steve said, patting the side of his mount's neck.

Master leave now? Aerilynn asked.

Soon, Steve replied, silently. He had learned from Arven that he should not have to respond verbally, and that had turned out to be the case. That was good—it made him look less like a fruitcake.

"Farewell, Dreamer," Arven said. "Give Erelvar my regards

and my condolences for the loss of Quarin. And give my love to my niece, Glorien."

"I shall, Majesty," Steve replied. "Farewell." With that, he nudged Aerilynn, gently, in the ribs. She walked from the trail into the forest, leaving Arven and Bralmendel behind.

As the forest closed in around them, the sky began to darken. As Steve watched, the sun slowly but visibly moved from west to east across the sky to set in Umbria. Weird . . .

Where does master want to go? Aerilynn asked.

The Umbrian forest east of Quarin, Steve replied. He pictured Erelvar's camp from memory and tried to send the image to her. He wasn't certain if he was successful, but she suddenly turned down a side trail that was thickly overgrown with brush.

The ride back was very much like his trip here with Nolrod. Aerilynn chose the trails, not he. Steve simply allowed himself to be carried, trusting the animal beneath him to find the way. Although the trails she chose were thickly overgrown, the branches and limbs never struck them. Steve had never ridden such a surefooted steed.

Soon they emerged from the trails into a clearing. Steve looked around—they had emerged in almost the very spot where he had first spoken with Nolrod. He smiled. This was going to be handy.

He dismounted and began to lead Aerilynn toward his tent. All he had to do was get alone with her and she could become Aerilynn again.

"Steven!" a voice called. Damn! He had hoped to make it back to his tent before anyone could see him.

Steve looked over to see Morfael hurrying toward him. Aerilynn nickered irritably. Steve was forced to agree with her. Still, what could he say? *Excuse me, Morfael, but I would like to be alone with my horse?* Not likely.

"Erelvar is waiting . . . for . . ." Morfael's words trailed off as he looked at Steven's horse.

"Where did you . . . ?" he began, and then stopped, signing himself.

"By the *Kanir*!" he exclaimed. "A Spirit horse! Aerilynn?"

Friend! Aerilynn's voice exclaimed happily in Steve's mind as she recognized Morfael.

"Yes," Steve replied. "It is Aerilynn, Morfael."

"Can she . . . change?" Morfael asked.

"Yes, but only at night, when we are alone," Steve said, petting Aerilynn's nose.

"Erelvar wants to see you," Morfael said. "But it can wait until morning."

"Thank you, Morfael."

"Good night, Steven," Morfael said. "Good night . . . Lady Aerilynn."

"He's with *who*?" Erelvar said.

"The Lady Aerilynn," Morfael replied. "She has returned as a Spirit Animal. A horse, in fact."

"Morfael," Glorien asked, "are you *certain*?"

"I knew it was she as soon as I looked in her eyes, my lady," Morfael assured her. "It *is* the Lady Aerilynn."

"And she can become herself?" Erelvar asked.

"Yes, but only alone with Steven and only at night, apparently."

"I want to see her," Glorien said.

"My lady, you cannot," Morfael told her. "She is in Steven's tent. If anyone enters she will become a horse again. Depending on what's happening that could be . . . embarrassing."

"Well, then, I can at least *speak* to her," Glorien replied. "I am going to Steven's tent. If she is within, I will speak with her from outside."

"My lady . . . ," Morfael began.

"I will *not* be denied this!" Glorien shouted. "I love her no less than Steven does. Stand aside, Morfael!"

"Yes, my lady," Morfael replied, stepping aside from in front of the tent's entrance as Glorien left.

"She is a headstrong woman," Erelvar said.

"Well, my lord," Morfael noted, smiling, "she has to be. After all, she is wed to you."

Steven inhaled the scent of Aerilynn's hair, deeply.

"I've missed you for so long," he told her.

"And I, you," she replied. "But I have seen you twice since our parting."

"Once in the forest," Steve said.

"And once in your dreams," Aerilynn told him.

"I don't ever want to lose you again," Steve said.

"Never, my love," she assured him. "Even death, yours and mine, has not kept us apart for long."

Steve was about to pull her face to his for a kiss when a voice called from outside the tent.

"Aerilynn?" Glorien called. Aerilynn gasped and Steve sat bolt upright. If she entered the tent . . . ! Never mind that they were both nude, Aerilynn would become a horse again.

"My lady!" Steve called. "Please, do not enter the tent!"

"Steven," Glorien replied, her voice wavering, "I know that I may not see her, but may I please speak with her? Please?"

"I am here, my lady," Aerilynn called. Then, in a whisper, "Steven, get dressed." Steve pulled on a fresh pair of trousers and a fresh tunic while Aerilynn wrapped herself in his blanket.

"It *is* you!" Glorien said. "Aerilynn, I've missed you so."

"You may enter, Lady Glorien," Aerilynn called.

"Aerilynn!" Steve whispered.

"Hush, Steven," Aerilynn told him. "I will stay in this form. The Lady Glorien is my mistress as you . . . are my master."

The flap to the tent opened and Glorien gingerly looked inside. Her eyes widened when she saw Aerilynn, and the tears that had been held back were released.

"Oh, Aerilynn!" Glorien cried, sitting down to embrace her former sword maiden.

Steve fidgeted a little while the two ladies embraced. Finally, he stood up.

"I'll leave you two alone for a moment," he began. Glorien rose and turned to face him.

"I shall not keep your lady from you for long, Steven," she said. Then she embraced him as well. "Thank you," she said. "Thank you for giving me this time with her."

"I have not forgotten how you shared your grief with me when we lost her, my lady," Steve replied. "I will never stand between you."

"Thank you," Glorien said again.

Steve stepped from the tent and closed the flap. Oh, well, this would probably be a good time to go see Erelvar. . . .

Chapter
-------- Nine ------------

FOR THE FIRST time in not quite a year—six years Quarin time—Steve fastened the straps on the Delvan plate that had been made for him. He was surprised at how well it fit. Apparently, he had regained more of his former muscle mass than he had realized. He had also forgotten how heavy the stuff was. He was wearing at least fifty pounds of steel.

Steve settled the Templar mantle over his shoulders, gathered up his helmet and stepped out of the tent. The grooms had almost finished outfitting Aerilynn in her new barding. The armor consisted of plate to protect her forequarters, with a mail skirt to protect her legs and hindquarters. Steve wondered whose horse was going without armor for this.

Heavy, Aerilynn's voice complained in his mind.

Safe, Steve admonished, although he certainly sympathized with her right now. He walked around her, testing the straps. She was unshod, but that was intentional. It would not do to have her change back into her Olvan form with horseshoe nails driven into her hands and feet. Glorien assured him that Aerilynn's . . . special nature would probably protect her hooves.

"Good morrow, Steven," a familiar voice called behind him.

"Morning, Arthwyr," Steve replied. Arthwyr was leading his own mount behind him.

"What a beautiful horse!" Arthwyr exclaimed, when he saw Aerilynn. "I have never seen a horse with eyes of that color before."

"She's . . . a gift from the Olvir," Steve told him. Arthwyr reached out to touch her nose and Aerilynn snapped at him. Only the Umbrian's quick reflexes saved him from being bitten.

Not friend! Aerilynn's voice said silently, but angrily.

"Be nice!" Steve ordered. Aerilynn's head and ears dropped at the admonishment.

"Spirited," Arthwyr observed. "A fine animal. I take it she does not bite at you, like that."

Only when I ask her to, Steve thought.

"No," he replied. "She's . . . nervous with non-Olvir, however."

"Obviously," Arthwyr agreed. "Are you ready to ride?"

"Yes. Do you know if the Delvan Fire has been sent to Olvanor yet?" Last night, Erelvar had agreed to send half the Delvan Fire to Theron's ships at dawn for transport across the Bitterwine. Steve wanted to be certain it got there in time. . . .

"Yes," Arthwyr replied. "I saw the wagons depart a few hours ago."

"Good," Steve said, placing his foot in the stirrup and lifting himself into the saddle. The armor made it more difficult; he was out of practice. Arthwyr mounted easily beside him.

Master heavy today, Aerilynn said.

Are you all right? Steve asked her.

Yes, Aerilynn replied. *Not too heavy.*

"Then let's ride to Aberstwyth," Steve said, both to Aerilynn and Arthwyr.

Lord Phelandor rode onto the surface of the bluff overlooking the remains of the city. By tomorrow evening the bridge to the Olvan quarter would be complete. This would not be the first time Phelandor had returned to Olvanor since his selection as one of the Twelve, but it would be the most satisfying.

Of all the things that Phelandor had lost since that selection, the one he missed the least was his sense of the Land. When he returned to Olvanor now, he could no longer feel the Land itself crying in rage at his presence.

Phelandor's anger still roiled at that memory. Rejected, and for what? For no other reason than he had dared to listen to a red-haired, green-eyed woman's promises of power and had dared to lie with her under a summer sky.

He had not known then that his newfound lover was the Dark One, although it would have made little difference if he had. *That* decision was not one of his regrets. Her promises of power had been genuine, beyond his wildest imaginings. And his life as her lover, until his body had died and that interest had died as well, was also beyond imagining.

It was no wonder that Jared wanted the Dreamer's life. They all did, with the possible exception of Heregurth. The junior Lord and Belevairn had never known the Mistress as lovers. All of the others, during their mortal lives, had been. Still, Jared was the one with the greatest right to vengeance. Only Daemor, if he still lived, would have possessed a greater claim.

However, Phelandor's vengeance would begin the morning after tomorrow. He would venture into Olvanor at the head of the most powerful force the Mistress had ever assembled. Then the land would *pay* for its rejection of him. . . .

"Aberstwyth," Erelvar said disgustedly. "And we still have not found a site suitable for our trap."

"The terrain just isn't rugged enough," Steve complained. "They could come at this town from any direction they wanted." Town was a loose description of Aberstwyth. All that was left of the once-proud city were the remains of a wall and a few dozen burned-out stone buildings. The refugees from Quarin packed the ruins to overflowing. When the Morvir reached this place it would be a massacre. . . .

"The refugees can't stay here," Steve said.

"There is nowhere else for them to go," Morfael objected.

"What about the old Taran holdings?" Steve asked. Clan Taran had been destroyed and driven from their territory in the war six years before.

"Those are on the plains," Erelvar said. "No defense at all."

"Maybe not, but the Dragon isn't coming that way," Steve pointed out.

"We did not run across any Morvir on our way down the river," Tsadhoq added. "They probably have no reason to secure the plains any more than they already have."

Erelvar thought for a moment.

"If we evacuate the refugees," he said, "can we set up our trap here?"

"No," Steve replied. "I already said, they can approach this town from any direction they choose. We have to press further in."

"But we have no idea where they will be going," Arthwyr objected. "They could go anywhere from here. South into clan Owein's lands; east, farther into Aldwyn territory—anywhere!"

"They will go to Castle Aldwyn," Steve said.

"How do you know?" Theron asked.

"Blitzkrieg," Steve replied. "Castle Aldwyn is the center of command for this territory. They will go there and destroy it. From there they will probably proceed to Castle Owein and destroy any fortifications along their route there."

"Blitzkrieg?"

"Lightning warfare," Steve replied. "You go for as much destruction along the deepest line of penetration you can. Everything you pass, you destroy—everyone you encounter, you kill. Ordinarily, follow-up troops move in behind the shock wave and occupy the territory that the blitz has cleared. Back in my world, a country named Germany conquered about as much land as the Northern Kingdoms occupy in a matter of days in this manner."

"And they won?" Morfael asked.

"No," Steve replied, smiling. "My country went in and kicked them back out of it. It took us a while, though."

"So your country conquered that land?" Morfael said.

"No, we gave it back to the people who lived there," Steve said. "They were our allies."

"This is all very interesting," Tsadhoq said, in a tone that indicated that he was not at all interested, "but we must find a place to set our trap. Let us travel on toward Castle Aldwyn."

"First," Steve said, "we have to get these people out of here and headed for clan Taran's old lands."

"We had best get started, then," Erelvar said. "I, Morfael and Arthwyr will each take a flank of *regir* and get the refugees moving. Theron—you and Tsadhoq march the army south, around Aberstwyth and continue toward Castle Aldwyn. If Steven finds a suitable ambush site along the way, stop and begin preparing it. We shall meet you in camp tonight."

"I stay with Steven," Arthwyr informed them. Steve turned to face him, surprised at his friend's defiant tone.

"You are Umbrian," Erelvar objected. "The people here will listen to you. Your help is needed here."

"I came to fight beside Steven," Arthwyr insisted. "I have

sworn an oath in the name of Uldon to aid him until this is finished."

"You did?" Steve asked.

"Yes," Arthwyr replied.

"Then you are his *felga*," Erelvar said.

"His sworn man," Arthwyr agreed. "Yes."

"Arthwyr," Steve said, "I . . . don't know what to say."

"You need say nothing, my lord," Arthwyr replied.

"But . . . these people need our help," Steve said.

"Do *you* wish me to stay and help Lord Erelvar organize the refugees, Steven?"

"I do," Steve replied.

"Very well," Arthwyr agreed.

"Thank you, Arthwyr," Steve said. "We'll . . . talk more later."

Jared sat down heavily in his chair at the head of the council table. Although his body was no longer capable of fatigue, he was mentally exhausted. He had spent the entire night attempting to master the first exercise of Power, as described in the *kaivir*'s library. He had met with little, if any, success.

The High Lord sighed. It was becoming increasingly obvious that the books themselves would not be enough to teach the *kaivir*'s art. A master was needed to guide the student in those areas that could not be set to paper.

There was only one apparent solution. Many of the lower-ranking *kaivir* had escaped the massacre at the Academy by the simple expedient of not having arrived before the attack. Up until now, all that were subsequently captured had been killed. Jared would have to order that ten be spared that fate. The rulers of Morvanor needed teachers.

The only problem would be convincing even the junior *kaivir* to cooperate. Actually, that should not be much of a problem. Refuse and be executed or teach and then be set free in the Coasts with a sizable quantity of gold.

Thinking of the Coasts reminded him that it was getting close to afternoon. It would soon be time for Jared's second audience with that pig Morgaine. With a sigh, Jared rose from his seat. Life had been so much simpler when the Mistress had led them. . . .

*   *   *

"The Dragon will have to come this way to get to Castle Aldwyn," Theron said. "Can we set the trap here?"

Steve stood in the stirrups and surveyed the terrain. They were still over a day's travel by horseback from Castle Aldwyn. Still, it appeared that Theron was correct. The road passed between two hills here. The far slopes of those hills were earthen cliffs, far too steep for the tank to negotiate.

Past those hills, the road wound south around another hill. Its near face was another earthen cliff, too steep for vehicles. The only problem was, if the army took position atop the far hill, the tank could climb one of the other hills to assault them, rather than sticking to the road.

They might not, though. The Morvir would have little reason to be cautious. After all, what could the Veran Guard and the Delvan Royal Guard do to the tank? The Morvir would probably just roll up to the hill and assault it from the road rather than negotiate their way up, and then back down, one of the other hills.

"I don't think we'll find a better site," Steve grudgingly admitted.

"So," Tsadhoq asked, "where do we dig?"

"Right between the two hills," Steve replied.

"Ten cubits wide, fifteen cubits long, fifteen cubits deep?" Tsadhoq asked.

"Uh . . . yeah," Steve replied, mentally converting Tsadhoq's figures into feet. That was roughly the fifteen by twenty by twenty that Steve had said would be necessary in council last night.

"And four *regir* need to be able to ride across the cover without falling in," Steve added. "Five should make it groan." That way one of the trucks wouldn't trigger their trap. Only the tank would be heavy enough to break through.

"That could be difficult," Tsadhoq said. "We can do it, but it will take some time."

"We also need to be able to remove the cover and put it back with just a few hours' notice," Steve added.

"Aye," Tsadhoq agreed. "So that we can place the Delvan Fire in the barrels. We had best get started. The sooner we get the trap laid, the sooner we can start fortifying that hilltop."

*   *   *

Arthwyr ap Madawc rode silently at the head of his knights. It had taken most of the afternoon to get the refugees organized and moving out of Aberstwyth. It would have taken longer, but telling them that the Dragon would be there in the next few days had made them move quickly.

They had left Aberstwyth several hours before and the sun had set shortly afterwards. Only the knowledge that an already-prepared camp would be waiting for them kept Arthwyr and his men moving. Dealing with the refugees had been exhausting work.

Still, it was a good thing that Steven had asked Arthwyr to help. As Erelvar had suspected, the Umbrians heeded Arthwyr's words over his own, even though many of these people had lived in Quarin for years.

It was also good that Steven had remembered clan Taran's holdings north of the river. The refugees would be safe there for a time. If Steven's plan to destroy the Dragon did not succeed it would not matter—no one would be safe anywhere.

Arthwyr had seen neither the Dragon nor the destruction it had wreaked, but Morfael had described both to him in detail. The fortress at Quarin had been reduced to rubble in less than half a day. The northeast and southwest quarters of the city had been destroyed from across the rivers. Arthwyr did not see how even Delvan Fire could destroy such a thing.

Steven seemed confident that it could, though. Still, it seemed to Arthwyr as though they were placing a great deal of hope on one trap. If *anything* went wrong the Dragon would roll over the legion and the Delvir as though they were not even there.

"Crossbows and knives in the dark," Arthwyr muttered.

"What was that, Arthwyr?" Erelvar asked.

"Your pardon, my lord," Arthwyr said. "I was thinking aloud."

"If it bears on our battle I would like to hear it," Erelvar said.

"If this trap fails, or even if it doesn't, I was thinking that the only way we can fight the Morvir is with crossbows from ambush and knives in the dark," Arthwyr explained.

"I agree," Erelvar said. "And your Umbrians will be the best able to carry out such a campaign."

"It would not be the first time, my lord," Arthwyr replied. Six years before, he and two hundred others had stalked a Morvan army of twelve thousand strong all the way to Castle Aldwyn. Only twenty of Arthwyr's countrymen had survived to reach Castle Aldwyn, but the Morvir and the goblins had lost ten times as many men as well as two catapults and all their supplies of oil. The same tactics could work here.

"Your force will not be part of the lure," Erelvar said. "You and Steven will be in hiding. If we fail to destroy the Dragon, your job will be to resort to crossbows and knives, as you say.

"Morfael," Erelvar added, "I want you and any other Olvir among the *regir* in that reserve force as well."

"Yes, my lord," Morfael replied.

"If we fail," Erelvar said, "you will be under Steven's command."

"We shall not fail, my lord," Morfael said.

"That may be . . . ," Erelvar began.

"Who goes there!" an unseen sentry shouted.

Arthwyr breathed a sigh of relief. They had finally reached the camp.

The stir of movement awakened Steve. He rolled over to see Aerilynn moving toward the tent flap. Only her hair covered her.

"Aerilynn?" he said. She turned at the sound of his voice, her silver hair sliding across the smooth curve of her hip.

"It is almost dawn," she said, smiling sadly. Steve climbed from the bedclothes, stepping toward her. She stepped into his embrace.

"I wish that you could stay . . . ," Steve began. Aerilynn placed her finger across his lips.

"Be grateful that we can be together at all, Steven," she admonished him gently. "Not many loves survive two deaths." Steve smiled and brushed a tear from the corner of her eye.

"Although I wish it, too," she admitted. Then she pressed her mouth against his for a hurried kiss.

"I *must* go," she said, pulling away from his embrace to step from the tent.

Steve watched from the tent as the first rays of dawn caressed her. She almost seemed to dissolve into the morning fog as her snow white hair swirled about her body. Soon, where Aerilynn had stood, there was a powerful white horse, with turquoise eyes.

He stepped from the tent, heedless of his own state of undress, and pulled the horse's head to him in an embrace.

"Until tonight, Aerilynn," he whispered.

Oats? Aerilynn's voice whispered in his mind. Steve laughed.

"Soon," he told her. "When the rest of the camp wakes up." With a final caress to her nose, Steve turned and stepped back into the tent.

It did not take him long to dress. Steve threw the tent flap back and stepped out into the early-morning light. He looked around for Aerilynn. She was nearby, grazing on the damp grass. She looked up and nickered at him and then went back to grazing.

"I'll get you your oats," he promised, smiling. Steve walked into the camp, in search of both the grooms and his own breakfast. He spared a glance toward the road below.

The Delvir had already excavated about half of the pit. Men were already back in the pit this morning excavating the bedrock beneath the road with picks, while others were dismantling three of the wagons to fashion a cover for it. Once they packed about six inches of dirt back on top of the decking, no one would be able to tell the pit from the rest of the road.

Steve watched for a moment. He hoped this trick worked. If it didn't, nothing would stop the Morvir from destroying everything in either Umbria or Olvanor—or both.

"All of our hopes rest on a hole in the ground," a voice said behind him. Steve turned to see Theron standing just behind him.

"Good morning, Theron," Steve said.

"That rock is going to slow them down," Steve observed. Theron smiled.

"Yes," he agreed. "They've only gained about a foot since dawn. At this rate they won't be finished until almost noon. Thank Lindra the Delvir came to our aid."

"You can say that again," Steve said. "Especially since they brought the naphtha with them."

"Naphtha?" Theron asked. "Ah, you mean the Delvan Fire. So, your people know about that, too?"

"Oh, sure," Steve replied. "My mother uses it to clean stains from clothing." Theron shook his head.

"Just when I think that nothing else you say will ever surprise me again, you prove me wrong," he observed. "Delvan Fire is the most potent weapon in the Delvan arsenal and your mother uses it on her laundry."

"Hey," Steve said, "you should try it sometime. Nothing gets tough stains out like naphtha. Just don't strike a spark while you're using it."

"Indeed not," Theron agreed.

"I wonder how the trap in Olvanor is coming along," Steve said.

"Fairly well, I should imagine," Theron said. "The Olvir are accustomed to trapping large game in pits."

"What?" Steve said. "What game do they have to trap in pits?"

"Oh, boars, buffalo, stags," Theron replied, "the odd legionnaire or two. There are usually spikes in the bottom for the latter."

"Are you at war with Olvanor?" Steve asked, horrified.

"What? Oh! No—that was centuries ago, when the Empire attempted to invade Olvanor."

"Oh, good," Steve replied, relieved.

"No, the Regency has attempted to win the trust of our Olvan neighbors ever since we split from the Empire," Theron added. "We have not had much success; the Olvir have long memories."

"That they do," Steve agreed. Of course, it helped that, if they remained in their own lands, an Olvan could hope to live for a couple of centuries. Over the millennia, the lore-masters had imbued the land with such Power that any native Olvan who resided in Olvanor aged *very* slowly.

"Have you eaten?" Theron asked. His question reminded Steve that he had started out in search of breakfast for himself and Aerilynn.

"No," he replied. "But I have to get Aerilynn some oats before I eat."

"Does Aerilynn . . . like oats?" Theron asked. Steve laughed.

"When she's a horse she loves them," he replied. "And she likes apples even better."

"How can she tolerate it?"

"When she's a horse she . . . thinks like a horse," Steve explained.

"I . . . see," Theron said. "Well, let us find Aerilynn some oats and then we shall breakfast together."

"Sounds good to me," Steve agreed.

Jared led Hilarin and Heregurth from the Gray Plain onto the bluff at Quarin. There was time, before their third meeting with King Morgaine, to inspect the progress at Quarin.

The twin spans of the causeway between Olvanor and the bluff had almost met. By Jared's estimate, Phelandor should be able to move his force into the Olvan quarter before sunset tonight. Very good.

"May I be of service, Dread Lords?" one the sentries atop the bluff asked as he approached them.

"Where are Lords Phelandor and Kephas?" Jared asked.

"They are with Lord Hhayim and Lord Selwyn in the northeastern quarter," the soldier replied.

"So the *regir* have arrived, then," Hilarin observed.

"Yes, Dread Lord," the sentry confirmed. "The lords are overseeing the distribution of the forces throughout the city."

"Have there been any more . . . problems since the Umbrian quarter was taken?" Jared asked.

"No, Dread Lord," the soldier replied, smiling. "The populace is quite . . . cowed, and the traitor has fled into Umbria."

"Thank you," Jared said. "You may return to your duties."

"Yes, Dread Lord," the sentry said, saluting before departing their presence.

"Shall we find the others?" Hilarin asked, once the sentry had left.

"No," Jared replied. "We must continue on to El-Adrid. Things are proceeding well enough here without us."

Steve walked toward the section of the camp where the Umbrian knights were quartered. It was past time for the talk he had promised Arthwyr last night.

He found Arthwyr talking with some of the knights under his command. Steve walked up behind him, intending to wait. The other knights fell silent as he approached and Arthwyr turned to face him.

"We shall talk later," Arthwyr said to the knight he had been speaking with. The man nodded to his lord and he and the other knights left.

"If I'm interrupting something, I can come back later," Steve said.

"No," Arthwyr replied. "My men are not happy with me for dragging them out here away from our own lands to defend clan Aldwyn from the Dragon. Especially since, from their viewpoint, the Aldwyns themselves are not here to do so."

"Lord Aldwyn is preparing to defend the castle . . . ," Steve began. Arthwyr held up his hand, stopping Steve's explanation.

"I am aware of that," Arthwyr said. "And, in fact, was just speaking your very words to my men. I shall deal with them. What did you wish to speak with me about?"

"I wanted to talk with you about this oath business," Steve replied. "You caught me kind of flat-footed with it yesterday."

"What of it?" Arthwyr asked. "I have sworn an oath to follow you and serve you until the Dragon is defeated."

"Why?" Steve asked. Arthwyr turned away, looking out across the hills. After a moment he drew a dagger from his belt.

"Do you recognize this, Steven?" Arthwyr asked, holding the dagger flat on his palm. Steve examined the weapon.

"Yes," he replied. "This is the dagger you helped me buy six years ago. The one I gave you when we parted at Quarin. I still have yours, as well."

"That is why," Arthwyr said.

"What? I . . . don't understand."

"We swore brotherhood then," Arthwyr explained. "Yet I allowed my duty to Umbria and to my clan to part us. As a result, the Lady Aerilynn was lost in battle and you were lost to a Morvan ambush a few months later." Arthwyr turned to face Steve. His eyes held an expression of determined anger.

"Now my brother has been returned to me," Arthwyr continued. "I will *not* fail you again. I will not abandon your cause because some old fools are too provincial to step outside their own lands to aid the greater whole."

"Even if it costs you your holdings?" Steve asked. "Perhaps even your clan?"

"No matter the cost," Arthwyr agreed. "Honor demands no less of me." It was Steve's turn to look away. After a moment he looked back at his friend—his brother.

"Thank you, Arthwyr," he said. "I pray that I live up to your trust in me."

Phelandor watched as the eight trucks rolled across the bridge into the Olvan quarter. He smiled. If the bridge could support the weight of eight trucks it could easily support the weight of the Dragon.

Still, it was best to be safe. The inspection crews followed behind the trucks, searching for signs of stress in the bridge's structure. The tank would not be sent across until their inspection was complete. From his vantage atop the southwest gatehouse Phelandor saw one of the crews mark a section of the bridge. Not a good sign . . .

No other sections had been marked by the time the crews finished their inspection. Phelandor awaited their report.

"Dread Lord," Captain Koreth reported, "the inspection crews report that the bridge is safe for the tank to cross."

"Send it across, Captain," Phelandor replied. Phelandor watched as Koreth relayed his orders to the tank crew. The field radios were fascinating devices. Koreth's little hand radio was powerful enough to allow him to converse with the tank crew several miles away.

The Dragon started across the bridge. Phelandor watched apprehensively as the tank approached the marked area. It passed without incident and soon the tank was safely in the Olvan quarter. The inspection crews followed behind, checking the bridge once again. Phelandor noticed that they spent more time than before at the marked section.

"Ask them what is wrong with that section they are inspecting," Phelandor ordered. Koreth spoke over the radio for a few minutes.

"The crews are simply being cautious, Dread Lord," Koreth informed him. "They found a cracked timber there earlier and are making certain that it has not grown any larger with the tank's passage."

"Has it?"

"No, Dread Lord."

"Good, send the ammunition transport across."

"Yes, Dread Lord."

Phelandor smiled. Tomorrow at dawn his campaign into Olvanor would begin. In a few days, Mencar would be little more than a pile of rubble.

Chapter
######### Ten ------------

"I FEEL LIKE a child being punished for spilling milk on the table," Erelvar grumbled. Steve tried hard not to snicker at the mental image that comment invoked.

"You must not turn around, dearest," Glorien said. "Otherwise, Aerilynn will become a horse again and there will be all manner of commotion."

At Aerilynn's suggestion, Steve had conveyed an invitation to Erelvar and the Lady Glorien to have dinner in Steve's tent. In the close confines of the camp, having only the Lady Glorien to his tent would have started more rumors than either Steve or Erelvar cared to deal with. However, that meant, for Aerilynn to be present, Erelvar had to eat his dinner facing away from the rest of them.

"I am aware of that," Erelvar said.

"Has the trap for the Dragon been finished yet, my lord?" Aerilynn asked, changing the subject.

"Nearly so," Erelvar replied. "Once the wooden cover is finished and tested, all that will remain is placing the Delvan Fire in the pit."

"Will the Delvan Fire actually destroy this horrible thing, Steven?" Aerilynn asked.

"Sixty gallons of naphtha?" Steve asked in reply. "Are you kidding? It'll be a barbecue."

"Let us hope you are correct, Steven," Glorien said. "Otherwise, nothing will save the Northern Kingdoms."

"Actually, the tank will run out of fuel and ammunition eventually," Steve assured her. "The Morvir have a large enough supply of both that they could practically destroy all of Umbria before that happens, though."

"Could we destroy those supplies?" Erelvar asked.

118

"I'm sure we could destroy the trucks easily enough," Steve replied. "A single gallon of naphtha, or even normal lamp oil, should be enough to destroy a truck. But the ammunition is being carried in the other armored vehicle. It would be no easier to destroy that than the Dragon."

"So we might as well destroy the Dragon," Erelvar concluded.

"Exactly," Steve agreed.

Dinner continued for another hour before Erelvar and Glorien decided to leave. Steve stepped outside with them, closing the tent flap behind him.

"Okay," Steve said. "We're safe." Erelvar turned around.

"Hello, Steven," he said sarcastically. " 'Tis nice to *see* you again."

"Sorry," Steve apologized. "But it's the only way for Aerilynn to join us. . . ."

"I know," Erelvar said, his tone softening. He placed a hand on Steve's shoulder.

"I am truly happy for you, my friend," he said. "Surely, Mortos has smiled on you to have Aerilynn returned to you in any manner."

"Yes," Glorien agreed. "And I believe we should now return to our own tent and let them have their time together, my lord."

"Agreed," Erelvar replied. "Good night, Steven."

"Good night, my lord, my lady."

As soon as Erelvar and Glorien turned to leave, Steve opened the flap and stepped back into his tent. Aerilynn smiled at him from the bedroll. Steve walked over and sat down beside her.

"Ready to go to sleep?" he asked, smiling. A delightfully wicked look crossed Aerilynn's face.

"You can sleep *later,* my lord," she said, placing her arms around him and pulling him to her.

The morning light finally woke Steven. He rolled over and ran his hand over the place where Aerilynn had lain the night before. He wished . . .

Be thankful for what you do *have,* he chided himself.

With a sigh, he rose from the bedroll and dressed. He had managed to acquire a few more of the white linen tunics and trousers. If he was a Templar now, he might as well dress the part. He settled the mantle over his shoulders and stepped outside.

The Delvir were just laying the cover over the pit when Steve walked to the edge of the hilltop to watch. Steve watched as, one by one, men walked out onto the cover. Eventually, twenty Delvir stood atop the pit. The cover held.

Excellent. Now, once the tank was confirmed to be in Umbria, the Delvir could pour the naphtha into the barrels at the bottom of the pit and bury the cover to make it look like the rest of the road.

Steve hoped that the preparations for the trap in Olvanor were going as well. Theron was certain that the Olvir would have no trouble preparing the pit, but Steve would feel better if he could check it out for himself.

He blinked as an unexpected idea occurred to him. Steve *could* check it out for himself. What had Arven said? Aerilynn would not tire and neither would Steve so long as he rode her. If that were true, then at full gallop he should be able to reach the forest outside Quarin by mid-morning. From there, he could be in Bralmendel in a few minutes.

"A rider approaches!" Steve heard the sentries call. Sure enough, a lone horseman soon appeared on the road between the hills. Steve pulled the binoculars from his pack. The man rode bareback, in the Olvan fashion.

The rider stopped as the sentries hailed him. There were a few moments of conversation and he continued on. Why had the Olvir sent a messenger?

Steve put the binoculars away. There was only *one* way to find the answer to that question.

"How long ago did the Dragon venture into Olvanor?" Erelvar asked.

"Last night," Morandil the messenger replied. "The Dragon crossed the bridge into the Olvan quarter last night. I was sent immediately and have ridden all night to get here."

Steve listened intently. The messenger's report had not been good. The bridge into the Olvan quarter had been finished yesterday, as estimated. Also, yesterday, five thousand Morvan cavalry had arrived at Quarin. *That* information was distress-

g; Steve had expected many more regular Morvan troops than
hat.

"Then the Dragon has not actually ventured into Olvanor,"
heron said. "It is only in the Olvan quarter of Quarin."

"When I left, no," the messenger confirmed. "However, it
as surely done so by now."

"I am not certain," Theron said to Erelvar. "The Morvir
ould still bring it into Umbria. They may have only moved it
o the Olvan quarter until the bridge into Umbria is prepared."

"No," Steve said. "They've got a lot more than eight trucks.
his looks more like they're splitting their force. The tank and
he ammunition transport are going into Olvanor along with
ight trucks. The remaining trucks, fifteen or so, will be
oming into Umbria. It makes sense."

"But Umbria has more promising targets for the Dragon,"
heron insisted. "There is very little in Olvanor for the Dragon
o attack."

"There is Mencar!" the messenger replied.

"That's not the point," Steve said.

"What is the point?" Erelvar asked.

"The Morvan infantry cannot make progress in Olvanor,"
Steve explained. "The Olvan hit-and-run tactics are perfect
against them. The Morvan infantry would suffer about equal
casualties with the Olvir.

"The tank, however, is another matter," Steve continued.
"The Olvan archers can do *nothing* to it. It can clear the
erritory ahead of the infantry, guaranteeing them safe passage.
Umbria, on the other hand, does not have the amount of cover
hat Olvanor has. Morvan infantry should do quite well here."

"So they destroy Bralmendel and Mencar," Theron said.
"While these would be tragic losses, to be certain, it will not
allow the Morvir to take Olvanor."

"I don't think they want to," Steve argued.

"Then why venture into Olvanor at all?" Theron shouted.

"This is not a war of conquest, Theron," Steve replied. "It is
a war of destruction. The Dread Lords' goal is not to conquer
he Northern Kingdoms. Not at this time, anyway. They want to
do as much damage as possible and pull out."

"Forgive me, Dreamer," Theron said, "but I would like to
know why you believe that."

"Because only five thousand Morvan cavalry arrived at Quarin yesterday."

"*Only* five thousand," Theron echoed.

"Yes," Steve replied angrily. "Only five thousand. Arthwyr would five thousand Morvir be able to hold the Aldwyns territory?"

"For a few days, perhaps," Arthwyr replied.

"And I think we all have a good idea of how well they would fare in Olvanor," Steve continued. "The Morvir sent in just enough strength to hold Quarin and maintain order. They have no intention of occupying the territory they invade."

"But . . . why?" Theron asked.

"Theron, what is the political situation in Morvanor?"

Theron began to answer and stopped.

"Right," Steve said. "Nobody knows! With the Mistress gone, for all we know, the Dread Lords are fighting it out for control. In any event, they will need time to get back on their feet. *That* is what this war is about now."

"If they do enough damage to Umbria, the Umbrians cannot attack them . . . ," Theron concluded.

"Precisely!" Steve agreed.

"But that makes it even *more* likely that they would send the Dragon into Umbria," Theron objected. "Olvanor would have no interest in leaving their land to attack Morvanor."

"The tank isn't being sent to Olvanor," Steve said.

"But you were just saying . . . ," Theron began.

"It is being sent to Validus," Steve interrupted. Theron fell silent.

"If the Morvir can do enough damage to the Regency, the Empire will come in and finish the job for them," Erelvar said.

"Exactly," Steve replied. "Oh, you can bet that the Morvir will destroy Bralmendel and Mencar on their way through. But that tank's *real* goal is Validus."

"And the Empire would not stop at the Regency," the Olvan messenger noted. "They would press on into Olvanor."

"Especially with the swath that the Morvir are going to be cutting through the Olvan forest," Steve added.

"I must return to Validus," Theron said, finding his voice again.

"Yes," Steve agreed. "You probably should. If you left today, you could probably make it back just ahead of the Morvir. Assuming we don't destroy the tank in Olvanor, that is."

"Excuse me," Theron said, rising from the table. "I must go and make preparations."

"Well," Erelvar said, once Theron had left, "I suppose the question now is what do *we* do?"

"I am riding to Olvanor," Steve replied. "Riding Aerilynn, I can make it to Bralmendel far ahead of that tank."

"Aerilynn?" Arthur asked. "You named your horse after the Lady Aerilynn?"

"Uh . . . well, not exactly . . . ," Steve began. Arthwyr's eyes grew wide.

"By Uldon's salty piss!" Arthwyr exclaimed. "The damned horse *is* Aerilynn! I *knew* that I had never seen a horse with turquoise eyes before!"

"We have more important things to discuss than Steven's horse," Erelvar interrupted.

"My apologies," Arthwyr replied. "I was . . . surprised."

"As I was saying," Steven began, "I can make it to Bralmendel ahead of the tank. I want to take some more of the Delvan Fire with me."

"How much?" Erelvar asked.

"At least a gallon per truck," Steve explained. "Maybe more. If we can burn their supplies, the Morvan weapons will stop working very shortly afterwards."

"Then we should do the same once they enter Umbria," Erelvar noted.

"Yes," Steve agreed. "It will be harder to do in Umbria, but if you can, the war will essentially be over."

"How many men do you want to take with you?" Erelvar asked.

"None," Steve replied. "They won't be able to follow me through the forest. Morandil here can accompany me back to Olvanor."

"I would be honored, Dreamer," Morandil replied.

"I ride with you," Arthwyr said.

"Arthwyr, you won't be able to follow me," Steve objected.

"You followed Nolrod to Bralmendel," Arthwyr replied. "I will stay close behind you once we enter the forest."

"If you lose sight of me even once, God only knows where you'll wind up," Steve argued.

"I shall take that chance," Arthwyr said.

"I shall ride behind him," Morandil offered. "There will be less chance of him losing the trail that way."

"Thank you," Steve said. "Erelvar, please have the Delvir load five gallons of the Delvan Fire onto each of our horses."

"Yes, and we shall prepare an ambush for the Morvan supply train," Erelvar said.

Steve nodded. Things were looking up. In a few days the Morvir would be deprived of all their modern weaponry. Then things would be back on an even footing.

A burst of gunfire sounded from farther back in the column. Phelandor cursed. Damn the Olvir—they had slowed his progress to a crawl once the Morvir had entered the forest. At this rate, half his force would be wounded before they made it to Mencar.

The Olvir had quickly realized that their weapons were useless against the Dragon. Phelandor had placed it at the head of the column to clear the way. Now the Olvir were circling back behind him to snipe at the men.

"Call a halt," Phelandor ordered, "and break out the flame-throwers." If need be, he would burn the entire forest between here and Mencar. . . .

"So," Arthwyr asked as they rode toward Quarin. "Is she always a horse?"

"No," Steve replied. "She can become herself at night—but only if we're alone."

"Sounds like the perfect woman," Arthwyr said, chuckling.

"What?"

"Available at night and cannot say one word during the day," Arthwyr replied. "Perfect."

"I take it you're joking," Steve said.

"I believe I am, but it does not sound . . . unappealing," Arthwyr said.

"Arthwyr, you're incorrigible."

"So I've been told, lad," Arthwyr agreed, laughing. They rode on in silence for a while. If Arthwyr and Morandil had not been with him, Steve would be halfway to Quarin by now. Unfortunately, their more mundane horses would never be able to maintain the pace.

"There is something I am dying of curiosity to ask," Arthwyr said, interrupting Steve's thoughts.

"What's that?" Steve asked, knowing he was going to regret this.

"Well," Arthwyr began, lowering his voice, presumably so that Morandil would not overhear, "have you ever done anything while she was . . . still a horse?"

"No!" Steve exclaimed. Arthwyr laughed.

"No wonder Aerilynn snapped at you," Steve said. Arthwyr only laughed louder.

"Lad, the way Lady Aerilynn felt about me, I am fortunate she did not knock me down and trample me," he replied.

"Hold!" Steve said, raising his hand. Arthwyr's jocular mood evaporated.

"What is it?" he asked.

"Maybe . . . nothing . . . ," Steve replied. Nestled between two hills was a small copse of trees. If the tiny grove was even a hundred yards across, Steve would be surprised. Still, if it *was* large enough, it could shave almost half a day off their travel time to Bralmendel.

Aerilynn, Steve thought, *is there a way to Bralmendel in that grove?*

Aerilynn carry master to Bralmendel? she asked.

Yes, Steve replied. Aerilynn tossed her head and snorted happily, before leaving the trail and heading toward the grove.

"Follow me," Steve called back to Arthwyr and Morandil. "Aerilynn knows a shortcut!"

For the second time in his life Prince Laerdon watched the forest burn. The lore-masters had worked for six years to restore the forest along the road the Morvir had cut through it. Now the Morvir burned it again along the same path.

Only now, they had sorcerous weapons to burn it for them. This invasion had gained more ground in one day than the previous one had gained in a sennight. At this rate, the Morvir would reach Bralmendel in the next day or two. And if the trap did not stop the Dragon there, they would reach Mencar a few days after that.

"Fall back!" Laerdon ordered. "We can do nothing more here. Fall back to Bralmendel!"

A damp carpet of leaves muffled the sound of the horses' hooves as they entered the grove. The light dimmed beneath the canopy of leaves overhead. Steve almost imagined that he could hear the trees whispering to them.

Aerilynn led them into the thickest vegetation. Arthwyr cursed quietly behind Steve. Steve smiled—apparently his Umbrian friend wasn't finding it as easy to keep up as he'd thought. Aerilynn's surefootedness kept Steve from suffering the worst effects of the limbs and branches.

The canopy overhead continued to thicken until Steve was certain they were no longer in the grove. There was no way the tiny grove he had found in Umbria could have contained the fifty-foot giants that grew around them now.

Steve could still hear Arthwyr and Morandil following behind him. Aerilynn splashed across a small creek and turned down another thickly overgrown trail. They should have left the far side of the grove by now, but Steve knew they were nowhere near that small copse of trees.

By the size of the nearly hundred-foot monsters that grew around them now, Steve guessed that they were deep in the heart of the Olvan forest. The ground grew more stony and less even. They should be nearing Bralmendel.

Sure enough, Aerilynn soon emerged onto a wider trail at the foot of the boulder-strewn hill. Steve reined her to a halt, looking behind him to see that Arthwyr and Morandil were still with him.

"Bralmendel," Steve announced.

"By the gods," Arthwyr breathed. "Two fortnights' travel— over in a few moments."

"'Tis easy when one knows the ways of the forests," Morandil said, although his hushed tone indicated that he, too, was impressed.

"Or when one's horse does," Steve replied, patting Aerilynn on the neck. "Come, we have an audience with King Arven."

*   *   *

Phelandor was pleased. Their rate of progress had effectively doubled once the flamethrowers and incendiary shells had been employed. The Morvir had also ceased taking casualties.

Then there was the psychological effect. Phelandor did not doubt that the mass destruction of the forest, in such a short time, was wreaking havoc with the Olvan morale.

Thousands, perhaps tens of thousands, of acres of forest had already been consumed by fire. The Morvir marched in the center of a burned swath hundreds of yards wide in either direction. At this rate they would reach Bralmendel in no more than two days—perhaps less.

Phelandor had discovered, during one of his advance reconnaissance trips, that Arven had gathered his forces atop the sacred mound. By the time Phelandor passed it by, Bralmendel would be littered from top to bottom with thousands of Olvan corpses.

He looked around, at the men under his command, and at the smoke in the distance from the raging fires he had kindled. Had the Mistress not fallen, had Belevairn not been slain, Phelandor had no doubt that Morvanor could have taken the world.

"We are coming, Arven," he said aloud to himself. "And nothing you can do will stop us."

"The Delvan Fire arrived this morning," Arven informed them. "We will place it in the pit on the morrow and then prepare for the Dragon's arrival."

Steve nodded. The only way they could have gotten the naphtha here this quickly was for Nolrod or another lore-master to bring it in himself. It was a good thing that they had.

The news upon their arrival had not been good. The tank *had* been sent into Olvanor and was, in fact, already halfway here. The Morvir were making much better progress than Steve had anticipated.

The invaders marched toward Bralmendel behind a wall of fire. A swath was being cut through the forest almost half a mile wide and the Olvir could do little more than flee before it. At this rate, the Morvir could reach the Regency within a fortnight if they weren't stopped here.

They would *have* to be stopped here. If they weren't, Mencar would be reduced to rubble, just as Quarin had been, and there would be thousands more deaths on Steve's conscience. The Dragon was going to meet a fiery death at the foot of *this* hill. It could not be allowed to go any farther.

"Is there anything else that can be done, Steven?" Arven was asking. Steven shook his head.

"Not unless the lore-masters can summon enough rain to quench the fire," he replied. "That could slow the Morvir and buy us some time. We could go back to striking from ambush, then."

"Nolrod and the others have been calling a storm since noon," Arven replied. "They have met with little success. It is the wrong season for such things."

"I can think of nothing else but to wait, then, Majesty," Steven replied. "Pray for rain and wait."

"*That* is the difficult part," Arven agreed.

Erelvar watched as the Delvir pronounced the pit filled. From where he stood, a scant ten feet or so away, one could not tell there had ever been a pit there. The surface of the packed earth road looked unbroken.

"We didn't march all the way from Deldwar to dig holes and fill them back up," Tsadhoq complained.

"I fear you will get your fill of action soon enough, Captain," Erelvar replied. "Have the mangonels been prepared?"

"Aye," Tsadhoq replied. "Three on the far hill and three on each of the flanking hills. Just crank them back, pour the Fire into the bottles, touch off the wicks and let fly."

"Will your men be able to escape after firing on the Morvan convoy?"

"They should be able to," Tsadhoq said, with more than a trace of doubt in his voice. "But if they are forced to flee after the first volley we will not have destroyed all of the . . . uh, the . . ."

"Trucks," Erelvar said, supplying the alien word.

"Aye."

"Nine of fifteen is not a bad casualty rate," Erelvar noted.

"Unless it's your side that's taking them," Tsadhoq agreed, smiling.

"And you are certain the Morvan scouts will not see them?" Erelvar asked.

"Not unless they search the damned hills," Tsadhoq assured him. "If the scouts just climb to the top of the hill and look out, we've got them covered well enow for that."

"We shall wait a quarter day east of here for your men to rejoin us before proceeding on to Castle Aldwyn," Erelvar told him. "We shall not await you longer than a quarter day after our scouts report the attack."

"So no lagging," Tsadhoq agreed. "Worry not, Morvan, we'll be there."

"So," Erelvar said, "now we wait."

"Aye, now we wait."

Chapter
-------- Eleven ------------

STEVE STEPPED OUT of his tent, drawing his hood over his head against the steady rain that had been soaking Bralmendel over the past day. Arven had presented him with the cloak yesterday, shortly after the rain had begun. It was white, trimmed in red with the Templar cross on the back.

When Steve had asked how Arven had managed to have it made so quickly, the Olvan king had simply smiled and reminded him that they stood on Bralmendel, as if that were explanation enough. However Arven had managed it, Steve found the gesture deeply moving.

The cloak shed the water like oilcloth, but had none of that material's stiffness or greasiness. Rather, it flowed and felt like the softest cotton. Truly a gift worthy of a king.

As Steve looked to the east, the clouds reflected a red glow from the horizon. Phelandor. According to Arven, the Dread Lord who led this force into Olvanor had once been Olvan himself. The fragments of Belevairn's memories left to Steve confirmed this. One would not have known it from his manner.

Lord Phelandor ravaged the land with a brutality Steve would not have thought any Olvan capable of—even one of the long-undead *Kaimordir*. In two days, he had burned a path through the forest half a mile wide and almost fifty miles long. Six years ago, it had taken Lord Daemor a fortnight to cover that same distance using axes and torches.

Phelandor's progress was slowing now, though. He was entering the area of the storm that the lore-masters had finally succeeded in calling. The forest, soaked by a day and a half of rain, was not quite so easy to burn as it had been. Still, he should be here long before nightfall.

*   *   *

Phelandor watched as the ammunition transport was once again forced to rescue trucks from the morass the forest floor had become. This rainstorm literally stank of the lore-masters' Power. Still, this would only slow his progress, it would by no means bring him to a halt.

Even with the delay this would cause him, the Dragon would arrive at Bralmendel shortly after midday. After that, Olvanor would have much fewer lore-masters to contend with. With the destruction of Bralmendel, the remaining lore-masters would have one less major source of Power as well. Mencar would be his within two days.

Jared stepped from the Gray Plain onto the bluff at Quarin. Hilarin and Heregurth emerged beside him. The negotiations with Morgaine were finally completed. An embassy was to be established both in El-Adrid and at Tar-Naurath, on the Northern Coast. Jared would be allowed to garrison 150 Morvir at each embassy. Any further negotiations at this point would be carried out by the new ambassadors, thank the Mistress.

Lord Kephas joined them atop the bluff shortly after their arrival.

"Greetings, High Lord," he said. Jared was already beginning to grow weary of that title and even more weary of the growing solicitousness on the part of the other Lords.

"Greetings, Lord Kephas," he replied.

"The bridge is almost completed," Kephas informed him. "We will be able to venture into Umbria on the morrow."

"Excellent," Jared said. "Has there been any word from Phelandor?"

"Yes, High Lord," Kephas replied. "Lord Phelandor has maintained contact with us by radio. He expects to engage the Olvir at Bralmendel this afternoon."

"Bralmendel?"

"The Olvir have entrenched themselves atop the sacred mound," Kephas explained.

"Yes," Jared acknowledged. "Atop the greatest site of Power in Olvanor."

"And us with no sorcerers of our own to defend against them," Hilarin whispered aside to him.

"That will change soon," Jared replied. "And the Dragon itself still carries the protection of the Mistress." Hilarin nodded in agreement.

"Hold off on the advance into Umbria," Jared ordered. "I want to hear the results of the battle at Bralmendel before I commit in Umbria."

"As you wish, High Lord," Kephas replied, bowing.

Jared was probably being overcautious, but he was uncomfortable with the situation in Olvanor. Things were progressing *too* smoothly.

"We have pulled back all of our forces onto the hilltop," Arven informed him. Steve nodded. The rain had let up about an hour before, but the sky was still heavily overcast. This late in the day it was pretty dark.

"Good," Steve replied. "I need to get in position. Did you place the decoys?"

"Yes . . . we did," Arven replied. "Are you . . . certain that this . . . will work?"

Steve smiled. One of his friends in college had been Afghan. As dark as it currently was from the overcast skies, and given the Olvan penchant for sniping from the shrubbery, the Morvir would be using infrared detection if they had it. In Afghanistan, the rebels would hang cans of urine from the trees to mislead the Soviet infrared. The T-55 was a Soviet tank, ergo . . .

"I think so, Arven," Steve replied. "I have it on fairly good authority that this trick works."

"Let us hope so," Arven said. "Your very life may depend upon it."

"Your report, Captain Koreth?" Phelandor asked.

"The northern face of the ridge is much too rough to take the tank around, Dread Lord," Koreth replied. "Especially as wet as the ground is. The southern face of the ridge is much gentler."

"Olvir?"

"Infrared shows a large number of targets in the trees," Koreth reported. "Especially along the gentler approach."

Phelandor nodded. Exactly as expected. He smiled—the presence of the *daegir* in the trees was of no consequence.

"Send the tank in first," Phelandor ordered. "We shall make our approach along the southern face of the ridge."

"Yes, Dread Lord."

Steve lay along the branch, sighting through the shotgun to where he knew the tank trap was set. There was a slim chance that the naphtha would not ignite when the tank fell onto it. Steve, and a magnesium flare, were going to make certain that it did.

He heard the tank long before he saw it. Finally the barrel emerged from behind the ridge, soon followed by the rest of the tank. Steve watched as it began to turn to face the slope of Bralmendel.

The diesel engine covered the sound of splintering wood as the nose of the tank began to dip. The tank crew almost saved it. Steve watched, horrified, as the treads stopped and then reversed. For an eternal instant, the tank teetered on the brink of the pit before finally nose-diving into the barrels of naphtha at the bottom.

Steve fired the flare as soon as the tank went over. The burning magnesium splattered over the tank armor just as it fell into the pit.

A huge ball of fire erupted from the pit, completely obscuring the tank from vision. Once the initial explosion had passed, Steve could see the tank, almost completely enveloped in flames. If that didn't do it, nothing would.

Shouts from below told him that the tank was *not* unescorted. Steve dropped from the tree limb to the ground and hurried up the hill, trying to use as much of the natural cover as possible. For some reason, he didn't think the Morvir would be happy with him if they caught up to him.

Arthwyr ap Madawc watched eagerly for some sign of Steven coming back up the hill. The . . . rifle rested in his arms like a crossbow. However, after practicing with it for half a day, Arthwyr knew that it was more accurate and much, much more deadly.

He glimpsed a figure moving quickly up the hill. Arthwyr put his eye to the . . . scope, as Steven had called it. Through the scope he could tell that it was Steven. Arthwyr lowered the rifle and watched the terrain behind his friend. He saw no sign of pursuit.

The fiery end of the Dragon had been seen by all atop Bralmendel. Now it was up to Prince Laerdon to carry out his portion of the assault. . . .

Prince Laerdon worked his away around behind the Morvan force in a mile-wide circle. Thank the land for the rain! It had prevented the Morvir from burning the last few miles of forest. Without the forest's cover, there would have been no way to get close enough for the Dreamer's plan to work.

There were only ten of them performing the actual attack. Another hundred were going to sacrifice themselves in a frontal assault on the supply train. Those hundred had volunteered to die so that Laerdon and his ten could destroy the Morvan supplies.

Ten *daegir* against the Morvan army. Still, Laerdon had done things even more insane in the last war against the Morvir. The old ache from the death of Adhelmen, his closest friend and the former commander of the *daegir,* rose to surface.

Laerdon turned his mind from that memory. *Now* was what mattered—not a war ended six years ago. But it had not ended. The Morvir were in the forests of Olvanor once again. Laerdon smiled—now it was time to repay that old debt.

He caught a glimpse of the Morvir's horseless supply wagons through the trees as well as the smaller dragon and metal wagon with the round back. Steven had said the cloth-backed wagons were the most important, and then the metal wagon. He had also said that they could not hope to harm the smaller dragon.

Laerdon took the blown-glass bottles and the metal flasks of Delvan Fire from his pack. About him, the *daegir* were doing likewise. They poured the Delvan Fire into the bottles and plugged them with rags stuffed securely into the bottles. Once this had been done, they put the bottles back into their packs—carefully. They then lit the rushes they had brought with them, set them in the damp earth, and waited.

They did not have to wait long. Soon, a flight of arrows landed among those guarding the supply train. Laerdon noticed with pleasure that several Morvir fell, never to rise again.

The Morvir responded immediately, leaving only a token force to guard the rear of the train. Laerdon drew his bow. Ten arrows flew from the forest and ten guards fell. Laerdon grabbed his torch and ran toward the supply train.

He grabbed a bottle from his pack, touched the wick to the burning torch he carried and hurled the missile in one fluid motion. The glass bottle flew through the open back of one of the wagons. Flame enveloped the crated cargo.

Laerdon hurled another bottle into the horseless wagon without lighting it. Soon the other wagons were also burning furiously as the *daegir* followed his example.

Laerdon lit another bottle and hurled it at the truck with the round metal back. Flames licked along its side as the Delvan Fire poured over it. Other missiles struck the metal wagon. The flames seemed to have little effect on it. . . .

The head of the *daega* to his left burst like a ripe melon and Laerdon heard the sharp crack that heralded the use of the Morvan weapons. The guards were returning from the diversionary attack.

"Retreat!" Laerdon shouted, turning to run. Another of the *daegir* cried out and fell, blood blossoming across his back. Laerdon and the others ran.

He had made it halfway to the forest when a searing pain ripped through his right leg. With a cry, Laerdon fell to the ground. Two of the *daegir* lifted him between them and dragged him the rest of the way to the cover of the trees. One paid for that act with his life.

Once within the cover of the forest, the survivors scattered, save for two who strove to carry their prince to safety. Laerdon's vision blurred and darkness enveloped him as they carried him through the forest.

Phelandor stared in horrified amazement at the fireball that erupted from the pit the Olvir had dug to trap the Dragon. For a moment he just stared. Then, heedless of his own safety, he spurred his mount forward to the edge of the pit.

The heat that rose from the pit was incredible. As Phelandor watched, the tank hatch fell open and one of the tank crew emerged, covered in flames and screaming. Phelandor drew his sidearm and shot the man.

A muffled explosion sounded from somewhere inside the tank, alerting Phelandor to the danger of his surroundings. He turned and galloped away from the pit. There was a short series of muffled explosions before all of the fuel and ammunition in the tank finally exploded at once.

Phelandor urged his mount out of reality and onto the Gray Plain to avoid the falling debris. After a few moments, he cautiously reemerged in the Olvan forest, prepared to flee again.

Small pockets of fire burned in the forest surrounding the pit. Phelandor turned to rejoin the main body of his troops.

"Dread Lord!" Captain Koreth said. "Are you all right?"

"Yes," Phelandor replied. "I am well."

"Shall we retreat?" Koreth asked.

"Retreat!" Phelandor shouted. Koreth stepped back a pace. "Before a rabble of Olvan hunters?" Phelandor shouted. "Never! Koreth, assemble your men and assault that hill! Use whatever means and tactics you deem necessary, but slay *everyone* on Bralmendel!"

"Y-yes, Dread Lord," Koreth responded.

"I am returning to the convoy to report this . . . this atrocity!"

"Yes, Dread Lord," Koreth replied. Phelandor rode onto the Gray Plain yet again. He might not be able to raze Mencar, but he could still cost the Olvir their rulers. . . .

The sight that greeted Phelandor's eyes when he emerged at the site of the convoy was even worse than the destruction of the Dragon at Bralmendel.

Pieces of burning trucks littered the convoy site. Clearly, from the way the backs of the trucks had been destroyed, the ammunition had exploded. Of the ammunition transport and the fuel truck, there was no sign. Also there did not seem to be enough wreckage to account for all of the trucks.

A second set of tread marks overlaid the marks left by the convoy's arrival. Phelandor followed them for approximately a mile to another clearing, to which the convoy had relocated.

The ammunition transport, the fuel truck and two trucks sat in the clearing. The fuel truck showed signs of fire damage. Phelandor waited for the commander of the platoon to report to him.

"Dread Lord!" Lieutenant Arvad said, saluting.

Phelandor returned the salute; he was beginning to find this custom tiring.

"What happened here, Lieutenant?" Phelandor asked.

"The Olvir made a suicide attack against the convoy, Dread Lord," Arvad reported. "At least a hundred made a frontal attack against the convoy while no more than a dozen snuck in with Molotovs."

"With what?"

"Molotov cocktails, Dread Lord," Arvad replied. "It's a terrorist weapon from the other world. A glass bottle filled with gasoline and a wick. They burned six of the trucks and almost got the fuel truck."

"Did they attack the transport?" Phelandor asked.

"No, Dread Lord," Arvad replied. "They ignored the ammunition transport completely. Lord, they seemed to know exactly where to strike. One would have to be much more familiar with our technology than the Olvir to plan such an attack."

"Yes," Phelandor agreed. He was fairly certain who the mastermind had been. . . .

Steve watched as the Morvir laid a ring of fire around Bralmendel. It didn't matter how wet the forest was, if you poured it on with the flamethrowers for long enough, it burned.

"We have to get out of here," Steve said to Arthwyr.

"We cannot just leave . . . ," Arthwyr began.

"It's that or die," Steve interrupted.

"Honor demands . . . ," Arthwyr began again.

"You may stay and die for your honor if you like, Arthwyr," Steve said. "I do not have that luxury. I have to find out if that convoy was destroyed and then I have to make sure the one in Umbria *gets* destroyed."

"How can we escape?" Arthwyr asked. "We are surrounded."

"We can only hope the forest on this hill is enough for Aerilynn to get us out of here," Steve replied. "But first I have to speak to Arven. Are you coming or staying?"

"I follow you, my lord," Arthwyr replied.

"I cannot abandon my people, Steven," Arven objected. "Not before the battle has even begun."

"This battle is already over, Majesty," Steve insisted. "I doubt that you will kill over a dozen of the Morvir and no one who stays will survive."

"I must stay," Arven repeated. "I have no choice, just as you have no choice but to leave." Steve blinked in surprise. He had not told Arven that he was leaving. . . .

"How . . . ?"

"This is but one battle," Arven explained. "Your part in it is over and you *must* see the destruction of this evil through to the end. Go, while you still may."

"Arven . . . ," Steve began.

"Go," Arven commanded. "Now, Dreamer! Your horses are prepared."

"As you wish, Majesty," Steve replied, sadly. "God be with you."

"And with you, Dreamer. Now go!"

Aerilynn led them down the side of the hill, into the thickest surviving patch of vegetation remaining. Unlike before, when Aerilynn had carried him, Steve felt a gut-wrenching pang when she chose a path. For a moment, just a moment, strange and malicious creatures peered at them from the foliage. Then they, and the pain in his stomach, were gone.

"What was *that*?" Steve asked.

Bad place, Aerilynn replied. *Only way out.*

Steve looked behind him. Arthwyr was still behind him, notably paler than usual.

"You okay?" Steve asked. Arthwyr nodded.

"Yes," he replied. "I . . . think so."

"Listen," Steve said. The sound and smell of the burning forest was gone. Arthwyr listened to the silence as some of the color returned to his face.

"Where do we go now, Steven?" Arthwyr asked.

"To find Prince Laerdon," Steve replied. *That is,* he thought, *if the prince is still alive.*

"The perimeter of the hill has been cleared, sir," one of the lieutenants reported.

"Good," Koreth replied. "Begin the advance and tell the men

not to spare the grenades. This is *not* going to be an easy battle, even with them."

The fire worked its way up the hill, away from Prince Delarian. He and a hundred of the *daegir* had secreted themselves in the trees far south of the foot of the hill. Delarian gestured his men forward. His orders were relayed, silently, through the trees.

Travelling upward, the fire was able to take hold in the sparse vegetation on the hillside. Back in this direction, the flames quickly died as the rain-soaked foliage refused to burn.

Delarian leaped from the limb he walked to another. His entire squad moved toward Bralmendel in this fashion. Soon he reached the end of the cover provided by the wood. Before him, the Morvir advanced up the hill.

Those atop Bralmendel fought bravely, but their efforts were almost useless against the Morvir. As Delarian took careful aim on a Morvan's back, an explosion shook the hillside.

Delarian let fly, almost simultaneously with the rest of his men. A hundred Morvir in the advancing force fell. He quickly nocked another arrow and fired it wildly into the mass of men before him as several of them turned to fire into the trees.

Whether his second arrow struck home, he never knew.

The man next to Koreth fell back with an arrow through his eye. Koreth fired his grenade launcher. The Olvir were providing fiercer resistance than he had anticipated. Much fiercer . . .

"Fall back!" he shouted into the radio headset he wore. "Regroup at the foot of the hill. We'll march back up under *heavy* grenade fire!"

Another explosion shook the hillside. Arven ducked the flying rock and debris that were as lethal as the explosions themselves. Even deprived of the Dragon, the Morvir were unstoppable.

No, he thought, *not unstoppable. Just costly.* The Olvir had already slain more than tenfold the number that Steven had claimed they could take. Unfortunately, the cost had been hundreds of Olvan lives thus far.

This was what he had sent his eldest son to destroy. The personal weapons that could wreak so much havoc. The Dragon had not been the true threat, just the most visible. He could only hope that Laerdon had been successful—and survived.

Three more explosions sent rock and gravel flying through the air. Several dozen more Olvir died. Arven drew his bow and let fly. A hundred yards away, a Morvan fell, pouring his blood into the land. All returned to the land eventually—even the Morvir, and even the *Kaimordir*.

Of that entity, of Phelandor, there was no sign. Were the Morvir now so powerful that their leaders could leave them unsupervised to attend to minor chores such as devastating a kingdom?

The Morvir massed for a charge up the hill. Arven smiled sadly. It was time to die. He would miss the land—the scent of the leafy carpet, the whispering of the great ones in the wind. He drew his bow again as the Morvir opened fire and began their advance up the hill.

The shaft never left the bow.

Chapter
-------- Twelve ------------

STEVE LISTENED TO the crunch of the leaves beneath Aerilynn's hooves. They had found the clearing, almost a mile back in the forest now, where the Morvan convoy had been attacked. Steve had counted the wreckage of six trucks, still burning.

Apparently the fuel truck and two other trucks had escaped. Of course, the armored vehicle that Steve suspected carried ammunition for the tank had also escaped. The Olvir could have done nothing to that.

Steve smiled. Without the tank, that ammunition would be next to useless. The Morvir would have no way to make use of it otherwise, and there would be no more tanks coming over to use it in the future.

Ahead of him, Arthwyr dismounted and checked the ground.

"The trail is fresher now," he said. "We must be getting close." Steve heard the sound of several wooden bows drawing.

"Very close, I'd say," he agreed. "Stand very still, Arthwyr."

Arthwyr stopped rising, immobile in a half-kneeling position. Steve slowly moved his arms out away from his sides.

"We are friends," he called into the trees.

"You are indeed," a familiar voice said at Steve's side. Steve started at the unexpected closeness.

"Nolrod!" he exclaimed.

"Greetings, Dreamer," he said. "You may relax. The bows of the Olvir are no longer drawn against you."

"What are you doing here?"

"Where should I be, but at the side of my king?" Nolrod asked.

"Arven?" Steve asked, hope rising suddenly within him. Nolrod shook his head, dashing the all-too-brief moment of hope.

"Laerdon," Nolrod replied. "He lies within this glen—sorely wounded, but alive."

"Will he . . . ?" Steve let the obvious question trail off.

"He will live," Nolrod assured him. "That is why I am here."

"Is there anything I can do?" Steve asked.

"Yes, there is."

"Name it," Steve said, firmly.

"Allow your steed to carry him to Mencar, if she will," Nolrod replied. "*She* can give him the strength to make that journey."

Master only! Aerilynn's voice cried in his mind. She whinnied and reared briefly.

"Aerilynn," Steve said calmly, patting her neck. "Aerilynn, the king needs you. Please?"

King? Aerilynn asked.

"Yes, the king of the Olvir needs you to carry him to Mencar or he may die."

Carry king, Aerilynn agreed. Steve patted her neck again in approval before dismounting to lead her into the glen.

Phelandor opened the door to the council chamber. Four others sat in the room with Lord Jared. All fell silent as he entered. Lord Jared rose from his chair.

"Phelandor," he said, his surprise showing in his voice. "Why are you not in Olvanor?"

"I have grave news, High Lord," Phelandor replied.

"I should expect so," Jared agreed. "Sit down and relay it to us."

Phelandor took his seat at the council table, aware that all eyes were upon him.

"The Dragon has been destroyed," he announced. There was a short, stunned pause before all the gathered Lords began talking at once.

"Destroyed! How?" Lord Fanchon exclaimed.

"Impossible!" Lord Kastor exclaimed.

"Incompetent fool," Phelandor heard Hhayim mutter, none too quietly.

"What are we going to do now?" Lord Eythan demanded.

"*Silence!*" Jared roared, striking the table with a hammer. The report echoed through the council chamber.

"Lord Phelandor," Jared continued once order had been restored to the room, "will be allowed to complete his report without interruption. Lord Phelandor . . ."

Phelandor nodded. Had he been mortal he would have wallowed at this point before continuing.

"The path to Bralmendel was trapped with a large pit," Phelandor said. "The cover of the pit was strong enough to support several men without giving away its presence."

"How could a pit destroy . . . ?" Fanchon began to interrupt. A blow on the tabletop from Jared's hammer stopped him.

"Continue, Lord Phelandor," Jared said.

"The bottom of this pit was filled with many barrels of Delvan Fire," Phelandor explained. "As soon as the tank landed on them, they exploded. Shortly afterwards, the tank's ammunition and fuel exploded, completely destroying it."

"This *is* grave news," Jared observed.

"There is more, High Lord," Phelandor added.

"Continue," Jared said.

"The Olvir made a suicide attack on the supply trucks," Phelandor said. "They used a . . . homemade weapon that my men tell me is common to the Dreamer's world to destroy most of my supplies."

"What weapon?" Jared asked, leaning forward intently.

"Lieutenant Arvad called them 'Molotov cocktails,' High Lord. Glass bottles, also filled with Delvan Fire and with cloth wicks. They destroyed six of the eight trucks in this manner."

"What of the assault on Bralmendel?" Jared asked. "Did you carry it out?"

"Yes, High Lord," Phelandor replied, brightening somewhat. "It was costly, but we eliminated all of the *daegir* as well as the Olvan royal family and several hundred tribesmen."

"How costly?" Jared asked.

"Almost . . . two hundred men, High Lord," Phelandor said. "But Mencar is now without defenders! We should be able to take it easily. . . ."

"No," Jared interrupted.

"High Lord?"

"Lord Phelandor," Jared said, "I want you to know that you are not completely to blame for this . . . farce."

"Th-thank you, High Lord," Phelandor replied.

"We have *all* been supreme in our arrogance," Jared contin ued. "We have all been too overconfident in the strength of ou new weapons to see their weaknesses. And what harm was it No one on *this* world knew of those weaknesses—save one."

"The Dreamer," Phelandor stated. He had already come to that conclusion himself.

"Precisely," Jared agreed. "However, even the Dreamer wa bound by prophecy. *He* could not destroy the Dragon—only the Arm of Death could do that. *Where* is Erelvar?"

"Still in Umbria as of last report, High Lord," Phelandor replied. "And I saw no sign of his presence in Olvanor."

"That cannot be," Jared said, musing aloud. "The prophecy of Uldon clearly states that *only* the Arm of Death could destroy the Dragon."

"The prophecy is obviously wrong . . . ," Fanchon began

"Nonsense!" Jared objected. "That prophecy has foretold *every* event that has happened to date. Such prophecies are neve *wrong*. Misunderstood, perhaps—but never simply *wrong*."

"What does it matter?" Hhayim asked. "The Dragon is destroyed. What shall we do now?"

"Indeed," Jared agreed. "Our chief concern now is the Dreamer. He knows that if he destroys our remaining supplies then we have no war. How long would it be before we ran ou of ammunition? One skirmish? Perhaps two? Certainly no long enough to take even one Umbrian fortress."

"What shall we do?" Fanchon asked. "It is almost impossible to defend against the type of suicide attacks that Olvir made against the convoy."

"We use the ammunition transport," Jared replied. "And we abandon our campaign in Olvanor. Phelandor, unload all of the tank ammunition and reload the transport with the supplies from the two remaining trucks. Then withdraw to Quarin."

"Yes, High Lord," Phelandor grudgingly agreed.

"Once the ammunition transport returns to Quarin, we shall load it with as many of the supplies as it will carry," Jared added. "Then that, the fuel truck and all of the infantry will proceed into Umbria."

"What of the Regency?" Hhayim asked. "That will leave them virtually untouched, especially since the Veran Guard has apparently left to return to Validus."

"Yes," Jared agreed. "The Dreamer has been very good at deducing our strategy to this point—or someone has. However, there is going to be a surprise waiting for the Veran Guard once they reach the inner sea—courtesy of our new allies. I do not believe *anyone* will be able to anticipate that."

Mencar was the closest thing that Steve had ever seen to a storybook castle. To his experienced eye, the walls and battlements were all perfectly functional but every single merlon was also a statue. Every support for the machicolation was a beautiful maiden or a snarling dragon or some other such adornment. Hell, it *was* a storybook castle, yet completely defensible.

At the base, the walls were as smooth as glass, to deny potential scalers any means of purchase at all. The forest had been moved back approximately a hundred feet all around the city. To look at it, however, one almost got the impression that the forest had never actually *been* there, not that it had been removed.

In the center of the city, the ornate defense works climbed up a hill easily as tall as Bralmendel. The entire city was probably only five miles across, if that. Still, it was impressive beyond belief. Every structure was a work of art, frescoed and carved in relief in such a way that one could almost imagine that one still walked through the wood.

But it was a wood peopled with fantastic creatures. Statues of unicorns and dragons mixed freely with renditions of more mundane forest animals. Strange that the mythical animals here paralleled those of his own world so closely.

As Steve led Aerilynn through the streets of Mencar he could not help but stare at everything he passed. It was hard to believe that this was the only city in the entirety of Olvanor. The bulk of the population lived in nomadic tent villages during the summer and in earthen lodges during the winter. Mencar was their one superb concession to civilization.

The gate of the palace was gilded with gold, with a carved representation of twin trees framing the entrance. The gates swung open as they approached. Steve glanced back to Nolrod, who simply nodded to him. Having received permission, Steve led Aerilynn into the palace.

He actually stopped, overcome with awe. Stone columns, carved into the shape of mighty oaks, supported the vaulted ceiling of the great hall. Overhead, thousands of shining stars sparkled at him from the jet black ceiling while sunlight streamed in from narrow windows, even though, outside, the clouds hid the sun.

And this was odd, Steve thought, remembering an old Robert Lewis Carroll verse, *because it was the middle of the night.* . . .

"Dreamer," Nolrod whispered in an amused tone. Steve shook his head, as if to clear it.

"Sorry," he whispered, leading Aerilynn farther into the palace. Women appeared around them, as if from nowhere, and helped Prince Laerdon down from the saddle. Four of the castle guard set down a cot on which the prince, no . . . the king, was laid. Steve saw that it had handles for exactly this purpose. The *daegir* lifted the cot like a stretcher and carried the still-unconscious king away.

"Will he be all right?" Steve asked.

"Yes, Dreamer," Nolrod replied. "Thanks to Aerilynn, he will recover much more quickly than he would had we been forced to wait in the forest. Now, if you will excuse me?"

"By all means," Steve replied. He watched as Nolrod left to tend to his king. Well . . . now what?

"What shall we do now, Steven?" Arthwyr asked, echoing his thoughts.

Steve sighed. There was only one answer to that question.

"We ride to Umbria," he replied.

"Perhaps, instead, you might stay and enjoy the hospitality of the palace for the night," a female voice suggested. Steve turned and saw what had to be the most beautiful woman he'd ever seen.

Reddish blond hair fell down her back from beneath the diamond tiara she wore. Her green eyes were shining emeralds and her ivory skin contrasted sharply against the black velvet gown she wore. She moved toward them with a fluidity that shamed both Aerilynn's and Glorien's Olvan grace. Steve dropped to one knee.

"Your Majesty," he said, knowing at an instinctive level who she *must* be.

"'Tis late," she added, placing her hand on Steve's shoulder, "and you have labored very hard today, Dreamer. Spend the night under our roof and regain your strength. Thy quest shall await you 'til the morrow."

That was true enough. It would take days for the Morvir to reach here, or to return to Quarin, whichever they chose. He and Arthwyr could certainly use a good night's sleep.

"As you wish, Majesty," Steve agreed.

A tinkling chime sounded from somewhere in the room. Steve and Aerilynn were instantly awake. Who would be calling on them at this hour? Aerilynn shrugged in response to the question in his eyes.

The room was dimly lit. Was it morning yet? It couldn't be—Aerilynn was still Aerilynn. He certainly felt rested, though. In fact, he felt more rested than he had since he had left his own world behind.

He rose from the bed and drew his cloak around him before going to answer the door. The grassy carpet of the room tickled his feet and was cool and damp with morning dew. It felt strangely refreshing.

Hope it doesn't frost in the winter, he thought with a smile. He doubted that it did. How the Olvir got the grass to grow indoors at all was completely beyond him. Not to mention, who trimmed it?

Steve opened the door a crack, careful so that she did not see Aerilynn. An Olvan woman waited outside. She smiled.

"I am sorry to disturb you at this hour, my lord," the woman apologized. "However, Queen Miriam would like to speak with you, and she insisted that it must be before morning."

"Of course," Steve replied. "Give me a moment to prepare."

"Yes, my lord."

Steve closed the door.

"I wonder what this is all about," he said to Aerilynn.

"Hurry," Aerilynn admonished him. "You must not keep her waiting."

The queen's chambers were carpeted in the same manner as Steve's room. The face of one wall of the sitting room had been fashioned to look like a rocky hillside, down which a spring tumbled to a sandy-bottomed pool in the floor. Steve examined the pool as he waited. There *had* to be a drain somewhere. . . .

"Do you like my bath?" a voice asked. Steve rose, turned and knelt before the queen. She had traded her black velvet mourning gown for a multilayered dress of a black, gauzy material. Steve could just barely glimpse a hint of her form through it.

"Good evening, Majesty," Steve said, bowing his head.

"You may rise, Dreamer," the queen replied. "And, please, call me Miriam—we do not often stand on formality outside of court in Mencar."

"Yes, Maj . . . Miriam," Steve replied. Then, in response to her earlier question, he added, "I was just trying to figure out where the drain was."

"Beneath the sand," Queen Miriam replied. "The sand purifies the water before it is drained away."

"I see," Steve said. He didn't ask what kept the sand from being sucked down the drain along with the water and clogging it up.

"I don't believe you summoned me here to discuss the engineering of your bath, Majesty . . . I mean, Miriam." The queen smiled.

"Indeed not," she agreed. "I have a request of you, Dreamer."

"Anything I may . . . ," Steve began. The queen raised a hand, interrupting him.

"Do not agree before you have heard," she admonished him. "You do not know our ways, and this may very well be a . . . task you are unwilling to perform."

"Very well," Steve agreed.

"I wish you to join me as host in the Ceremony of Parting tomorrow."

"That doesn't seem like an odious task . . . Miriam," Steve said.

"It will take most of the day," Miriam explained. "I know you are eager to be away."

"Not eager to be away," Steve objected. "More like eager to get on with my own tasks. But I have a debt to your husband, Majesty. I can spare the time."

"There is more to hear before you decide," Miriam said.

"And I believe you will wish to speak with Aerilynn, although I am certain of what her answer will be."

"That's why you wanted to see me before morning," Steve noted.

"That is correct," Miriam confirmed.

"Go on," Steve urged.

"The Ceremony of Parting is . . . different for a king," Miriam explained. "For most, it is a private thing. I am asking you to host Arven's spirit for one last farewell to his people."

"I would *be* Arven?" Steve asked. This was a new twist on the old 'king for a day' bit. *Dead* king for a day . . .

"Yes," Miriam replied.

"That is . . . different," Steve agreed. "Still, as I said, I owe Arven a debt. I can think of no better way to repay it."

"I agree," Miriam said, nodding. "But you still have not heard . . . all there is to hear."

"There's more?"

"Indeed. As I said, for a king the ceremony is more public. But there is a private part as well," she said. Her expression saddened.

"You would host Arven's spirit for a final farewell to me as well," she finished, quietly.

Steve began to say that that didn't seem too much to ask, when he realized exactly what she meant. After all, how would *he* want to say his last farewell to Aerilynn after his death?

"You . . . mean . . . ?" Steve said, pointing first at himself, then at Miriam, and then finally back at himself. The queen simply nodded.

Steve walked down the hall to their room. Miriam's pain had been so well hidden earlier. Tonight it had been laid bare.

Steve knew that pain well. He had lived with it for half a year, after Aerilynn's death. He would have given *anything* for one more time in her arms. How could he refuse Miriam's request—especially since he was largely responsible for Arven's death? But how could he grant it?

He opened the door to their room and slipped in quietly. Aerilynn sat up in the bed and smiled. Her smile quickly vanished.

"Steven?" she asked. "What is wrong? You look as though something terrible has happened. Is there news of the Morvir?"

"No," Steve said, forcing a smile. "Nothing like that." He sat heavily on the bed. Aerilynn put her arms around him from behind.

"Tell me," she said. "Tell me what troubles you so."

"I've been asked to . . . do something," he said.

"What could the queen ask of you that would be so terrible?"

"Aerilynn," Steve said, "I love you."

"I know, dearest," she replied. "What did Queen Miriam ask of you?"

"She wants me to be her . . . host for the Ceremony of Parting," Steve replied.

"Steven!" Aerilynn exclaimed excitedly. "That is wonderful! You must be . . . Steven?"

"You think it's 'wonderful'?" Steve asked.

"Yes," Aerilynn replied. "Are you afraid, dearest? Are you afraid of allowing Arven's spirit to enter you?"

"No," Steve said. "That part doesn't bother me."

"Then what?"

"Aerilynn, do you . . . know what would be . . . expected of me?"

"Yes," Aerilynn replied, nodding.

"*Everything* that would be expected of me?"

"Yes . . . ?" Aerilynn replied again. The way she slowly drew the word out made it clear that she wasn't understanding the problem.

"It . . . wouldn't bother you?" Steve asked.

"What?"

"Me and . . . Miriam . . . you know."

Aerilynn stared at him for a moment. Then comprehension appeared on her face, quickly followed by amusement. She fell back onto her pillow, laughing.

"What's so funny?" Steve asked.

"Oh, Steven!" she said. "I am the most fortunate woman in all of Olvanor."

"Say what?"

"No other man in Olvanor would even *dream* of refusing Queen Miriam's request. But you would, simply because you are worried that I might be jealous."

"Aerilynn, I love you," Steve said. "I won't do anything that might hurt you or that might . . . make me lose you. I went . . . too long without you."

"My love," Aerilynn said, sitting up and placing her arm over his shoulder, "I would never leave you for easing the queen's suffering. 'Tis not like you are going to go . . . whoring with Arthwyr. You have been asked to be host for the queen, Steven. I am *proud* of that!"

"Proud?"

"Yes! Of all the men in Olvanor, mine is the one that the queen herself has deemed worthy to be her host. Please accept, Steven—for her sake. She is my queen."

"As you wish, my lady," Steve replied.

Steve knocked lightly on the door to the queen's chambers. A handmaid admitted him. Miriam was in the sitting room, staring into the distance. For a moment Steve just watched her. She was certainly beautiful, but now her features were filled with sorrow.

"Your Majesty," Steve said softly.

"Yes, Steven?" she replied without turning. He smiled—Miriam had known he was there all along.

"It will be my honor to serve as your host," Steve said.

A sob escaped her. Steve involuntarily took a step toward her and stopped.

"Please?" she asked. Steve walked over and knelt by her chair. He put his arms around her while she wept against his shoulder. After a time, the tears passed.

"Thank you," she said, caressing his cheek and smiling sadly. "Now go. I would not keep you from *your* love."

Prince Theron stood in the prow of the lead galley. With the aid of the current, they had left the mouth of the Bitterwine just before sunset. The wind, however, was against them. They had been forced to lower the sails and rely only on the oars.

Still, they were making good progress, so far as they could tell in the dark. The Dreamer's star had almost faded to the brilliance of a normal star, although it still outshone any other star in the sky. However, it did not illuminate the night as it once had.

A sliver of the waxing moon was beginning to rise. Soon they would have more light with which to judge their progress. Theron estimated that the Veran Guard would reach Validus by tomorrow evening. It would be good to be able to check their actual progress.

Suddenly, a fiery glow appeared near the surface of the water. It arced up into the air as a ball of fire. Theron briefly glimpsed a ship silhouetted against the flames before it rose. *Pirates!*

The missile struck the second galley, spreading burning oil across the entire deck. The light illuminated the Nymran fleet. No other missiles were launched. Perhaps it was a lone pirate and, now that he had seen that he was facing twenty galleys, he had decided to withdraw.

"Pirates!" a crewman shouted, pointing to fore and port. Theron turned in time to see a pirate galley emerge from the darkness on a collision course. The gleaming brass of its ram reflected the firelight of the burning trireme.

The impact threw Theron from his feet, but not before he could see that other pirate galleys were emerging from the darkness from the seaward side of the fleet. This could *not* be coincidence! The coastal pirates must have known the Nymran fleet was on this course.

Theron rose to his feet and drew his sword as the implications sank in. *Someone* in Morvanor had formed an alliance with the Coasts.

"There's the prince!" one of the swarming pirates shouted in their bastard Nymran tongue.

"Take 'im alive or Morgaine'll 'ave our 'eads," someone else replied. Excellent! That gave Theron an advantage. They would be trying *not* to kill him.

Another of the small pirate galleys rammed them. As Theron was thrown back he felt the railing strike him in the back before he tumbled over it to fall to the sea below.

The water closed over him as his armor tried to drag him to the bottom. Theron dropped his sword, fumbling with the wet leather straps. The salt burned his eyes. The metal-and-leather skirt dropped away, but his breastplate still threatened to carry him to a watery death.

The straps were already swollen with the salt water. Theron's lungs began to burn with the thirst for air. Finally, the stubborn straps gave way and Theron let the heavy, bronze breastplate fall from his body.

He kicked in the direction his mind told him was up, praying to Lindra that he was correct. He had heard of men who had swum to their death after getting disoriented underwater. His lungs screamed for him to breathe.

Theron's head broke the surface of the water and he gasped in a deep breath of air. He was far too close to the battle. Ignoring his protesting lungs, Theron took a deep breath and dived under, swimming toward shore.

He broke the surface when his lungs would no longer be denied. He had gained perhaps a hundred feet toward shore. More important, he was now well out of the range of illumination that the burning galley provided.

A wave lifted him and carried him toward the distant shore. Theron turned and swam with it. It must be leagues to the Olvan shore. Even if he reached it, there was a good chance that the Olvir would kill him for trespassing on their lands.

What seemed like several hours later, Theron dragged himself up onto the beach. His stomach retched in rebellion against the amount of seawater he had swallowed. After the convulsions had stopped he collapsed onto the sand. He was not conscious to feel the hands that gently lifted him and carried him into the forest.

Chapter
-------- Thirteen ------------

ARTHWYR AP MADAWC WAS not amused. He had risen shortly after dawn only to find Steven's room empty. Actually, it was not empty. His possessions were there. Also, Aerilynn was in her stall, so Arthwyr knew that Steven was still in Mencar. He was just nowhere that Arthwyr could find him.

To make matters worse, the palace—the entire city, in fact—was livelier than a nest of angry hornets. No one had so much as heard his attempts to interrupt them, let alone given him any answers.

Arthwyr singled out a male servant and approached him.

"Excuse me," he began, but the Olvan was oblivious to him. Arthwyr caught the man's arm as he moved away and pulled him against a wall.

"I said, 'excuse me,'" Arthwyr repeated. The Olvan's eyes were wide with surprise.

"I am trying to find my liege who has mysteriously disappeared," Arthwyr continued. "And if I do not get some answers from someone *very* soon I am going to search the palace myself!"

"That will not be necessary, Arthwyr ap Madawc," a voice said behind him. Arthwyr turned to see three of the palace guard standing behind him. He released his hold on the servant, who then hurried away, glaring at Arthwyr's back.

"I am pleased to hear that," Arthwyr replied. "Where is Master Wilkinson?"

"He is with Queen Miriam," the guard replied, "preparing for the Ceremony of Parting."

"Preparing for what?"

"The Ceremony of Parting," the guard repeated. "It is . . . akin to your funerals."

154

"For the king," Arthwyr deduced.

"That is correct."

"Well, then, by the gods, why did someone not tell me?"

"We were not aware of your relationship to the Dreamer," the guard explained. "You have our apologies. *Daega* Leyvan will be assigned to you for the remainder of the day to answer any of your questions."

You mean, to keep me from causing any more trouble, Arthwyr thought. That was all right—it did give him someone to question if need be.

"Thank you," Arthwyr replied. "My apologies as well for the commotion." The guard captain smiled.

"You do not mean that," he said. "And neither would I if my liege had turned up missing. Good day to you. Enjoy the ceremony."

"Has the priest of Mortos been summoned?" Miriam asked.

"Yes, Majesty," one of the handmaidens replied. "He will arrive shortly."

"Good," she acknowledged. "Hold still, Steven!"

"How do you people get anything done?" Steven asked. "It takes all day just to get dressed!" Miriam laughed.

"You sound like Arven already," Miriam chided. "He also hated preparing for his addresses. He loved to speak with his people, but . . ." Her voice trailed off.

"Majesty?" one of the handmaidens asked.

"'Tis all right," she said softly. "Just . . . a cinder in my eye."

"Yes, Majesty," the handmaid replied, sounding not at all convinced. Then Steven spoke—in Nymran, to the shock and dismay of the servants.

"*Are* you all right?" he asked.

"Now is not the time for grief," Miriam replied, also in Nymran. "That will come . . . later."

"Very good, by the way," she added. "You have deduced quite correctly that few of the servants speak this tongue. Arven would also speak to me in Nymran when we wished privacy.

"There!" she announced, returning to the Olvan tongue.

"Finally!" Steven replied, also in Olvan. Miriam noticed that the servants exchanged startled glances. If Steven were not careful, he would have the servants convinced that Arven had already joined with him.

He was so like Arven, in many ways. Miriam ran her fingers down the back of her husband's tunic that Steven now wore as a wave of melancholy washed over her. The similarities had startled her when he had carried her son home last night. His bearing, his manner, his . . . openness were so like Arven's. It had made the choice, which had been so difficult, suddenly so obvious.

Judging from Steven's own statements, he also had need of this joining. The Dreamer felt that he was in some way at fault for Arven's death. The only one, other than Steven, who could absolve him of that was Arven himself. This way, perhaps Steven could receive that absolution.

"The priest has arrived, Majesty," one of the handmaidens announced. Miriam smiled, taking her hand from Steven's back.

"'Tis time, Steven," she said.

Steve blinked in the morning sunlight as he walked out onto the balcony. Mencar had seemed picturesque in yesterday's overcast skies. In the clear sunlight, it was nothing less than magical. The walls of the city sparkled as if thousands of diamonds had been ground into powder and embedded in the walls.

Below him, thousand of Olvir were gathered to say farewell to their king. Steve wasn't certain how he felt about this. He had gotten a taste of possession once, when he had been cursed with the presence of Belevairn's persona in his own mind. He never would have dreamed that he would ever *volunteer* to undergo that again. Yet here he was.

Steve could feel the Power as the priest began the ritual. This was not like the Power that he knew from Belevairn's memories. Rather than gathering it from his surroundings, the priest received it from . . . another source. As he had done with Theron, Steve opened himself and allowed Power to flow through him as well, adding his offering to the priest of Mortos.

The priest of Mortos gave Steve the slightest nod of acknowledgment and continued the ritual. Finally, after much prayer and invocation of the Lord of the Dead, the priest laid his hands upon Steve's brow.

Steve gasped as darkness consumed his vision and dizziness consumed his senses. He could barely feel as the *daegir* on either side of him caught his arms to keep his body from falling to the balcony floor.

Mencar was replaced by a vision of a great wood. Steve stood by a stream. Across the stream stood a figure he knew well—Arven. The king reached his hand across, toward Steve.

Steve gathered his resolve and walked to the edge of the stream. He reached across, and grasped Arven's proffered hand.

Arven stood next to him. The stream was gone and they stood together in a dense forest.

"I must admit that I am surprised at Miriam's choice of host," Arven said, breaking the absolute stillness of the forest. "But I must also admit that I concur wholeheartedly."

"It was the least I could do," Steve replied.

"Least? I think not, Steven," Arven disagreed. "Few not of the people would have the courage to accept the role of host."

"I mean . . . the least I could do to make up for the damage I have caused," Steve explained. "Both to you *and* to Olvanor."

"Yes," Arven replied. "You *do* blame yourself for all of the evils that your world's weapons have done here, do you not?"

"I am responsible," Steve began.

"Nonsense," Arven objected. "Did you seek out Belevairn and offer him these weapons?"

"No!" Steve replied. "Of course not!"

"I thought not," Arven said. "As I understand it, Belevairn was forced to slay you to obtain it. To me that seems the highest sacrifice one could make to *protect* Olvanor—and myself."

"Well . . ."

"Are you more powerful than Death, then, Dreamer?"

"No, Majesty," Steve replied.

"Then why do you assume the responsibilities of the *Kanir* when you have not their Power? Release this guilt, Dreamer. 'Tis not yours to bear. The evils of the Morvir rest solely on their souls—not yours."

"I left you to die, Arven!" Steve objected.

"On my order!" Arven replied. "Your quest is more important than a battle on a hilltop. The destruction of the Dragon is more important by far than the life of a king. And as you yourself are well aware, death is not the end of all things."

"I left because I was afraid," Steve objected. "The quest just gave me a way out. Besides, the Dragon has already been destroyed."

"You are wrong, Dreamer," Arven replied. "You pursued Belevairn alone across your own world at great risk to yourself. You surrendered yourself to his Morvan troops to save your sister's life. You are not a man who fears death, Dreamer, however much you might like to believe that you are. If the quest had not called, you would have remained and fought beside us. And the Dragon is *not* yet destroyed. It has been sorely wounded—but it yet lives."

"What . . . ?" Steve began.

"That is enough," Arven interrupted. "All that remains is for you to ponder my words. Now, however, the people of Olvanor await us."

Arven opened his arms to Steve as if for an embrace. Steve stepped into his arms and the two of them flowed together. Again, darkness and dizziness overwhelmed him.

Miriam watched as Steven regained his footing and gently shrugged out of the supportive hold of the *daegir*. He removed the crown from its velvet pillow and placed it on his head. As the crowd below cheered their king for one final time, he turned and Miriam gazed into Arven's eyes.

"Arven . . . ," she began.

"Later, my love," Arven interrupted. "The people have need of us now."

Arven turned back to the crowd assembled below and raised his arms.

Arven/Steven gazed down at the crowd below. The crowd fell silent as the pair lifted their arms. This was completely unlike what Steven had experienced with Belevairn. Then Belevairn had been an intrusive presence in his mind.

Now the two of them had become one mind, one consciousness. Each still possessed his own individuality, but the lines that divided them no longer existed. One's thought was echoed in the other's mind. They were one.

"People of Olvanor," Arven/Steven announced, "it is with deep sorrow and joy that I must bid all of you farewell. I sorrow in that I will no longer share in the lives of my people and my loved ones. I take joy in that I go now to the Halls of Mortos to join with the many loved ones who have gone before me. But I shall miss you.

"As many of you know, the Dragon has been destroyed," Arven/Steven added. "The man responsible for that destruction now stands before you as well as I. He is a dear friend, who has opened his heart to me that I may speak with you one last time."

That was no sacrifice, Steven/Arven thought.

"But this is not his only sacrifice," Arven/Steven continued. "The battle at Bralmendel was costly. Mine shall not be the only Ceremony of Parting that takes place today. Each of those lives weighs as heavy on his heart as they do on mine, for he holds all men as dear as I hold my own people.

"For our benefit, he left his home, so far as he knows never to return there. He left his family, his friends and his countrymen to journey here and destroy the Dragon and its Dark Mistress. And he has done so!

"The Morvir retreat toward Quarin even as we speak," Arven/Steven told the people. Steven/Arven was surprised. He has not heard any reports on the movements of the Morvir. How had Arven learned of this?

"Without the sacrifice of this man, whose body I now share, they would be almost to Mencar by now. Our shining jewel in the heart of the forest would soon be a burning crypt. So today, as we part and you cheer for my joy and my sorrow, let your voices also rise for he who has also parted from everything he holds dear to ride to our defense." Arven/Steven paused.

A cheer rose from the people, building slowly at first and then rising into an ear-shattering cry that went on and on and on. . . .

There was a touch on their arm. Arven/Steven turned toward Miriam. There were tears in her eyes.

"They are cheering you," she said. "Both of you."

"I know," Steven/Arven replied softly, hardly daring to believe it. "I . . . know."

Steven/Arven looked back toward the crowd below. These

people did not blame him for giving the Morvir the weapons that had destroyed so much of their homeland. They cheered him as the man who had given up all he loved to save them.

Because that is exactly what you did, Arven/Steven thought.

Yes, Steven/Arven agreed. *That* is *what I did.* Tears came to their eyes as Steven and Arven shared the love of the people.

After what seemed like hours, the cheer finally began to die away. Arven/Steven lifted their arms. The crowd fell silent.

"Chieftains of Olvanor," Arven/Steven said. "My final audience will now be held in the Great Hall. Farewell, my people."

As they turned to proceed to the Great Hall, Steven/Arven could hear the cheer rise up again behind them.

Theron's eyes fluttered open. For a moment he just stared at the sunlight sifting through the leafy canopy overhead, wondering where he was. Then memory returned and he sat up, only to find a firm hand on his chest, pushing him back down.

"Rest," said a soft, female voice. Theron looked up into the eyes of a young Olvan woman. At least she *appeared* young. It was difficult to tell with the Olvir.

He looked around. They were in a large, yet completely covered, clearing. Around him, he could see scores of his men, lying on grass mats as they were tended by Olvan women.

"Thank you," he said. His voice came out as a hoarse croak.

"Drink," the woman said, lifting him and holding a cup full of foul-smelling broth to his lips. Theron drank deeply. It tasted as bad as it smelled, but filled him with warmth.

"Thank you," Theron said again. This time his voice sounded more normal.

"You are welcome," the Olvan woman replied, smiling and nodding once.

"Why . . . have you . . . helped us?" Theron asked hesitantly.

"We help all those whom the sea sends to us as it has sent you," she replied, smiling.

"Besides," a harsher male voice said near him, "invaders do not usually drag themselves onto the beach naked and retching, if that is what you are truly asking."

"I . . . suppose not," Theron agreed, turning to see an

Olvan elder in the garb of a tribal chieftain. "We must journey to Validus at once."

"You will not be journeying anywhere for a few days," the chieftain replied. "Some of your men are still unconscious. Some of them are severely wounded."

"Wounded?" Theron said, beginning to rise. "I must . . . tend to . . ."

"You are exhausted," the woman said, pushing him back down onto the mat.

"I am . . . a . . . healer," Theron objected.

"You are too tired," his nurse insisted. "Your men are well tended—none are in danger of death."

"Rest," the chieftain agreed. "The battle has sapped your strength."

"Did . . . you see . . . ?" Theron began.

"No," the chieftain replied. "The battle was too far from shore for us to see. All we saw was the glow of fire on the horizon. However, no Nymran ships have come seeking you. I believe the pirates won."

Theron nodded. The chieftain was correct. If the Nymran fleet had won the battle, they would have searched the shores for survivors. The pirates knew better than to beach on Olvan shores for *any* reason.

"I must . . . journey to . . . Validus," Theron insisted. "The . . . Dragon is . . . on its way . . . there."

"The Dragon is destroyed," the chieftain told him. "The Morvir retreat toward Quarin. That means you can stay and rest for a few days more. I have sent word to Mencar of your presence. I cannot allow you to leave before I hear from the queen."

"Lindra . . . be praised," Theron sighed. At least that was one concern removed from his mind. The warmth of the broth was spreading from his stomach, enveloping his entire body. Soon he felt himself drifting off to sleep.

"Keep them asleep," the chieftain ordered, "until we know what is to be done with them."

"Yes, lord," the nurse replied.

Another chieftain was called to approach the throne. Most were present simply to pay their last respects to their king.

Some few had matters for which they wished to seek the wisdom of their king one final time, and a very few had brought matters of great importance. Steven/Arven was impressed with the patience and wisdom the king displayed. Especially since he knew that most of the king's mind was on . . . other matters.

"Majesty," the chieftain said, kneeling on the steps to the throne.

"The crown welcomes the chieftain of the Red Hawks," Arven/Steven replied.

"Majesty, your memory shall live in song forever among my tribe and the tribe of my brother," the chieftain said in greeting.

"The loyalty and love of both the Red Hawks and the Silver Hawks is well known," Arven/Steven agreed.

"Majesty, I have just received word from my brother of a . . . distressing incident."

"What is that?" Arven/Steven asked.

"A fleet of Nymran ships was sunk by pirates off my brother's coast," the chieftain replied. "Many Nymrans were washed onto the beach and rescued. My brother seeks guidance as to what should be done with them."

"Sunk!" Steven/Arven cried. "What of Prince Theron?"

"The prince is well, Majesty," the chieftain replied, surprised.

"My . . . apologies," Arven/Steven replied as Steven/Arven stepped back to allow the king to speak. "I knew of the Nymran fleet and its mission. I was . . . distressed to learn that it had been sunk."

"Yes, Majesty."

"The Nymrans shall be allowed safe passage through Olvanor," Arven/Steven ordered. "Any tribe that assists them shall be compensated by the crown. Are they still among the Silver Hawks?"

"Yes, Majesty," the chieftain replied. "They are likely to be for a few days yet. Many of them are wounded."

"How many were rescued?"

"Almost three hundred, Majesty."

Steven/Arven shuddered. Three hundred survivors out of three thousand men. That would be a severe blow to the

Regency. The Veran Guard was its only standing legion. Reserves would have to be called in. . . .

"Thank you, Red Hawk," Arven/Steven replied. The chieftain departed, bowing, as the next chieftain was called forward.

Laerdon's eyes slowly opened, heavy with the fatigue of his injury. Nolrod had done well with the boy; his wounds were almost healed over. Unfortunately, such rapid healing exhausted the body.

"F-Father?" he asked, staring into Steven's eyes. Arven/Steven nodded. Laerdon grasped their hand and pulled it to his face. Arven/Steven knelt beside the bed.

"Be strong, my son," he said. "Grieve not for me—I am at peace and we shall be together again soon. Believe me, the years shall pass much more swiftly than you think."

"Father!" Laerdon cried out with a sob.

Arven/Steven leaned over and gathered his son into his arms for a final embrace.

"You are king now, Laerdon," he said. "Rule wisely, with an open heart and an open mind. I know you will do well."

"I . . . will . . . try," Laerdon replied.

"Listen carefully to Nolrod," Arven/Steven advised. "But make your own decisions. *You* are king, and if Nolrod feels you are leaning too heavily on his counsel he will depart."

"Y-yes, Father."

"Rest now, my son," Arven/Steven said softly. "I would not have you join me in the Halls of Mortos too soon."

Arven/Steven knelt by the bed and held his son until the sobs passed and the exhausted youth once again entered the sweet oblivion of sleep. With tears in his eyes, he kissed the young man's forehead and left.

The handmaids had been dismissed by the time Arven/Steven returned to Miriam's quarters. He opened the door and stepped inside, examining the sitting room.

The small waterfall splashed into the bathing pond. Its soft melody played throughout the room. He stepped in, gently closing the door behind him.

She was waiting in the bedroom. She rose and walked over to him as he entered. Arven/Steven smiled. She was wearing the diaphanous golden gown she had had made to wear for him on their hundredth year together.

"My queen," he said, breathlessly. She laid a finger across his mouth. He kissed it.

With practiced skill, her fingers moved across his garments, undoing the fastenings that had taken so long to put in place. His lips sought hers as she pressed against him.

It began gently at first. Then, with a passion that only desperation could bring, she gave herself to him. Her mouth devoured his as if by the strength of her passion she could keep him there, forever.

Arven/Steven stopped—withdrew from her embrace.

"Ar-Arven . . . ?" she said.

"This is not my queen," he said. "This desperate passion is not like you, my love."

She began to weep. Arven/Steven stepped forward and took her into his arms.

"I shall miss you as well," he said. "But we shall not be apart forever. And, Miriam, it is so beautiful there."

"Tell me," Miriam said, wiping her eyes.

"Imagine a land more ancient than even our own," Arven/Steven said with wonder in his voice. "A land with even more Power than Olvanor, where the very trees sing. A land where *all* men—Olvan, Delvan, Umbrian, Nymran and even Morvan—are at peace and are one with the land and with the *Kanir*. Where all the rivers are as cold and as clean as the purest mountain stream. I shall be there to welcome you when you arrive, my queen."

"Arven, I love you," Miriam said, pillowing her head on his shoulder.

"And I you, my dearest," Arven/Steven assured her. "And that love will endure forever."

When they resumed, the gentleness, the tenderness that Arven remembered had returned. All too soon, the moment was over.

"Good-bye, my queen," Arven/Steven said. "I shall await your arrival."

"I shall never take another," Miriam said.

"Yes, you shall," Arven/Steven chided her. "That is the way

of life. And when he arrives in the Halls of Mortos, we shall both be there to greet him. Good-bye, my queen."

"Good-bye . . . Arven," Miriam sobbed.

Steve could feel Arven separate from him.

Stay with her, Arven's voice said inside him. *Comfort her and give her all the love in your heart tonight—for me as well as for her.*

I shall, Arven, Steven promised. *I do love her.*

After seeing her through my eyes, how could you not? Arven replied. *Farewell, my friend—my dearest, yet briefest friend. Give my love to Glorien when next you see her.*

I shall, Steve promised. *Farewell.* And then, like a candle blown out by the wind, Arven's presence was gone. Steve gently stroked Miriam's hair.

"Arven?" she asked.

"No," Steve replied. "He is gone . . . my queen." He held her tightly to him as she wept.

Chapter
-------- **Fourteen** ------------

STEVE'S EYES OPENED. The sound of soft breathing next to him told him that Aerilynn had not left yet. It must be just before dawn. He rolled over and slipped his arm around her.

The voice that moaned pleasantly was *not* Aerilynn's. Steve raised up on an elbow. Golden hair fanned out across the pillow—Miriam. He caressed her cheek. Her eyes fluttered open.

She smiled up at him, clasping her hand over his.

"I have to go," Steve said.

"Mmm," Miriam replied. "Where?"

"First to the Silver Hawks," Steve replied. "Then to Umbria to rejoin Erelvar."

"Aerilynn can take you to the Silver Hawks in a matter of moments," Miriam said, snuggling up against his arm. "How long will it take you to rejoin Erelvar?"

"Not long," Steve replied. "A few hours."

"Good," Miriam said, pulling his head down toward hers. "Then we have time for a proper good-bye. . . ."

Arthwyr ap Madawc waited impatiently. It was almost mid-morning and there was still no sign of Steven. Arthwyr was beginning to wonder if Arven had decided to take up *permanent* residence in Steven's body.

That was not a pleasant thought, all joking aside. Arthwyr was wondering what he would do if that turned out to be the case when Steven finally arrived. Arthwyr kneeled, for Queen Miriam was with him as well.

"Farewell, Steven," Arthwyr heard the queen say. "Would that you could remain with us for a few more days, but I know that cannot be."

That good, eh? Arthwyr thought.

"Good-bye, Miriam," Steven replied. Arthwyr was grateful that his head was bowed. That way, no one would see his surprise from Steven's casual use of the queen's name—*without* title.

"Please, take this with you," the queen said, "as a token of our . . . friendship. You will also find it helpful with the Silver Hawks."

"But, Majesty," Steven objected, "this is—"

"Arven's ring, yes," Miriam finished. "It is . . . not uncommon for the king's host to carry his seal. Laerdon's ring is now the royal seal, but this will identify you to any tribesman in Olvanor."

There was a long pause. From Arthwyr's position, he could see their feet move closer together, then part. Had Steven just kissed her? Arthwyr dared not look up.

"Farewell, Steven," the queen said.

"Good-bye, my queen," Steven replied. The queen's feet turned and walked away.

"You can get up now, Arthwyr," Steven said. "She's gone." Arthwyr rose to his feet.

"I was beginning to think you two were going to leave me there all morning," he complained.

"Sorry about that," Steven replied. "I don't know why she ignored you like that."

"You jest," Arthwyr said. Any fool should realize that the queen had wanted privacy, and so long as Arthwyr's eyes were firmly rooted to the floor, she had it.

"No . . . ," Steven assured him. Arthwyr shook his head.

"One of these days," he said, "you must tell me your secret."

"Secret?" Steven asked.

"We are a bit slow, this morning, are we not, my liege?" Arthwyr observed. "Your secret with these highborn Olvan women."

"That's simple," Steven replied, acridly. "I *respect* them."

"Respect?" Arthwyr noted. "Hmm, I shall have to try that sometime."

"Arthwyr," Steven said, shaking his head, "you're hopeless."

"Yes, my liege."

"Come on," Steven said, climbing into the saddle, "we have places to go, and not much time to get to all of them." Arthwyr mounted his steed.

"Do not blame *me,*" Arthwyr replied, smiling. "After all, am not the one who slept late."

Theron awoke once more under the leafy canopy. He fel' rested, alert. This time, no hand restrained him when he rose

The majority of the survivors were up and about as well Theron smiled. Many of them did not look comfortable in the tribal Olvan clothing they had been given. Some few were actually in armor. Those must have arrived later. The only way someone in armor could have possibly reached the shore was by floating on wreckage.

Theron singled out one of the *triarii* and approached him The man's insignia identified him as a decurion. He quickly rose to attention as Theron approached.

"At ease," Theron said once he was within easy speaking distance. "Report, decurion. Who is the ranking officer here?"

"There are none present above the rank of decurion, Imperator," the man replied. That was not good. Kupris and the other officers must be dead or captured. Hopefully, most were dead. The Coastal pirates had a standing market in the Empire for Validan officers. The fate of any man sold to them would not be pleasant. . . .

"What happened?" Theron asked. "I was thrown into the sea when the attack began."

"Praise to Lindra, and to Uldon, for that, Highness," the decurion replied.

"Yours was the only vessel boarded," the decurion continued. "The damned pirates just rammed the other galleys and sank them. Then what few men were able to doff their armor and swim to the surface were fished out of the sea in nets like tuna."

"How did you escape?" Theron asked.

"By the grace of the *Kanir*, Imperator," the decurion replied. "I thought I was going to drown for certain. My ship carried me all the way to the bottom. Then I was caught by the mast when it broke and carried back to the surface. I and a few others clung to the mast until it washed ashore." Theron nodded.

"A miraculous rescue, indeed," he agreed. "How many have survived?"

"Slightly more than twelve score, Imperator," the soldier replied. "One of the magi is among them. He is not yet conscious."

That was good news, at least. Theron would tend to the magi first among the wounded. He thought for a moment. He would need four centurions and a score of decurions to organize this force.

"You are promoted to centurion," Theron told the decurion. "What is your name?"

"Hektor, Imperator!"

"Gather all the decurions who have survived," he ordered. "I am going to see if our rescuers will grant us the use of a tent or whatever."

"Yes, Imperator!" The new centurion saluted. Theron placed his right fist against his chest in return. Once the men were organized, he would lead them down to the sea to find whatever equipment might have washed ashore from the battle. In all likelihood there was not going to be much.

The forest around Mencar seemed so much more . . . alive than it had before. Steve was aware of every bird, every tree in a completely different way. He stopped at the edge of the clearing around Mencar. It was more than a little overwhelming.

He felt a movement within the wood and glanced up. The startled expression on the face of the Olvan warrior was comical. He had not expected this outlander to see him on his rounds about the city.

But then, Steve realized, he was not exactly an outlander anymore. Joining with Arven had caused the land to accept him as one of its own. As such, he now had a . . . sense of the land and what it held. He could feel the . . . life of the wood.

Steve nudged Aerilynn in the ribs and guided her among the trees. He could almost pick out the trail she followed for himself. Almost. The sense within him enabled him to know when they changed regions.

Soon they emerged into a clearing. Men moved busily about the clearing—Nymrans. They were sorting through what looked like a pile of wreckage. Steve felt, rather than heard, movement in the trees above him. He looked up, seeing only leaves but knowing that he looked a Olvan *laegir* in the eye.

"Where is Silver Hawk?" Steve asked. His eyes tracked the unseen movement as the Olvan descended. Soon the tribesman dropped to the forest floor.

"How did you know he was there?" Arthwyr whispered. Steve ignored him for the moment.

"Who *are* you?" the Olvan asked. Steve merely held out the hand that now carried Arven's ring in reply.

"Forgive me, lord," the Olvan said, dropping to one knee.

"No forgiveness is necessary," Steve replied. "I am obviously not of Olvan birth."

"I had heard that the Dreamer had served as Arven's host," the tribesman insisted. "And what other not of the people would know the ways of the land?"

"Very well," Steve agreed. "You are forgiven. Where is Silver Hawk?"

"He is with the Nymran prince in the tent," the man replied.

"Thank you," Steve replied. He urged Aerilynn across the clearing. The Nymrans stopped to watch them cross as they passed.

"How did you know where that Olvan was in the trees?" Arthwyr asked, once they were out of earshot.

"Where *else* would Olvan guards be?" Steve asked in reply. He didn't really want to explain all of this to Arthwyr.

Steve dismounted once they reached the tent. Arthwyr dismounted beside him.

Stay, Steve thought to Aerilynn as he dropped the reins to the ground.

Stay, Aerilynn agreed. Steve walked up to one of the Nymran legionnaires who guarded the tent.

"Master Wilkinson of Quarin to see Prince Theron," he said, speaking in Nymran.

The guard turned and entered the tent. Steve examined it carefully. This *was* a Nymran tent, but it was not Theron's command tent. Rather, it was one of the legion's ten-men bivouac tents.

The flap of the tent opened and Theron looked out, surprise plain on his face.

"Steven!" he said. "Please, come in, both of you."

"I'm glad to see you're all right," Steve said as he entered the tent. The chief of the Silver Hawks was indeed here, as well as five Nymrans. Judging by his garb, one of them was a magi. His eyes narrowed suspiciously when he saw Steve.

"Highness," he said, "this man is warded."

"I knew that," Theron replied, dismissing the magi's concern with a wave of his hand. "He has been ever since he returned."

"I am?" Steve asked. "I have?" Theron turned to face him.

"You did not know?" Theron asked.

"No!" Steve replied.

"Interesting," Theron observed. "Especially since Felinor claimed that you are the one maintaining it. He was quite certain of that.

"Enough of that, though," Theron said. "What news do you have for me?"

"The tank has been destroyed," Steve told him. "The Morvir are retreating back to Quarin, but most of the royal family and the royal guard are dead."

"That confirms what I've learned from the Olvir," Theron replied, nodding. "However, the prophecy states that only the Arm of Death could slay the Dragon. I do not understand. . . ." Theron let the comment trail off.

"I've been told that the Dragon has *not* been destroyed," Steve added.

"By whom?" Theron asked.

"By Arven, during the Ceremony of Parting," Steve explained. "He said that the Dragon had not been destroyed, just badly wounded."

"That *would* seem to be a reliable source," Theron agreed. "But you are certain the tank is destroyed?"

"It blew itself into a million pieces," Steve assured him. "All the king's horses and all the king's men won't be able to put *that* tank together again."

"I beg your pardon?" Theron asked.

"Just paraphrasing an old nursery rhyme from my world," Steve explained. "There is no way that tank will ever roll again. I don't understand what Arven meant, either."

"There is only one explanation," Theron mused.

"And that is?"

"The . . . tank was not the Dragon," Theron explained. "Or, at least, not all of it."

"The Morvan army!" Steve exclaimed.

"And *they* are headed straight toward Erelvar," Theron agreed.

"I have to warn Erelvar!" Steve said.

"Yes," Theron said. "He must be told. But you have some time before the Morvir are ready to move into Umbria."

"Yes," Steve agreed. "What about you? What happened?"

"The Coastal pirates were laying in wait for us," Theron said disgustedly. "A fleet of pirate galleys rammed our triremes and sank us. We are fortunate that as many as did survived."

"So, no weapons from my world were involved," Steve observed.

"No," Theron agreed. "Just pirate galleys. They knew where we would be, though. Someone in Morvanor has forged an alliance with the Coasts."

Steve nodded. That would not be good news to carry back to Erelvar, but there was no denying it. Only the Morvir could have given the pirates the information on Theron's whereabouts.

"I am glad you sought me out, Dreamer," Theron added. "I have need of you."

"How so?"

"You can aid me in healing my injured men," Theron explained. "If nothing else, you can supplement my Power. I need to get these three centuries headed toward Validus as soon as possible."

"I'll help any way I can," Steve assured him.

It was just after noon by the time Theron had finished healing the wounded men. The experience had proven educational on a number of fronts. Not only had Steve been able to observe Theron's use of the Power in healing, but he had discovered something new in his own access to it.

Before, Steve had seemed to draw the Power from someplace *inside* himself. Now, not only did the Power come from within, but he could feel it flow into him from the land itself as well. Apparently, his acceptance by the land extended to that level as well.

"Your . . . Power is great, Steven," Theron said. Even with Steve aiding his effort, Theron had been exhausted by the end of it.

"I could . . . not have done it . . . without you," Theron said. Steve laid a hand on Theron's shoulder and opened himself again to the Power. Now, however, he forced it into Theron, replenishing him. Theron blinked in surprise.

"I'm glad I could help," Steve said. In spite of the long work and his efforts now, Steve did not feel overly fatigued.

"I have to rejoin Erelvar now, however," Steve added. "Unless there is something else you need of me?"

"N-no," Theron replied. "My . . . thanks for your help." Steve nodded. Theron sounded much better—less exhausted.

"Anytime," Steve said. "Come on, Arthwyr. We've got to get moving."

"Yes, my liege," Arthwyr replied. They mounted their steeds.

"Farewell, Steven," Theron said. "Good fortune in Umbria."

"Thanks," Steve replied. "We're going to need it."

Jared watched as the remnants of the Olvan spearhead returned to Quarin. The ammunition transport led the column, followed by the two surviving trucks and last by three hundred of the original five hundred men that had ventured into Olvanor.

Even so, for such a small force they had accomplished much. Almost all of the Olvan royal family had been destroyed, along with virtually all of the elite Mencarian army. True, the cost was great, but it could have been much, much worse.

It was a pity that the Dragon would not be loosed in the Regency. Even so, the Regency would not be a threat to Morvanor for some time now. Their new allies had proven quite useful—more so than Jared would have thought. The entire Veran Guard, or most of it, was now either at the bottom of the Inner Sea or sold into slavery in the Empire, which was already preparing to move against Validus.

Jared was still confused as to how the Dragon had been destroyed in Olvanor. According to the prophecy of Uldon, only the Arm of Death was able to accomplish that. Jared had deliberately driven Erelvar into Umbria by attacking the northwest quarter of the city and then sent the tank into Olvanor to avoid just that. What little intelligence they had claimed that Erelvar was still in Umbria.

Jared shook his head. Somehow, someone *other* than the Arm of Death had destroyed the Dragon. How this had come to be was beyond him. Perhaps Erelvar had found some way to travel to Olvanor in time to destroy the Dragon himself. . . .

No, that did not seem likely. It was much more likely that some element of the prophecy was being misunderstood. . . .

"Greetings, High Lord," Phelandor's voice said behind him.

"Greetings, Lord Phelandor," Jared acknowledged. "What is your report?"

"We were able to retreat from Olvanor without incident," Phelandor replied. "We were forced to leave behind two cases of tank ammunition, but I ordered it buried and it is well hidden."

Jared shrugged. "It is useless without the tank," he said. "You could have left *all* of it. It consumed more fuel to return it here."

"I . . . did not think of that," Phelandor replied.

"It does not matter," Jared said. "Since we are taking only the ammunition transport, we have more than enough fuel to carry out our objective."

"Yes, High Lord," Phelandor agreed.

"I have decided to personally take command of the Umbrian campaign," Jared added. "I would like you and Kephas to stay on as sub-commanders, for there will undoubtedly be times when I am called away to Morvanor."

"Yes . . . High Lord," Phelandor replied.

Steve could sense when they arrived in Umbria. The life of the forest seemed less . . . intense. Steve could still sense it, as he had in the forest around Mencar, but it was not the same.

Is this it? Steve asked.

Yes, Aerilynn silently replied. *Small forest.*

Steve had asked Aerilynn to return them to the small copse of trees they had used to leave Umbria. Hopefully, Erelvar had not travelled very far from his last position. Even so, with Arthwyr's tracking skills, it shouldn't be too hard to follow an army.

For that matter, Steve could probably find it without *any* knowledge of tracking. An army didn't exactly march through without disturbing the local countryside.

They left the small forest and, in a few minutes, they were back on the road to Castle Aldwyn. The road looked much as it had when they left. After almost an hour's ride they came to the site Steven had selected for the tank trap.

He stopped in the middle of the road. There was, literally, no sign that the Delvir had ever fortified the hill ahead of them.

"Are . . . we in the right place?" Steve asked.

"Without question," Arthwyr confirmed.

"Where is . . . ," Steve began.

"The wall?" Arthwyr finished.

They began to ride to the top of the hill. However, as they circled around to climb the less steep far side, they were hailed by Delvan sentries.

"Halt!" the voice commanded. "Who goes' there?"

"The Dreamer," Steve replied. "I wish to see Captain Tsadhoq." There was a pause, presumably while the sentries discussed what was to be done. Eventually, one of the Delvan sentries emerged from the light brush of the hillside. He looked Steve up and down carefully.

"Captain Tsadhoq is nae here," he finally said, apparently satisfied with Steve's identity. "He is with the main body of the Guard an hour down the road."

"Thank you," Steve said. He and Arthwyr turned back for the road.

Jared watched as the Morvir unloaded the trucks into the ammunition transport. They were only going to get about four truckloads into the transport. It seemed that there would be no way to avoid sending the trucks in to resupply the army. Still, the territory they would be sent through would have already been taken. That should help prevent any attacks against the convoys.

Jared felt a stir in the Power as someone emerged from the Gray Plain behind him. He turned to see Lord Hilarin riding up alongside him. Jared smiled beneath his mask. Apparently his efforts, untutored as they might be, were heightening his awareness of the Power, after all.

"I have news, High Lord," Hilarin said, "of the Dreamer."

"The Dreamer?" Jared replied, turning his attention more fully from the loading.

"Yes, High Lord," Hilarin said. "Alas, I fear it is not good news."

"Go on."

"The Dreamer is warded from detection," Hilarin explained. "He cannot be found by sorcery."

"How have you learned this?"

"Let us say that I owe Master Levas a favor," Hilarin replied. Jared nodded his understanding. If a *kaiva* of the third order could not locate the Dreamer, then he could not be located by sorcery.

"He will be with Erelvar," Jared stated. "When we destroy them, we will have him as well."

"Yes, High Lord," Hilarin agreed.

They had learned from Tsadhoq that Erelvar was camped about another three hours down the road. Steve wasn't certain what the idea behind this staggered camp structure was.

Arthwyr had reluctantly agreed to let Steve ride on ahead. Steve had immediately urged Aerilynn into a gallop, quickly leaving Arthwyr's mortal horse behind. Under Aerilynn's tireless hooves the three-hour ride had been reduced to a single hour. Arthwyr could catch up while Steve met with Erelvar.

As King Arven had said, neither she nor Steve were fatigued by the ride. They could ride all the way to Delgroth and back at this pace without stopping, Steve was certain. Of course, sleep deprivation had many effects in addition to physical fatigue. Steve wondered if Aerilynn's Power would compensate for those as well.

Steve slowed Aerilynn to a walk as the camp came into view. The sentries passed him through after only a cursory challenge. These men knew him.

"Arthwyr ap Madawc is about two hours behind me," Steve forewarned them. "Send him to Lord Erelvar's tent when he arrives."

"We shall watch for him, my lord," the sentry assured him.

Steve rode into the camp. He smiled when he saw that Erelvar's tent, and his own, was set up on the edge of a small grove of trees. If only Steve had known, he could have saved hours of travel.

Erelvar met Steve as he approached the tent.

"Steven!" Erelvar said in greeting. "What news have you from Olvanor?"

"Mixed, I'm afraid," Steve replied.

"The Dragon?"

"The tank was destroyed," Steve answered as he stepped into

Erelvar's tent. "Along with six of the eight supply trucks and almost two hundred Morvir."

"That seems like excellent news," Erelvar observed.

"Steven!" Glorien said happily as Steve stepped into the main room of the tent. Then her gaze fell on the ring that he wore. Her hand moved to her mouth as her eyes widened in horror.

"Arven, and most of Olvanor's army, are dead," Steve said.

"No," Glorien whispered.

"I served as host during the Ceremony of Parting, my lady," Steve continued. "Arven asked me to give you his love."

"Oh, no—no," Glorien repeated.

"You hosted Arven?" Erelvar asked.

"Yes," Steve replied.

"Would you again? For Glorien?"

"Of course, but there is no priest. . . ."

"Arven, King of Olvanor!" Erelvar commanded. "The Arm of Death bids you. Come forth!"

Steve gasped. Unlike before, when the priest had performed the ritual, there was no gentle transition—the Power of the Champion of Mortos ripped through the barriers between life and death like a sword. Steve staggered beneath the psychic impact.

I am here, Arven's voice said in Steve's mind.

Yeah, Steve thought back, *so I noticed. Come on out.*

"Niece," Arven said. "Do not grieve so. I am still with you."

"Uncle?" Glorien said, rising and stepping toward him. Arven held out his—Steven's—arms to her. She stepped into his embrace.

"It is I," Arven assured her. "I am still with you, and you will join me in time. This is but a temporary parting, I promise you. I must go, now. Steven has much to discuss with Erelvar."

"Good-bye, Uncle," Glorien said.

"Good-bye, *felgae,*" Arven said. "I am proud of you. I always have been."

And Arven was gone as quickly as he had arrived. Steve stepped out of Glorien's embrace.

"Thank you, Steven," she said.

"Of course," Steve replied. Then to Erelvar, "How about a little warning next time?"

"I thought it best to do it quickly," Erelvar replied. "What I do is not like the hosting."

That was true. During the hosting, Arven and Steve had been joined, almost of one mind. This had been more like what he had experienced with Belevairn—another person taking his body while Steve had watched.

"You said the news you brought was mixed," Erelvar said, interrupting Steve's thoughts. "What else is there?"

"Two more things," Steve replied. "Theron's fleet was sunk by pirates off the Olvan coast."

"What!" Erelvar said. "Is Theron . . . ?"

"Theron survived," Steve assured him, "by sheer luck. Most of the Veran Guard was destroyed. The pirates knew where to find them. Theron believes that Morvanor has allied with the Coasts, whatever that means."

"The Coasts were once Nymran penal colonies," Erelvar explained. "They managed to wrest their autonomy from the Empire and have been pirates ever since. The Northern Coast practically borders Morvanor. If they *have* allied with Morvanor, this could have serious consequences in the long run."

"It seems to have had pretty serious consequences in the short run," Steve noted. "Almost the entire Veran Guard has been destroyed. Theron has about three hundred men left."

"Yes," Erelvar agreed. "That will not be good for Validus. The Empire is certain to move against them. You said there were *two* things. I am almost hesitant to ask what the second is."

"The tank was not the Dragon," Steve said. "At least, not all of it."

"What do you mean?" Erelvar asked.

"Erelvar," Steve asked, "who was prophesied to destroy the Dragon?"

"I . . . was," Erelvar replied.

"Right! But the tank has been destroyed—*I* destroyed it."

"That is against the prophecy!" Erelvar said, realizing the implications.

"Which means that the tank must not have been the Dragon," Steve concluded.

"Then . . . what *is* the Dragon?"

"The tank was *part* of it," Steve explained. "The Morvan army is the rest of it—and the whole damned thing is on its way here."

Chapter
-------- Fifteen ------------

HIGH LORD JARED watched as the army prepared to move out. At Jared's order, the force had been divided—half the Morvir to the front and half in back with the ammunition transport and the fuel truck safely nestled between them. No pit would catch the ammunition transport in Umbria as the tank had been caught in Olvanor.

Phelandor and Kephas had already been sent to scout ahead. Jared wanted to be certain that no surprises awaited the Morvir on the road to Castle Aldwyn. The Dreamer had done enough damage to their plans. Of all the Northern Kingdoms, the attack against Umbria was the most vital to Morvanor's defense.

After the Delvir, the Umbrians were the people most likely to move against Morvanor. With the Delvan royal guard in Umbria, that made this campaign doubly important. Outside of the nearly impregnable Delvan strongholds, the Royal Guard would die as easily as the Umbrians.

"We are ready, Dread Lord," one of the captains reported, saluting with the open hand in the Earth fashion. It was Garth, commander of what would have been Jared's company had the Mistress not been defeated. Jared returned the salute.

"Move out," he commanded.

Captain Garth spun on his heel and marched back to his place at the head of his lead company.

"Battaaal-ion!" he shouted. "Move out!" Jared Company began to march, followed by Daemor Company and Kephas Company. The ammunition transport and fuel truck fell in behind them, followed by Fanchon Company and the remains of Phelandor Company.

There was a group with an interesting story to tell. Somehow the Olvir had contrived a trap capable of destroying the T-55. Not that that in itself was all that difficult. The method they had used was a fairly standard one—on Earth. The attack against the supply convoy with Molotov cocktails was also a standard Earth tactic.

The Olvir *could* have reasoned those tactics out on their own. It was not impossible for them to have realized that fire, particularly Delvan Fire, was their only possible effective weapon against the tank. Not likely, but possible.

One thing was *not* possible, however. One of the companies that had trained on Earth before Jared Company had served briefly in Afghanistan against the Soviet backed forces. There they had learned an Afghan trick for defeating infrared guidance on Soviet aircraft.

The Afghans would fill cans with urine and hang them in trees near their camps at night. Then, when the Soviet-supplied fighters would come in to strike the camp, they would hit the decoy targets first, giving the rebels enough warning to at least have a hope of escaping.

According to Phelandor Company, the tank's infrared had detected scores of targets in the trees around Bralmendel. Once the battle was over, Phelandor Company had searched the surrounding forest. They had found several metal flasks full of urine.

Someone with a knowledge of Earth weaponry had directed the defense of Bralmendel. Garth had a pretty good idea of who that someone must be.

His last mission on Earth had been a hostage exchange. A young woman, captured by Lord Belevairn, had been exchanged for her brother, the Dreamer. Garth and Lieutenant Dalin had escorted the Dreamer from the city of Guatemala to their base in Nicaragua, where they had left him in Lord Belevairn's custody.

Shortly after that, the five companies had returned to Delgroth and Hilarin Company had been sent to Earth for their month of field training. Since then, Garth had neither seen nor heard mention of Lord Belevairn. Somehow the Dreamer *must* have escaped and managed to find his way here.

Furthermore, the Dread Lords knew this. Why else would Hhayim Company, which had just begun its year of basic training, have been sent to join them in Quarin? Why else, after withdrawing from Olvanor, would the Special Forces be ordered to load all of the supplies into the armored ammunition transport before heading into Umbria? Why else would the transport and the fuel truck be sandwiched between the five companies for protection?

There was no doubt in Garth's mind. The Dreamer was about and the Dread Lords knew it. He suspected that all was not well with the Mistress, either. Hhayim Company had seen the fires of Delgroth unleashed. Somehow, even without that, Garth just *knew* that she was gone. And there were other clues as well.

Lord Daemor, like Belevairn, was conspicuously absent and the other Lords deferred to Lord Jared as Garth had never seen them do before. Somehow, the balance of power in Morvanor had shifted to Lord Jared.

Still, if one of the Dread Lords were to rule in Morvanor, Garth could not think of a better one than Jared. Lord Jared had personally rescued Garth from an ambush in Umbria six years ago. Unlike all of the other Dread Lords, Jared still had *some* shred of his humanity left.

Even so, it would probably be best if Garth did not advertise his understanding of the situation. In Morvanor, it was not a good thing to know more than one's commanders *wanted* one to know. Still, he could keep an eye out for *familiar* faces among the enemy. . . .

"You are going *where*?" Arthwyr asked, incredulously.

"I am going to take a quick trip to Quarin to see what the Morvir are up to," Steve repeated. "On Aerilynn, I can make it there and back in a few minutes. If you don't want to come along . . ."

"Not if you are going to dress like that," Arthwyr replied.

"Huh? What's wrong with how I'm dressed?"

"Nothing," Arthwyr replied. "If one is going to temple! But white is not exactly the color of choice for sneaking about the forest, my lord! You might as well fire off some of those . . . flares of yours!"

"Oh," Steve acknowledged. "Well . . . Aerilynn's whiter than my clothes, and we *have* to take her."

"I believe we can do something about that as well," Arthwyr insisted. "Come, my lord."

Steve had to hand it to Arthwyr; he had no idea where the Umbrian knight had managed to dig up the green-and-brown *bardé*. With that draped over her, the only white that showed on Aerilynn was around her eyes and her feet.

"Sir Bowen was reluctant to part with this," Arthwyr told him. "I assured him that it would be returned safely."

"Happy now?" Steve asked, smiling. He had traded his own white garments for a green tunic with a tan undertunic.

"Less unhappy," Arthwyr conceded. "At least now we shall not stand out like beacons."

"Let's get going," Steve said, mounting.

Hot, Aerilynn's mental voice said in objection to the *bardé*.

Safe, Steve countered. *Take us to the forest outside Quarin on the Umbrian side.*

Aerilynn obediently walked into the small copse of trees near which Erelvar had chosen to camp. As the trees closed over them, Steve could feel the subtle shifts that told him that Aerilynn was already walking trails not quite of this world.

Steve glanced behind him. Arthwyr followed closely behind. Steve wasn't worried; the Umbrian was developing a knack for this. He turned his attention back to the trails Aerilynn was following.

The forest around Quarin was more like the Olvan forest than those deeper in. Steve was beginning to understand why the Olvir never left their own lands. After being immersed in a forest so full of life for so long, it must be depressing to enter a normal wood.

The forest around them now cried out in anguish. Steve cast out with his new senses: what were the Morvir doing? He turned Aerilynn toward where he felt the center of the disturbance, unconsciously nudging her back into the ways of the forest.

They reached the injured area of the forest quickly. Through the trees, Steve could see the cause of the forest's anguish. The ammunition transport ripped its way through the underbrush, widening the narrow road that led to Quarin. The fuel truck

ollowed and both were nestled in the midst of several
ompanies of Morvir. There was no sign of the other trucks.

This was *not* good. The Dread Lords had outmaneuvered
hem. The supplies for the invasion were being carried in that
rmored vehicle instead of the trucks. Molotov cocktails would
lo very little to the ammunition transport and it was obvious
hat the Morvir were not going to let anyone close enough to
ven try.

Steve doubted that the pit tactic would work again, either.
The Morvir were going to be expecting that now. At this point
he soldiers, instead of the supplies, were the most vulnerable
arget and they weren't all that vulnerable.

"Arthwyr," Steve said, "meet me back north of the Quarin
gatehouse in the forest."

"What?" Arthwyr said. "What are you going to do?"

"Buy us some time," he said. "If I don't get there by sun-
down, you have to make it to Erelvar ahead of these people."

"I am not leaving you . . . ," Arthwyr began.

"You have sworn an oath!" Steve hissed between his teeth.
"Now do as I command!"

"Yes, my lord," Arthwyr agreed. He turned his mount and
rode back toward Quarin. Steve dug his remaining few hand
grenades out of his saddlebags. This *had* to be the craziest stunt
he had ever thought of.

Lord Jared rode high above the battalion, watching carefully.
The forest had been searched carefully prior to their departure,
but Jared was not going to take any risks.

Movement from below caught his eye. A lone horseman
charged the flank of the battalion. Jared quickly surveyed the
surrounding forest. There was no other sign of attack. What
fool would . . .

Jared realized with horror who the horseman *must* be just as
two explosions erupted among the Morvir flanking the ammunition transport. The Dreamer!

Jared drew his sword and called the Mistress's fire, hurling
it earthward even as he descended. The Dreamer had to be
stopped before he reached the transport!

*   *   *

Steve pulled the pin from another grenade. Three left—he would have to make them count. Aerilynn galloped toward the transport. They would have only seconds before the Morvi responded. Steve hurled the grenade under the transport's left tread.

He was reaching for another grenade when Aerilynn literally leapt to the left. A bolt of fire struck the ground where she had been. Steve looked up to the right—Jared! Damn! He hadn't even *thought* of the Dread Lords!

Steve hurled his grenade at the fuel truck. Only as it left his hand did he think to wonder whether or not he had pulled the pin. He hoped that he had. . . .

Aerilynn galloped across the front of the ammunition transport. The tread rolled over the grenade Steve had thrown. Steve spurred her harder, pulling the last grenade from the folds of his tunic. This had to be the one that would get him out of here. . . .

The grenade under the transport's thread detonated. The left side of the transport actually lifted almost an inch from the blast. Steve pulled the pin from his last grenade and hurled it into the Morvir ahead of him.

The men who had been preparing to fire on him leapt and ran for their own safety. Behind him, the grenade that had landed atop the fuel truck exploded. He *had* remembered to pull the pin!

The grenade ahead of him exploded, clearing his path to the forest. This just might work! He dug his heels into Aerilynn's sides as he glanced back.

He barely noticed the burning fuel truck or the limping transport. All he saw was the black, nightmarish horse behind him and the one who rode it. Jared was almost on top of him!

Steve turned back as Aerilynn leapt from the road into the trees.

Away, Steve commanded. *Quickly!*

Steve's stomach lurched as a violent shift of reality swept over him. They were in the Olvan forest! Steve could feel the life of the wood soar beyond what it had been in Umbria.

Another violent shift knotted his stomach as Steve looked back. Jared was *still* behind him! Steve turned back as another reality shift passed. Aerilynn was trying everything she could to lose their pursuer. Steve just hung on for the ride. His armor sure would be nice to have right now. . . .

Aerilynn leapt from one trail to another. Two violent shifts in quick succession threatened to squeeze Steve's stomach like a wringer. He swallowed the bile that rose in his throat, fighting off the nausea.

Aerilynn slowed to a walk and Steve sat up, looking around. Jared was nowhere to be seen. Steve smiled. With the *goremka,* Jared would not be lost for long. Still, it was *bound* to be annoying!

The Dreamer had disappeared! One moment, Jared had been right behind him. Then the Dreamer's steed had leapt through the brush and disappeared.

Jared dismounted and examined the ground. The horse had left no sign for him to follow. It was simply gone. That was not possible! Jared had felt no use of the Power!

He remounted and looked about. This was *not* the forest around Quarin! This terrain looked more like . . . Olvanor. Jared quickly urged his mount onto the Gray Plain. He had to return to the battalion and assess the damage. . . .

Arthwyr found Steven waiting for him at the rendezvous. To his relief, his friend did not seem to be harmed.

"Was it worth it?" he asked.

"Definitely," Steven replied. "I destroyed the fuel truck and damaged the transport."

"Transport?"

"The little dragon," Steve explained. "I think they'll be able to repair it, but it should buy us a day or so."

Arthwyr sighed, shaking his head. Only Steven could assault an enemy force over a thousand strong and escape unscathed. Anyone else would have died like the fool he was.

"Where to now?" he asked.

"Back to warn Erelvar," Steven replied. "The situation has changed, and not for the better."

Garth squeezed the handle on the fire extinguisher, filling the ruptured compartment of the fuel truck with carbon dioxide. Other crews attacked the flames on the outside of the truck with extinguishers and water.

Thank the Mistress that this truck had been carrying diesel *and* that the driver had not lost his head. If he had not driven it out of the pool of flame before abandoning the cab, all of their fuel would have been lost. If the truck had been full of gasoline . . . well, Garth would rather not think about that.

As it was, the fuel in the center compartment would have to be dumped. This attack had cost them a third of their fuel supply. It had taken a brave man to execute such a daring attack.

Garth had gotten just enough of a glimpse of their attacker to be certain who he was. The Dreamer, the man that Garth and Dalin had taken as captive to Lord Belevairn. At this point, he would have to admit to Lord Jared that he knew what was happening. Until Garth had actually seen the Dreamer, he could pretend that he did not know what was happening. Now . . .

The fire extinguisher in his hand sputtered and died. The interior of the compartment was now filled with a cold fog. The rest of the crew had put out the flames on the sides of the truck.

"Pull the truck over there and dump the center compartment," Garth ordered, pointing to a small creek that ran alongside the road. "Be careful—it's still hot."

He turned back to the repair crew that was inspecting the damage to the ammunition transport. If only this damn thing were armed! Losing the tank in Olvanor had been a heavy blow.

"Report!" Garth ordered.

"The tread has suffered minor damage to several links," the sergeant in charge told him. "We can have it fixed by morning. Faster if we could get some of the links from the other transport in Quarin."

"I will see what I can do," Garth replied. If Lord Jared would carry him back to Quarin, Garth could bring one of the trucks out, pick up a crew and go back to get the links. That would also give him the opportunity to speak with Lord Jared.

The damage could have been worse, Jared supposed. Upon his return he could immediately tell that the fuel truck had not been completely destroyed. In fact, it seemed to still be operational. He saw Captain Garth over by the transport.

"Captain Garth!" Jared called. Garth turned and walked over to him, saluting.

"Your report, Captain," Jared said.

"The fuel truck is operational, Dread Lord," Garth replied, "but we have lost a third of our fuel. The ammunition transport has suffered minor damage to one of its treads. We can have it repaired by morning."

"No sooner?" Jared asked. He wanted to get out of this forest and onto open ground, where such attacks would be more difficult.

"Possibly, Lord," Garth said, "with your help."

"How can I help?"

"If you could take me to Quarin, I could bring a truck out to carry a crew back to Quarin. If some of the tread links from the other transport survived undamaged, it would speed the repairs."

"How likely is that?"

"Almost certain, Dread Lord," Garth replied. "Even one undamaged link would speed our efforts."

"Very well," Jared agreed, reaching down. Garth mounted behind Jared. The captain remained silent until they arrived at Quarin and were once more on solid ground.

"I shall expect your return within the hour," Jared said once Garth had dismounted. He turned to depart.

"Dread Lord," Garth said, interrupting him.

"Yes?"

"Lord, there is something else I wish to speak with you about now that we are away from the army."

Jared had been expecting something like this. The Special Forces would be very confused about having been attacked with Earth weapons. Unfortunately, Jared had not been able to contrive a plausible explanation as of yet.

"What is it, Captain?" Jared asked.

"Lord, I recognized the man who attacked the column," Garth said.

"*What?*" Jared exclaimed.

"Yes, Lord," Garth replied.

"How do you know this man?" Jared demanded.

"My last mission on Earth was a hostage exchange," Garth explained. "Lord Belevairn had captured a young girl, and her brother had agreed to surrender himself in exchange for her. Lord Belevairn claimed that this man was the Dreamer."

"Did he surrender to you?" Jared asked. This was *not* good. If this story had not yet spread, Jared would more than likely have no choice but to kill Garth.

"Yes, Lord," Garth replied.

"What was done with him?"

"We brought him back, captive, to Lord Belevairn, Dread Lord," Garth explained. "Lord Belevairn was going to take him to Delgroth after he returned us through the void."

"Damned fool!" Jared exclaimed. "He should have killed him as he was ordered!"

"Lord?" Garth asked. Jared looked down at him.

"Yes, Captain?" he said.

"The Mistress is . . . gone, is she not?"

Jared sighed. Garth had just sealed his own death.

"Yes, Captain," he said, grasping the hilt of his sword beneath his cloak.

"Lord!" Garth exclaimed, falling to his knees. "Please tell me it is you that now rules Morvanor and not Daemor or one of the others!"

Jared paused, taken aback by the unexpected display.

"The Council of Ten now rules Morvanor," Jared replied. "The other Lords have appointed me as High Lord of that council."

"Thank the Mistress!" Garth exclaimed.

"Why?" Jared asked.

"High Lord, you, alone among the Lords, will keep Morvanor for *Her*," Garth replied. "You alone will preserve us to serve again on the day of Her return. The others would follow their own desires—but not you!"

Jared released the hilt of his sword. Behind the mask his eyes narrowed. Such devotion to the Mistress was almost unheard of. Fear, yes, but not *this*. Unless . . . Jared knew the Mistress had held plans to add a thirteenth from among the Special Forces.

"Captain Garth?" Jared said, his voice low and threatening.

"Yes, Drea . . . High Lord?"

"Did you have an . . . audience with the Mistress on your return from Earth?"

"Y-yes, High Lord," Garth replied.

"Concerning what?"

"I . . . I cannot say," Garth stammered.

"Did she let the shadows fall for you?" Jared asked, his voice dropping even lower.

"I . . . cannot . . ."

"Did she?" Jared shouted.

"Yes!" Garth cried, flinching. "Y-yes, High Lord."

"Noooo!" Jared screamed in anguish and rage as his sword flew from its scabbard. Fire blazed white hot along its length as Jared's eyes flared brilliant red behind his mask. Jared knew the ritual. He *knew*! She had taken him by the hand and drawn him to her. Then she had wrapped the chains around his soul that could *never* be broken.

No! the memory of a command spoken long ago echoed in his mind. *I love you no less, my Jared.*

Jared blinked. It was no longer Daemor he saw before him, smug and full of himself with the Mistress' affections. It was Garth, calmly standing at parade rest with his eyes closed, waiting for the blow to fall.

The fire on the blade flickered and died. Jared let his arm fall, and then his head. Had he been mortal . . . he would have wept.

"As you were, Captain," he said, softly.

"H-High Lord?" Garth stammered. "Are you . . . ?" Garth let the question trail away.

"I am . . . well," Jared replied. "I cannot kill you. You are the . . . last one *she* touched. We are all that is left of her now."

"Y-yes, High Lord."

"Was she as . . . beautiful as I remember?" Jared asked.

"Beyond belief, Lord," Garth replied. Jared flinched at the sympathy in the man's voice. Sympathy for *him*? Jared shook his head. There were matters that must be tended to without delay.

"What," Jared asked, "shall we tell the men . . . Lord Garth?"

*   *   *

Steven had apparently not escaped as unscathed as Arthwyr had originally thought. By the time they had made it back to camp, he was as pale as a corpse and slumped over Aerilynn's back. In any other situation, Arthwyr would have stopped and tended to him. Now he knew the best thing was to get him to Erelvar and the healers.

They emerged from the trees in the midst of the camp. Thank the gods for that horse! Arthwyr jumped down from the saddle and ran to Erelvar's tent.

"Get the healer!" he shouted at the guard who stood outside the tent. The man looked absolutely stunned at their appearance.

"Move it, man!" Arthwyr said. "Or I'll kick your arse out of the way and get Erelvar himself!"

"What's going on out here?" Lord Erelvar demanded, stepping outside. His eyes fell on Steven's form slumped over Aerilynn's neck.

"Go!" Erelvar commanded the guard. The man was off like a shot from a crossbow. Erelvar and Arthwyr gently lifted Steven down from the saddle. He cried out when they started to lay him on his back.

They turned him over. There was a small bloodstain on the back of his tunic and the cloth was ripped. Arthwyr tore away the garment. A small piece of metal was embedded in Steven's back, near the spine. He had apparently never felt it.

Arthwyr had seen such things before. Men struck from behind by arrows who never noticed the wound until either the battle ended or they fell dead. But with an arrow, their companions could tell what had happened. This had gone unnoticed until Steven had begun to falter.

"He's bleeding inside," Erelvar said. Then he grabbed Arthwyr's wrist before the Umbrian could pull the shard from Steven's back.

"No!" Erelvar said. "He could die in seconds if you do that! Wait for Felinor."

The *magus* arrived quickly. He knelt by Steven and examined him. Then he closed his eyes and moved his hands over the wound.

"He has lost much blood," Felinor finally announced.

"I *never* would have guessed," Arthwyr spat. "What can you do for him, sorcerer?"

"Not as much as a true healer could," Felinor said. "Would that Prince Theron were still here." He looked closely at Erelvar and then at Arthwyr. Arthwyr felt a tingle pass over his body that smacked of sorcery.

"Your blood can help him," Felinor announced. "I will have to remove the fragment and he will lose even more blood before I can seal the wound."

"If it will save him," Arthwyr said, "take every drop."

"Fortunately," Felinor replied, "I shall only need a few pints."

Steve blinked. He was lying in a tent—*his* tent. It was late, or dark at any rate. He started to sit and a burning pain flared up along his entire back. He cried out.

"Be still, my love," a familiar voice said from the darkness. Soon the light of a candle lit the tent.

"Aerilynn?" Steve asked. He felt so *weak*.

"Yes," she said, mopping his brow with a damp cloth. "Rest. You were sorely wounded in the battle today."

"But—I . . . never felt . . . a thing," Steve protested.

"That happens sometimes," Aerilynn replied. "Rest."

Steve had something else to say but he couldn't think of it right now. He drifted off to sleep.

Chapter -------- Sixteen ------------

"THE TRANSPORT HAS been repaired, Dread Lord," Garth reported.

"Excellent," Jared replied. The sun was just beginning to rise over the horizon. They had lost an entire afternoon's march. Curse the Dreamer!

"How are the rumors among the men?" Jared asked.

"Much reduced, Dread Lord," Captain Garth replied. Jared nodded. With Garth's help he had fabricated an explanation for yesterday's events.

Garth had told the men that the Dreamer had escaped from Delgroth—that the Mistress had released the fires of the mountain to destroy him, but somehow he had escaped her wrath. Lord Belevairn had been killed by the Dreamer during his escape and the path to Earth was lost until Lord Daemor could find it again.

The tale explained everything. The Dreamer's presence, the absence of both Lord Belevairn and Lord Daemor as well as the eruption of Delgroth. Most important, it kept the secret of the Mistress's . . . absence from the one group they dared not tell. Garth's . . . special status had also been omitted from the report.

That was still a problem. Jared was certain that none of the other Lords would accept Garth's position as one of the Twelve. A *Kaimorda* without mask or steed? Not likely. Still, something would have to be done. There was only one thing that Jared could think of. . . .

"Captain Garth?" he said.

"Yes, Lord?"

"By order of the Mistress," Jared began, "you are hereby promoted to the rank of marshal and placed in command of the Special Forces. Here are your insignia and commission."

Jared slid a document across the table. The document was sealed with the Divine Seal.

"How . . . ?" Garth asked.

"Daemor and I each carried one such commission," Jared explained. "For emergencies. Even the other Lords will not know that this was not issued by the Mistress."

"Thank you, High Lord."

"Take command of your force, Marshal Garth," Jared ordered. "I want Castle Aldwyn reduced to rubble in three days."

"As you command, High Lord."

The bright morning sunlight filtered through the tent, waking him. Steve cried out—it felt as though a knife had been thrust into his back.

"Be still, my liege," Arthwyr said, gently pinning his shoulders. "If you move about too much, you will tear the wound open again."

"Where . . . ?" Steve asked.

"We are in Erelvar's camp," Arthwyr replied. "You must rest. . . ."

"No . . . time," Steve argued, trying to sit up. Arthwyr pinned him down.

"You must lie still!"

"No," Steve said. He had to tell Erelvar about the Morvan army. There was no time to rest.

Steve relaxed back onto the bedroll. His back felt as though it were on fire. Arthwyr was right—he couldn't do anything with this wound. Steve took a deep breath in through his nose and held it. Then he forced it out through his mouth.

A world away, a priest had once hypnotized Steve as the prelude to exorcising Belevairn. Steve took another deep breath in through his nose, slowly counting to ten before forcing it out through his mouth. The pain eased a little.

Steve opened himself, as he had with Theron in the clearing. As it had then, the Power flowed into him.

Our Father, Steve began silently, *who art in Heaven* . . .

He directed the Power as he had seen Theron do with the wounded men in his camp. The remaining pain in his back faded as the Power suffused the wound. Now he had to *heal* it.

Lead us not into temptation . . .

Steve could almost see the torn tissues. Some work had already been done with the Power. It was sloppy, incomplete— but it was enough to keep him alive. Without the little that had been done, Steve would be dead.

. . . but deliver us from evil . . .

The tissues knitted together. The weak wall of the great artery that ran along the spine strengthened. Steve moved the Power outward. Muscle tissue grew and rebonded. He moved outward again—the skin mended over the wound, sealing it against infection.

For Thine is the Power . . .

A final wash of the Power removed all traces of infection from the healed wound. He would be weak from blood loss for a day or so, but that was all. He had healed the wound—he *was* a healer!

"Amen," Steve said aloud.

"Steven?" Arthwyr asked, concern in his voice.

"I have to see Erelvar," Steve replied, sitting up before Arthwyr could react.

"Your wound—"

"Is healed," Steve interrupted. "Check it yourself."

Arthwyr moved to where he could see Steve's back. After a moment he sat back and solemnly signed himself.

"You are a healer," he said quietly.

"I am now," Steve agreed. "Where are my clothes?"

"This is grave news," Erelvar said. Steve had quickly informed him of the new organization of the Morvan column.

"Yes," Steve agreed. "With all of their supplies in that transport, there's no way to destroy them."

"You destroyed the Dra . . . the tank," Erelvar objected. "This . . . transport is much weaker. . . ."

"The Morvir aren't going to fall for another pit trap—if you'll pardon the expression," Steve explained. "And there's no way we're going to get close enough to dump enough Delvan Fire on that thing with Molotovs."

"So what can we do?" Erelvar asked.

"I don't know," Steve replied. "I just don't know."

"Then may the *Kanir* preserve us," Erelvar said.

* * *

Jared dismounted and walked from the stable into the council chamber. This was going to be an interesting session of the Council, to say the least. Hopefully, allowing the Dreamer to escape was not going to have too much effect on his standing with the other Lords.

All of the Lords had gathered for this meeting. They fell silent as he entered and took his place at the head of the table.

"What is the news from the Coasts?" Jared asked.

"The Nymran fleet has been sunk," Hilarin replied. "Many of the officers have been captured. However, Prince Theron was not among them. He may have survived, but it is most likely that he drowned when his ship was destroyed."

"Excellent," Jared said, nodding. "This alliance may prove more fruitful than we had expected."

"It would seem so, High Lord," Hilarin agreed.

"What of the *kaivir*, Lord Hhayim?" Jared asked. "Have you been able to capture any survivors?"

"A handful, High Lord," Hhayim replied. "We have located one *kaiva* of the first order and three initiates. All are under heavy guard."

"Excellent," Jared replied. "I will speak with them and assign them after Council."

"Who are they to be assigned to?" Phelandor asked.

"The *kaiva* of the first order shall be mine," Jared replied. "Beyond that, I believe our two ambassadors should each receive a tutor. In their position, sorcerous training is most necessary. The third shall be assigned by vote of the Council. Are there any objections?"

"No, High Lord," Phelandor replied. The others nodded their agreement.

"Good," Jared said. "Now, I have . . . several matters to report to the Council."

The Council listened intently as Jared relayed the tale of the Dreamer's attack on the column. They were silent throughout his description of the attack itself and the damage done to the column. Finally, Jared described his own unsuccessful pursuit of the Dreamer and his consternation at finding himself deep in Olvanor once the Dreamer had eluded him.

"I can explain neither how he disappeared nor how I found

myself deep in Olvanor," Jared concluded. He waited, uncomfortably, for the other Lords to respond. Lord Phelandor was the first to speak.

"The Dreamer has learned the way of the forest," he said.

"What do you mean?" Jared asked.

"The lore-masters of Olvanor can travel throughout Olvanor, perhaps throughout the world, in moments by following the forest ways," Phelandor replied. "There have been tales of lore-masters who travelled to the lands of the dead in this fashion. Be glad you lost him on *this* world, High Lord."

"How is this possible?" Jared exclaimed. Phelandor shrugged.

"It simply *is*," he replied.

"Where would he have learned this . . . way of the forest?"

"We know he was at Bralmendel," Phelandor surmised. "That *was* one of the most sacred sites in Olvanor."

"True," Jared replied.

"The only question I have," Hhayim said, "is how does this affect us? How must we change our plans in light of this knowledge?"

"Our plans stand," Jared replied.

"What of the Special Forces?" Hilarin asked. "Surely they are aware that something is amiss."

"Yes," Jared replied. "In fact, Garth *recognized* the Dreamer. It seems that Belevairn had once captured him on Earth. Garth and one other were his guards."

"Have they been killed?" Hilarin asked.

"No," Jared replied. "Garth now knows the truth. It was he who helped me devise the explanation we have given the others."

"High Lord!" Hilarin objected. "How do you know this man can be trusted?"

"Because he is bound to the Mistress as firmly as you and I, Hilarin."

"What?"

"The Mistress had planned to add another Lord from the Special Forces," Jared explained. "She apparently chose Garth for that honor and had already performed the Bonding with him." Silence greeted this announcement.

"Garth is one of us . . . ," Hilarin observed.

"No!" Kephas objected. "We *cannot* add another Lord to the Council."

"But the Mistress . . . ," Heregurth began.

"Enough!" Jared shouted. "Garth will *not* be added to the Council. He is *not* of the *Kaimordir*. The Mistress was defeated before he was masked *or* given a steed. Of what use is a Lord who will die in forty years?"

"True," Hhayim agreed. "Still, he *is* the only member of the Special Forces who can be trusted."

"Precisely," Jared agreed. "Besides, the Mistress herself gave us an answer to this problem."

"What is that?" Hilarin asked.

"This," Jared said, dropping Garth's commission on the council table.

"Garth has been carrying this document with him, sealed, since he was Bonded," Jared lied. "When I told him the truth of our situation, he produced it, thinking it 'might be important.' "

"There has not been a marshal in Morvanor for over fifty years," Hilarin observed.

"I have placed Marshal Garth in command of the Special Forces," Jared continued.

"This is all well and good," Hhayim commented, "but it still does not answer my original question. Where does the invasion stand?"

"It proceeds," Jared replied. "The Special Forces have passed the ruins of Aberstwyth. In two days, Castle Aldwyn will fall under attack."

Steve shifted in the saddle. His back, where the shrapnel had lodged, was stiff and sore. Apparently his first attempt at healing had not been completely successful.

It had taken the entire morning to get the army reassembled and on the march toward Castle Aldwyn. In all that time, Steve still had no ideas on how to stop the Morvir before they reached the castle. So far, the only thing he'd come up with had been to attempt a raid on Quarin for whatever armaments were guarded there. The transport would hold only four or five truckloads of supplies. The rest had to be back at Quarin. One rocket launcher could solve their whole problem.

The problem was how to get in, get the supplies and get out alive. Unfortunately, no solution seemed apparent. Steve could only hope, and pray, that a solution presented itself before the Morvir destroyed most of Umbria.

Laerdon stood on his father's balcony looking out over the city. However, it was *his* balcony now, as was the crown that rested on his head.

He was not ready for this. The throne should not have been his for another century at least. Even then, in a normal succession, his father would have ceded the throne to him and remained as his advisor. But the Morvir had taken Arven from them before his time.

Laerdon felt a hand on his shoulder.

"Hello, Mother," he said.

"Do you find the crown heavy, my son?" she asked.

"Far beyond its weight," he agreed. "I am not worthy. . . ."

"You are the king!" she interrupted. Laerdon flinched at the sudden harshness in her voice. "Do not *ever* doubt your worth, your right, to wear it. Its weight will make you strong—unless you allow it to break you."

"I am . . . afraid . . . ," Laerdon said, letting his words trail off, unspoken.

"Of failing?" Miriam asked. "You shall not fail. Of erring? Arven made *many* errors as king. But he learned from them, as you shall."

"I miss him," Laerdon said.

"We all do," Miriam agreed.

"Majesty!" a voice reached them from inside the palace.

"A king never rests," Miriam said. "You are needed, Majesty."

With a sigh, Laerdon turned and walked back into the palace. A guard stood in the doorway to his chambers.

"Yes?" Laerdon asked.

"Pardon the interruption, Majesty," the guard said. "The lore-master wishes to speak with you. He says it is of the utmost importance."

"Let him enter," Laerdon said. It seemed odd to have to *allow* Nolrod to enter his chambers. For all of Laerdon's life,

he lore-master had simply appeared from nowhere at will—
usually at the most inconvenient of times.

"Good even, Majesty," Nolrod said, dropping to one knee as
he entered.

"Rise, old friend," Laerdon said. "What brings you to us this
late?"

"Majesty," Nolrod began, "two wooden crates were found
buried near Bralmendel. They were filled with these."

Laerdon took the heavy object from Nolrod. It was a strange
thing. A large cylinder of brass formed one end of the
otherworldly device. The other end was a rounded cone of
some grayish metal. The thing weighed almost two stone and
was half Laerdon's height.

"Find the Dreamer," Laerdon ordered. "Take this to him. He
will know what should be done with them."

"As you command, Majesty," Nolrod replied. Laerdon
watched as the lore-master departed.

"You need have no fear, my son," his mother said behind
him. Laerdon turned to face her.

"You will make a fine king," she said.

"Shall we make camp, my lord?" Morfael asked.

"No," Erelvar said. "If we march through the night, we can
make Castle Aldwyn by morning. The men can rest there."

"Yes, my lord," Morfael replied. The terrain had grown
considerably more rugged after the half day's march. Morfael
was concerned that travelling after dark was inviting disaster.

He glanced up to the sky. The Dreamer's star was little more
than a very bright star now. It offered none of the illumination
that it once had. The moon would be up soon, however. That
should offer more light.

"Might we stop for dinner at least, my lord?" Morfael
suggested. "The moon would be up by the time we finish and
there would be less chance of accident." Erelvar was silent for
a moment, thinking.

"Very well," he said. "You are probably right. Halt the
march."

"Yes, my lord," Morfael agreed.

*   *   *

Steve sighed with relief once the halt was called. He might not tire while he rode Aerilynn, but the magic involved didn' keep him from getting hungry.

Apparently they were going to stop only for dinner. Erelvar did not order the camp to be raised. He must want to make the castle by morning.

That made sense. The army could spend the day setting up their camp at the castle and then rest up for the coming battle

Thinking of the battle made his mood drop. All the rest in the world wouldn't help against the Morvir. Once they arrived, whoever did not flee would die. It was that simple. The defenders might be able to kill a few score of the attackers, but that would be all. Then it would be on to the next castle— Castle Owein. The Morvir might be able to march all the way through Umbria just on the strength of the weapons they had with them.

Steve sat on a nearby rock. What could he do? If Steve didn't come up with some idea, and soon, hundreds, perhaps thousands more would die at Castle Aldwyn, just like Bralmendel. Steve *had* to keep that from happening. There must be something they could do!

Someone set a plate down in front of him. Steve looked up to see Morfael.

"You look like a man with the weight of the world on his shoulders," Morfael observed.

"Good," Steve replied. "I *feel* like a man with the weight of the world on his shoulders."

"Might I join you?"

"Please," Steve said. Morfael sat on another rock, facing him.

"What troubles you, Steven?" Morfael asked.

"This battle," Steve replied. "It's hopeless, Morfael."

"Is our situation that desperate?" Morfael said. "Surely the castle will provide some defense. . . ."

"You weren't at Bralmendel," Steve replied, shaking his head. "There were three thousand men defending that hill. Only a handful of them survived, and the Morvir didn't even use their heaviest weapons. From the accounts I heard, they used nothing more powerful than grenades."

"Those are the little balls that explode?" Morfael asked.

"Yes," Steve replied. "They have weapons that are *much* more powerful than that."

"Then at the very least we shall make them use them," Morfael said. "You yourself have said they will run out eventually."

"They could kill thousands—tens of thousands—before that happens!" Steve objected. "They could practically burn Umbria to the ground just with what they have!"

"Steven," Morfael said, "you are a priest now, are you not?"

"Sort of," Steve replied. "Actually, I'm more of a . . . consecrated knight."

"As is Erelvar."

"Uh, yeah . . . I suppose so." Steve had never thought of it like that.

"Then you are also a priest," Morfael concluded. "As such, do you not think that you should have a little faith? We *shall* triumph."

Steve simply stared at Morfael for a moment. Morfael was right—Steve had healed himself with his faith this morning. He had been reunited with Aerilynn against all hope by faith. He had assaulted the Morvan army on faith. Now he should trust that a solution would be found—on faith.

"You are right, Morfael," Steve agreed. "We shall triumph—the *Kanir* will see to it."

"As they always have, Dreamer," a newly familiar voice said behind Steve.

"Nolrod!" Steve said, smiling and standing to turn and face his new/old friend. His smile was replaced with a look of astonishment when he saw the tank shell that the lore-master was carrying.

"Where on earth did you get *that*!" Steve exclaimed.

"What is it?" Erelvar asked, eyeing the tank shell critically.

"Our salvation," Steve said.

"What does it do?" Erelvar asked.

"These are the weapons the Dragon was firing at Quarin, Erelvar," Steve explained. "These are what destroyed your fortress."

"These?"

"Yes, fired from the tank's cannon," Steve explained. "Each time the . . . snout fired, it was firing one of these."

"But we have no . . . cannon," Erelvar protested.

"No. If we did this would be a *lot* easier," Steve agreed. "However, these are still the most powerful explosives we've been able to get our hands on. Light a fire under them and they'll blow up *real* good."

"Like the little balls?" Erelvar asked.

"No, like the explosion that knocked down your gatehouse!" Steve exclaimed. Erelvar's eyebrows lifted.

"Can we use them from a distance?" he asked. There was a touch of excitement in his voice.

"No," Steve replied. "As you said, we don't have a cannon—which is why the Morvir just left them lying around. We have to put them where we want them." Erelvar thought for a moment.

"How many of these do you have?" he asked, turning to Nolrod.

"A full score, Lord Erelvar," Nolrod replied.

"If these were set on a cliffside above the Morvan army . . . ," Erelvar said.

"They ought to start one hell of an avalanche," Steve finished. "That transport wouldn't take too well to having a few hundred tons of rock dumped on it."

"I doubt that the soldiers would enjoy it, either," Arthwyr noted.

"There are many ways of starting avalanches," Nolrod observed. "The Morvir will be scouting the tops of the cliffs farther in."

"That's true," Steve agreed. "We would be better off blowing the road out from under them. Arthwyr, does the road have any drop-offs?"

"Yes," the Umbrian replied. "A few hours ahead the road starts climbing into the hills where Castle Aldwyn lies. There are several such . . . drop-offs."

"If we blow the road out from under them, the transport will tumble down the cliff," Steve said. "Then we can all watch it go 'splat' on the bottom."

"If we do this from below, the men who set the shells will die," Erelvar said.

"Not if the fires are lit with burning quarrels," Arthwyr disagreed. "My men can hit squirrels from fifty yards."

"And then run like hell," Steve said.

"Aye," Arthwyr agreed.

"Then that is our plan," Erelvar agreed. "Nolrod, can you take Steven to where these weapons are located?"

"Easily."

"Good," Erelvar replied. "Steven, make all possible speed back to us."

"I'll be back before you know it," Steve said.

"In the meantime, we shall find a suitable cliff," Erelvar said. "May the *Kanir* ride with you."

"They have been so far," Steve noted.

Chapter
-------- Seventeen -----------

GARTH WATCHED AS his troops broke camp. To have been promoted to marshal and placed in command of this force was a great honor. It saddened him to know that this invasion was for no other purpose than to destroy the Special Forces, but he understood Jared's reasoning. Morvanor must be preserved.

The first rays of dawn broke over the horizon. Garth watched as the sun slowly climbed into the sky. Tonight, they would camp around Castle Aldwyn. Tomorrow, it would be nothing more than a pile of rubble. With any luck, the traitor and the Delvan Royal Guard would be there as well. And the Dreamer—especially the Dreamer.

Garth could hardly believe that the small, unassuming man he had met on Earth was responsible for the defeat of the Mistress and the fall of Delgroth. The man certainly did not lack courage. That had been evident on Earth when he had faced, and insulted, Lord Belevairn. It had been dramatically proven when he assaulted this force alone. But to destroy Delgroth!

Of course, that had not been his own power. Any of the Special Forces could have done the same with the right weapons. The *Kaimordir* were right to fear them. Morvanor must be preserved—for the Mistress.

Staring into the rising sun, Garth could almost see her. Red hair spilling around the alabaster face, dominated by those penetrating green eyes. She had stolen his heart more thoroughly than any mortal woman ever could. She had wrapped her chains around him and taken him to realms of ecstasy he had not even imagined existed. And she was gone.

The emptiness that knowledge created in him was something he had never experienced. He had experienced its shadow on

Earth with Maria. The pain that settled in his chest now was a hundred times worse.

The Dreamer would pay for that. Garth swore, if he ever got the chance, the Dreamer would pay *dearly* for that loss.

"The column is ready, Marshal Garth," Captain Dalin reported.

"Sound the march," Garth commanded. A puzzled expression at the harshness in Garth's voice briefly crossed the captain's face before he turned to relay the orders.

The Dreamer would *pay*.

Steve watched as the sun climbed toward noon. The army was exhausted. They had worked all night setting the charges on the selected cliffside and were now marching to Castle Aldwyn.

Arthwyr claimed that there were some low hills around the castle that Erelvar's army could camp on and fortify. So, once they made camp, rest would not come for some time. If things went wrong, they would not get to rest at all before the Morvir arrived. Of course, if things went wrong it would not matter.

Steve just hoped that Arthwyr was able to pull off his mission *and* get out alive.

Arthwyr ap Madawc waited in the thin forest below the cliff. The targets on the cliffside were clearly visible from here, if one knew what to look for. Those on the road above would see only clumps of bushes clinging to the cliffside.

Twenty men, to destroy an army a thousand strong. It brought back memories. Memories of six years ago, when Arthwyr had led another twenty men to attack the Morvan army's supplies before they could reach Castle Aldwyn.

"Better watch it, lad," he muttered to himself. "Saving the Aldwyns is getting to be a habit."

A strange, rumbling sound reached him. It was very similar to the Dragon's growl. The Morvan army was approaching on the road above. Arthwyr lit the rush torch set in the ground next to him. Soon now—very soon.

Jared watched as the column approached the cliffside. This was the ideal spot for an ambush from above. Fortunately, he already had men atop the cliff. No enemy presence had been found.

The road skirted the cliff, above and below, for almost two hundred feet before once again nestling between two hills. Even though they had found nothing atop the cliffs, Jared would feel better once the army was past them.

Jared had stopped by to check on the army's progress with the intention of leaving immediately. Now, however, he wanted to wait until the army was safely past the cliff. *Then* he could return to Morvanor.

Arthwyr waited for the armored war machine to reach the second target. Ten shells had been placed along the cliffside under the road. When it reached the second target, the archers would fire.

It reached the second target. Arthwyr gently squeezed the trigger of the crossbow and the burning quarrel flew toward the cliffs. Arthwyr smiled as his bolt flew squarely into the center of the dry brush. *Now* it was time to "run like hell" as Steven had said.

He mounted his horse and galloped away from the cliff. At this point he did not particularly care if the Morvir saw him.

High above the convoy, Jared glimpsed movement in the valley below the road. He turned his attention downward in time to catch a glimpse of armored riders galloping through the trees. Enemy scouts?

Jared turned his mount and rode out over the valley. The force seemed too small to be of consequence. Still, a force no larger than that had caused severe problems in this area six years ago. However, there was little the Umbrians could do to *this* force.

Jared was about to turn back and report this to Marshal Garth when he noticed several wisps of smoke emerge from the cliffside. As he watched, flames appeared in several patches of brush on the cliffside. Why had the Umbrians set fire to the cliffside? The flames from such small patches of brush would never reach the column. If not for Jared's aerial view he might never have noticed them.

*   *   *

The shell was wedged deep into the rock, carefully placed there by Delvan hands. It had warmed in the heat of the noonday sun, but far from dangerously so. Now, however, the flames from the burning brush around it licked against its sides. It was hot enough to burn anyone who tried to touch it, but it was still not hot enough to explode.

A small metal flask next to the shell ruptured from the heat of the fire. Burning naphtha filled the crevice in which it was hidden. The temperature of the shell quickly climbed far beyond the ignition point of the powder within the casing. . . .

A series of explosions suddenly ripped open the cliffside below. To Jared's horror, the cliffs crumbled away like clay. Robbed of its foundation, the road began to crumble as well.

Jared watched helplessly as the road fell away from beneath the transport and the fuel truck. The two vehicles, and several hundred men, joined the avalanche cascading down the hillside.

The two vehicles landed together at the bottom of the cliff. Burning diesel poured over the transport. Recovering from his surprise, Jared quickly backed away, placing the hill between himself and the impending explosion.

Soon a massive fireball erupted from the valley floor. *Where* had the Dreamer gotten explosives of that strength? When Wilkinson had attacked the column himself, he had carried nothing more potent than hand grenades. Hand grenades were not capable of *this*.

Jared cautiously returned to the column. At first glance almost all of the army was missing. Only the smallest portion of the vanguard had reached the safety of the undamaged road.

On closer inspection, it was apparent that much more of the force had survived. They were currently in the process of climbing back up to the road. It would be a few hours before they could assess the full extent of the damage.

One thing Jared did know, however. The weapons they needed to destroy the castle had just been lost. More would have to be shipped from Quarin in the trucks. . . .

*   *   *

Garth watched as most of his army fell into the crevasse tha
fell open behind him. The vibration of the avalanche wa
shaking more debris loose from above.

"Take cover!" Garth ordered just before a massive explosio
shook the entire hillside. The bucking earth knocked Gart
from his feet. The munitions in the transport must hav
exploded.

As quickly as he could, Garth pressed his back against th
cliff, taking what shelter he could from the debris that cascade
down on them from above. This *had* to be the Dreamer's doing
But where had he gotten the explosives?

Even if Wilkinson possessed the knowledge to make blac
powder, there had been nowhere near enough time to manu
facture the quantity that would have been necessary to demol
ish the cliffside. Garth flinched as a boulder larger than he wa
smashed into the road next to him before tumbling on down th
cliff face.

Eventually, the cascade from above slackened. Garth waite
a moment before standing and moving away from the cliff fac
The sight that waited for him was not a pleasant one. Abou
half the vanguard of the army had reached the relative safety o
the road beyond the mined area. Two hundred men in all—
many dead or injured from the avalanche.

Everyone and everything other than that had been caught i
the collapse of the road. This was not good, to say the leas
Garth doubted that enough men would be left to take Castl
Aldwyn, let alone march through Umbria. The Dreamer ha
just successfully destroyed the invasion.

The walls of Castle Aldwyn came into view as the vanguar
of Erelvar's army approached. While nowhere near as impres
sive as Quarin had been, Castle Aldwyn didn't look like a
pushover, either.

The main keep was protected by both an inner and an oute
wall. The outer wall looked newer than the rest of the castle
Steve could see that stables, barracks and other building
occupied the space between the inner and outer walls. Presum
ably these, and the outer wall, had been added to the origina
fortress.

As Arthwyr had said, several hills surrounded the castle

although none were as high as that occupied by Castle Aldwyn itself. Even with the Morvir's modern weapons, this castle would not fall without cost.

To Steve's surprise, one of the hills was already occupied. Men worked digging a trench about midway up the hill, piling the earth and rubble they excavated uphill of the trench. From the depth of the trench, Steve guessed they must have been at it for a few days now.

Erelvar called a halt and the army came to a stop before this hill. The hill was ideally situated to threaten the road. Any force that attacked the castle would have to pass its archers. Similarly, due to the lay of the land, any force that attacked the hill would expose itself to attack from the castle.

"Morfael," Erelvar asked, "is that not Cai Aldwyn atop the hill?"

"Yes, my lord," Morfael replied. The figure in question apparently saw them and began to approach their force. Erelvar, Tsadhoq and Steven rode forward to meet him.

"Greetings, Lord Aldwyn," Erelvar said when they had met.

"Good e'en, Lord Erelvar," Lord Aldwyn replied. "I hope you do not mind my taking the liberty of placing your force for you. This hill seemed the ideal position."

"Aye," Erelvar agreed. "It is the one I would have chosen. My thanks for beginning work on the fortification for us."

"Once your scouts reached me with word of your plans, I began immediately," Cai explained. "If our combined forces are to have any hope of survival, let alone victory, we shall have to have made every preparation possible."

"Aye," Captain Tsadhoq agreed. "With your permission, Lord Aldwyn, my men and I shall take over directing the labor."

"Of course," Lord Aldwyn agreed. "None can match the Delvir in working with stone and earth."

"The army is at your disposal, Captain Tsadhoq," Erelvar added. "We have until tomorrow to prepare this camp for battle."

"We'll do whate'er we can," Tsadhoq said. "'Tis nae much time, though."

"Would you and your commanders care to join me in the

castle?" Lord Aldwyn asked. "We have much to discuss ere the Morvir arrive."

"That we do," Erelvar agreed. "Lead on, Lord Aldwyn."

Steve glanced back toward the hill as they rode to the castle. With Cai having given them a two-day head start on the labor, they should be able to fortify the hill pretty well.

It was a pity that it wasn't going to do any good.

"Your report, Marshal?" Jared asked when Garth entered his tent. The surviving force had made camp atop the hill adjacent to the ambush site while they licked their wounds and assessed their situation.

In response, Garth laid a ruptured brass cylinder on the council table.

"We know where they got the explosives now," Garth said.

"What . . . is it?" Jared asked.

"The remains of a tank's shell casing, Lord," Garth replied. "As a shell, it's worthless without the tank to fire it. As a bomb . . ." Garth shrugged. Its effectiveness had been adequately proven this afternoon.

Jared turned to Phelandor. He had recalled Kephas and Phelandor as sub-commanders. From now on, one of the Ten would be with the army at *all* times.

"How many of these did you leave in Olvanor?" Jared asked.

"Only two cases, Lord Jared," Phelandor replied. "I am glad now that I did not leave them *all* behind as I was ordered."

"How many *is* that?" Jared asked.

"A score total, Lord Jared," Phelandor said.

"They used ten of those on this trap," Garth said. "We can tell from the blast patterns where they were planted in the cliff face."

"So," Jared observed, "they still *have* ten of these things!"

"We shall have to be very careful during the rest of our approach to Castle Aldwyn," Garth said.

"What are our casualties, Marshal?" Jared asked.

"Over three hundred are dead and almost four hundred are too wounded to march," Garth replied. "The remaining five hundred have almost all sustained minor to moderate injuries."

"Have the trucks arrived from Quarin?" Jared asked.

"Yes, Lord," Garth said. "Three truckloads of munitions just arrived."

"Can you be prepared to move out in the morning?"

"Yes, Dread Lord."

"Good," Jared said. "By midday tomorrow we will assault Castle Aldwyn."

"When will King Botewylf's army arrive?" Erelvar asked.

"Two days hence," Lord Aldwyn replied. "The *king* is leading a force of five thousand." Steve turned from the narrow window through which he was watching the sun set. Derision had been more than plain in Cai Aldwyn's voice.

"You don't sound as though you put much hope in the king," Steve noted.

"Dryw ap Botewylf is no king," Cai spat. Steve raised an eyebrow. The denotive "ap" was not used for the head of a clan. Cai was no longer Cai "ap" Aldwyn once he became the clan chief. He was simply Cai Aldwyn or "the Aldwyn."

"Why do you say that?" Steve asked. "If he is personally leading an army to *this* battle he must be pretty brave."

"He is a mere boy!" Cai replied. "He has barely seen sixteen summers!"

Sixteen, Steve thought, sadly. At sixteen, Steve had thought life was giving him a tough break because he couldn't get a date for the school dance. He would never have been able to cope with the type of obligation that Dryw Botewylf lived under.

"I am only four years older than him, then," Steve noted. "Does that make my presence here worthless?"

"Dryw ap Botewylf is a pampered whelp!" Cai objected. "Nothing like yourself!"

Steve actually laughed out loud. Cai threw a confused look at Erelvar, who was doing his best not to laugh himself.

"Erelvar," Steve said, "will you please tell Lord Aldwyn what your first opinion of me was?"

"I had never met a weaker, more spoiled and whining, useless brat in my life," Erelvar replied. Cai's eyes widened. He looked anxiously between Steve and Erelvar. Duels had been fought over slighter words in Umbria.

"Morfael?" Steve asked. "Was Erelvar wrong?"

"He was not . . . completely correct," Morfael answered diplomatically.

"The sad thing," Steve added, "is that he *was*! I was helpless! Nevertheless, Erelvar stood by me until I became a man."

"A man that I am proud to call my friend," Erelvar added.

"But you are the Dreamer!" Cai objected. "And he *knew* that!"

"And Dryw Botewylf is your *king*!" Steve replied. "And you know that as well. King Dryw shows more promise at sixteen summers than I did at nineteen. Give him the chance to *be* a king, Cai."

"Well said!" Arthwyr's voice said from the doorway to Aldwyn's chambers.

"Arthwyr!" Steve exclaimed. "How did the ambush go?"

"Quite well," Arthwyr replied, smiling and walking into the council room. "The whole cliff face crumbled away like a child's mud castle. Then the two engines fell into the slide and were both destroyed in a great ball of fire."

"Congratulations, Arthwyr," Lord Aldwyn said, smiling. He rose and grasped Arthwyr's hand.

"Once again Castle Aldwyn owes its salvation to the Madawcs," he said. Arthwyr shook his head somberly.

"'Tis not over yet, Cai," he said.

"But you said that the Morvan engines had been destroyed."

"Aye," Arthwyr agreed. "But not the army, Lord Aldwyn. I tarried behind awhile to spy on the Morvir. Most of their force is still intact."

"How many?"

"Between five and seven hundred," Arthwyr replied.

"But they have no more weapons," Cai objected.

"Oh yes they do," Steve said. "They still have about fourteen truckloads of arms. They just don't have the armored transport to haul them around in anymore."

"We can destroy the trucks," Erelvar noted.

"More easily than the transport," Steve agreed. "However, we have no one between here and Quarin to sabotage their supply lines."

"What do you recommend?" Erelvar asked.

"Arthwyr already told us the best way to fight these people,"

Steve replied. "With crossbows and with knives in the dark. We should abandon the castle and scatter."

"Never!" Lord Aldwyn shouted. "By the *Kanir*, I shall *not* flee and leave the front gate open for them!"

"It makes little difference if you leave the gate open or if they blow it open," Steve answered calmly. "Except that, if the castle is manned, all of the defenders will die. Besides, if we do this right, they'll never make it to the castle."

"How do you propose to do that?" Erelvar asked.

"Lord Aldwyn has almost a thousand men here—all of them with crossbows, if I am correct." Steve looked over to Cai, who nodded his affirmation.

"We can use an old, very old, trick on them," Steve continued. "It's called a foxhole. . . ."

It was very late by the time Steve made it back to his tent. Of course, it would be even later by the time the Delvir made it back to camp after digging the foxholes in the locations Steve had selected.

He wasn't completely happy with the compromise that had been reached this afternoon. Two hundred fifty of Lord Aldwyn's men would be foxholed fifty yards off the road with the remainder manning the castle. The Delvir and Erelvar's infantry were going to man the fortified hill, as originally planned. Erelvar's cavalry would be stationed in front of the castle's main gate.

The plan was that the men in the foxholes would fire two quick volleys into the flank of the attacking force. Each man would have two crossbows loaded and ready to fire, courtesy of Erelvar's *regir*. They were to then maintain fire on the Morvir while Erelvar's cavalry charged. Steve sighed; people were going to die simply so that Lord Aldwyn could keep the bulk of his force in the castle.

Still, as Tsadhoq had pointed out, a thousand holes in the ground would be damned hard to hide. This was probably the best solution, but it was also the most dangerous for the defenders.

"You are troubled, my love," Aerilynn's voice said from the tent's entrance.

"Aerilynn!" Steve said, sitting up. "I'm sorry—I forgot all about you!"

"'Tis all right," she said, stepping into the tent and closing the flap. "You have been planning tomorrow's battle."

"Yes, and it doesn't look good."

"You fear we will be defeated," Aerilynn observed.

"No," Steve replied. "But I fear our losses will be severe. Aerilynn?"

"Yes, my love?"

"I . . . want you to . . . leave here," Steve said, haltingly.

"Steven!" Aerilynn objected.

"I can get Erelvar to give me another horse," Steve added quickly. "I don't want you to die in tomorrow's battle! *Please,* Aerilynn."

"No!" Aerilynn said. "I will not be condemned to live out my days without you, or as a dumb animal. We shall survive or not *together!*"

"But . . ."

"No! Steven, I was sent back to aid in your quest. I shall not be robbed of that and, if you are sent to the Halls of Mortos, I wish to be there with you. Would you abandon me? If I asked you to leave tonight, would you go?"

"No," Steve replied. "I couldn't leave you to die."

"Neither can I," Aerilynn asserted. "Come, my love. Lie with me tonight. Tomorrow we go into battle together."

"Eat, drink and be merry," Steve replied.

"What is that?"

"An old saying from my world," Steve explained. "Eat, drink and be merry, for tomorrow we die."

"Well," Aerilynn said, placing her arms around him, "we have both eaten and drunk . . ."

"I second the motion," Steve agreed, smiling.

Chapter
------- Eighteen ------------

THE FIRST, FAINT light of dawn found the army on the march. Garth had selected a force of exactly five hundred from the survivors of the avalanche. That left almost thirty able-bodied men behind with the wounded.

He could have included them on the assault, but thirty men would make little difference there. If the Dreamer led an attack on their rear, however, those thirty men could well prevent the wounded from being massacred. Lord Jared had agreed that it was a worthwhile precaution.

Garth glanced upward at the thought of Jared. Three airborne figures paced the army. There would be no repetition of yesterday's trap. The *Kaimordir* would personally inspect all the cliff faces, both above and below the army, that they must pass before reaching the castle.

As Garth watched, the three gathered for a midair conference. According to Lord Jared, the Mistress had intended to make him one of the Twelve. Garth wondered what it would be like to ride one of the demon steeds through the air.

One of the Dread Lords separated from the others and vanished. The remaining two moved to either flank of the army and began pacing it again. From this distance there was no way to tell who had left, but Garth guessed that Lord Jared was returning to Morvanor.

He returned his attention to the army around him. They had a long march to Castle Aldwyn ahead of them yet.

For the second time since his return to Quarin, Steve was wearing the Delvan plate armor. Aerilynn was once again clad in borrowed armor. She snorted and pawed the ground. Steve could feel her impatience as it mirrored his own.

215

It was not so much an eagerness for the coming battle as it was a desire to have it over with. That feeling was echoed by every man there, Steve was certain.

"Have our scouts yet returned?" Erelvar asked Morfael.

"Not yet, my lord," Morfael replied. "We should be hearing from them shortly."

"Good," Erelvar began, "this waiting is—"

A commotion from the men around them interrupted him. Steve followed the pointing fingers up to the sky, already knowing what he would see.

One of the Twelve sat high in the air above them, its steed's hooves firmly planted in nothing. Whoever it was, he had the sense to sit well out of range of their crossbows. Steve unhooked the strap on his saddle holster and drew his rifle. One of his silver bullets ought to provide the Dread Lord with an unpleasant surprise.

As he raised the rifle to sight through the scope, the figure turned and vanished. Steve doubted that he had been seen at this distance. It was just dumb luck.

"Damn!" he said.

"Could you have killed him?" Erelvar asked.

"Possibly," Steve said. "The bullets in this rifle have been blessed."

"Too bad," Erelvar said. "Now they will receive their scout's report before ours can return."

Phelandor shuddered. That had been close. Through his binoculars he had seen a figure below raise a rifle to its shoulder. He had not forgotten the consecrated bullets he had found in the armoire in Quarin. If Phelandor had been studying another part of the force at that moment he would quite possibly be dead now.

He emerged a little ahead of the army. He turned and rode back to where Jared and Kephas rode alongside the force.

"What preparations have they made?" Jared asked.

"One hill has been *heavily* fortified," Phelandor replied. "Delvan work. The Delvir and Erelvar's infantry are holding that position. They are about two thousand strong. Erelvar's cavalry are in position outside the main gate of the castle. All of the castle garrison seemed to be in place on the walls."

"Seemed to be?" Jared asked.

"I was forced to withdraw before I could make an accurate count," Phelandor answered.

"Forced to withdraw?" Kephas asked. "Surely you stayed out of bowshot!"

"Of course I did!" Phelandor replied angrily. "Rifle shot is another matter."

"The Dreamer?" Jared asked.

"I would presume so. I did not wish to discover if he has any more of those consecrated bullets."

"Indeed not," Jared agreed. "Still, the entire castle complement seemed to be present?"

"The walls are certainly well manned."

"Good," Jared said, nodding. "Erelvar is using conventional tactics. As long as we are wary of explosives planted in our path, our victory is assured."

"Let us hope so, High Lord," Phelandor cautioned.

Brys ap Aldwyn shifted in his hole. He had been waiting here since before dawn. In his hands he held a loaded crossbow. At his feet, another loaded crossbow waited. His orders were to fire two shots quickly and then maintain fire.

Brys was not certain what he thought of waiting to pop out of a hole in the ground like a child's toy. Somehow, it did not seem an honorable way to do battle. It was not as though he were fighting an honorable opponent, however.

He shuddered, although the dawn chill had long passed. The Dreamer had gathered them all together that morning before they were sent to their posts. He had placed a melon on a stump and then fired his weapon at it while they watched. The melon had exploded into hundreds of pieces.

"That was your head," he had calmly explained to them. "The Morvir have weapons even more powerful than this, so keep your damned heads *down*! When you reload your second crossbow get back down in your hole to do it! Always give them as small a target as possible. Does everybody understand?"

They had, all too well. Brys lifted his head up, hoping that the uprooted bush that covered his hole would hide him. He peered through the branches. There was still no sign of the Morvir.

Good—maybe they would not come. . . .

*   *   *

Garth surveyed the road ahead through his field glasses.
Here the road began its final ascent toward Castle Aldwyn.
They were in a wide place, almost a valley, between two hills.
Ahead the hills began to crowd the road until they rose on
either side of it like cliffs.

Beyond the miniature canyon, the road turned sharply to the
right. Around that turn the Delvir waited atop their hill. Past
another bend to the left sat Erelvar's forces and Castle Aldwyn.
Garth smelled a trap.

Still, the Dread Lords had found no enemy presence atop the
hills flanking the road, and the low brush of the valley was too
short to hide any force whatsoever. The army should not come
under fire until they made the bend.

"Your command, Lord Jared?" Garth asked.

"Signal the advance," Jared replied. "Halt before the turn and
send men to lay down covering fire before advancing further."

"As you command, Dread Lord."

Brys ap Aldwyn swallowed hard as the Morvir began their
march across the field. Soon the trumpets would sound and
they would all die, burst like melons.

Still, if he were about to die, he would take as many of the
Morvir with him as possible. The Morvir might kill him, but
Castle Aldwyn would not fall to the Mistress's bastards.

"For hearth and home," he whispered.

The army was almost to the mouth of the canyon when the
trumpets sounded. Garth reined his horse to a halt and held up his
hand, halting the advance. He did not relish the thought of being
caught in another avalanche. Where had the signal come from?

He was studying the canyon when the army behind him
erupted into chaos. Garth spun in time to see a hail of arrows
flying toward them. He dived from the saddle, using the horse
as protection from the missiles.

The brush in the valley had concealed holes dug into the
ground. Foxholes! Archers now pelted the Morvan army from
their hiding places. Another volley flew toward them.

Garth's horse staggered and fell, several quarrels embedded
in her corpse—one through the eye. Garth leapt behind the

body, pulling a grenade from his belt and drawing his side arm. Curse him for a fool! He should have scoured the valley!

He hurled the grenade wildly and fired at a crossbowman who was reloading his weapon. The man jerked and fell back into his foxhole. Garth had to re-form his troops well enough to get out of here!

"Get the trucks *out* of here!" he shouted into his headset. "Trucks, pull back! Sergeants, form up your squads!"

As Brys ap Aldwyn hurriedly fitted another quarrel into the crossbow, something small and round fell into his foxhole to land at his feet.

Brys froze, looking at the . . . thing. It was small and its surface was oddly pebbled. There was some type of handle at one end. It was undoubtedly one of the Morvan weapons.

Whatever it was, he had best get rid of it—quickly. Brys reached down to pick the object up. There was a brilliant flash and an unimaginable force slammed into him as burning metal ripped through his body.

Brys screamed—and then stopped. The pain had gone. He opened his eyes.

Brys was no longer in the foxhole. Instead he stood naked on a featureless plain in the midst of a dense, gray fog. A figure in white armor on a white horse rode up to him.

"Brys ap Aldwyn," the man said, "it is time to go."

"W-where am I?" Brys asked.

"You are dead," the figure calmly told him. "I have come to guide you to your reward. Follow me." The figure turned to leave.

"L-Lord Mortos?" Brys asked. The figure's horse turned back and Brys looked up into the face of Death.

"Yes, Brys ap Aldwyn?"

"Did . . . did I die well, Lord?" he asked.

The man on the horse smiled warmly.

"You died *gloriously*, Brys," he replied.

Aerilynn's hooves churned the road as the cavalry charged past the Delvan position. The archers should have fired their second volley by now. That meant that by the time the cavalry reached the Morvir most of the archers would probably be dead and the Morvir would be re-forming.

Great, Steve thought. *That means I'm at the head of the Charge of the Light Brigade here.* Instead of cannons, Erelvar's cavalry was going to be charging into automatic-weapon fire—and maybe a hand grenade or two for good measure.

They passed the Delvir and reached the bend at the top of the small defile that led down into the valley.

Yep, Steve thought as he leaned into Aerilynn's turn. *Into the Valley of Death rode the two fifty . . .*

The cavalry literally thundered down the defile, the hoofbeats of over two hundred horses reverberating from the stone walls beside them. As Steve had guessed, the Morvir were beginning to re-form, although apparently more of the archers were still alive than he would have thought. A thin but steady hail of missiles still sought the Morvir, who had almost withdrawn out of range.

Still, over two hundred of the Morvir were able to fight. As the cavalry charged, Steve saw death in their hands. Two hundred fifty cavalry against two hundred men with machine guns—no contest. They were all dead men.

Then the Morvir did something that Steve had thought he would never see. Something that literally gave the battle to Erelvar's cavalry.

They turned and ran.

Garth looked toward the canyon with a start upon hearing the thunderous sound of the cavalry charge. The Morvir had regrouped and were almost withdrawn from the valley.

The charge was nowhere near as large as it had sounded. The walls of the canyon amplified it and directed *all* of the sound toward them. It should be simple for them to repel. . . .

The army routed. One moment Garth stood at the head of two hundred men and the next he stood alone, watching his men flee.

"Stand fast, you fools!" Garth shouted into his headset. "We outnumber them! Stand fast! STAND FAST!"

It was useless. The men, reduced from five hundred to two hundred and already in retreat, had panicked at the magnified sound of the cavalry charge.

Garth turned back to face the charge. There was no hope of escaping the horses. He loaded a grenade into the launcher of the assault rifle he had claimed from one of the corpses.

Perhaps he could turn the charge, panic the horse. If not, he would die like a man.

As he raised the rifle to fire, a strong hand grabbed him by the collar and hoisted him from the ground. Garth involuntarily released the rifle, allowing it to fall. The ground fell away beneath him as Lord Jared hauled Garth up and laid him across the *goremka*'s neck.

"This is getting to be a habit, Marshal," Jared said. "I shan't always be here to pluck you from the field. See that it doesn't happen again."

"Y-yes, High Lord," Garth replied as they left for the Gray Plain.

One man remained behind to face the charge. Steve drew his .45 as the man raised his rifle. That one man could break the charge, could give the fleeing Morvir time to regroup. Steve wasn't going to give him the chance to fire, if he could help it.

As Steve took aim, one of the Dread Lords charged down and plucked the man from the battlefield. As he hauled the man across the saddle, the *goremka* and its riders vanished into nothingness.

Steve blinked. Who had that been? Who was important enough to warrant a personal rescue by one of the Twelve?

Steve reholstered the revolver. It didn't matter. Right now they had a charge to complete. The cavalry was rapidly overtaking the fleeing Morvir.

A handful of the enemy stopped and turned to face the charge. They dropped to one knee and fired, before Steve could redraw his pistol. Steve ducked involuntarily as the crack of passing bullets rang in his ears.

Someone to his right fell from the saddle. Steve wondered briefly who that had been. Was it someone he knew? Then the cavalry trampled the three Morvir who had stopped to fire.

The remaining Morvir stopped in a belated attempt to regroup. The cavalry slammed into them. In these close quarters, the firearms were little more useful than the swords carried by the knights. A few more riders and horses fell, but not many.

The charge broke, as planned. Usually, the cavalry would charge on past the enemy in a situation like this to wheel and reattack. Against firearms, that strategy would be suicide. Far better to stay in close quarters where the knights' weapons were almost as effective as the assault rifles.

Random bursts of gunfire mixed with the screams of wounded horses and men. Steve drew his sword in time to slice through the neck of a man who was taking aim at Erelvar. The corpse fell to the ground and was lost in the forest of horses' legs that churned the ground into bloody mud.

Steve flinched from an explosion far to his left. One of the Morvir must have thrown a grenade! For an instant there was a small clearing in the midst of the battle. The press of combat quickly filled the brief gap.

Aerilynn reared beneath him. Steve leaned forward, clinging to the reins. Anyone who fell from the saddle in *this* battle would quickly find himself trampled into the mud.

Aerilynn landed on the Morvan who had taken aim at Steve. Steve felt, rather than heard, the sickening crunch of bone as her hooves landed on the man's skull. Steve wheeled her about, scanning the battleground for targets.

The sounds of gunfire had died away. Around him he could see only Erelvar's cavalry, scanning the battlefield as he was, looking for the enemy. Steve sighed and let his sword arm drop. It was over.

They emerged into the air above the hospital camp. Garth had managed to assume a slightly more dignified position behind Lord Jared. Phelandor and Kephas were already awaiting them on the ground.

"What do we do now, High Lord?" Phelandor asked once Jared had rejoined them. Jared dismounted and helped Garth down from the *goremka*.

"We withdraw," Jared replied. "And we destroy Castle Aldwyn and the Delvan Royal Guard. Erelvar's force is not as important, but we shall attempt to destroy it as well."

"How?"

"Phelandor," Jared commanded, "return to Morvanor and summon the remaining Lords. Kephas, travel to the Coasts and summon Hilarin and Heregurth. *We* shall complete the attack, just as we did at the Academy."

"Yes, High Lord," they replied.

"Marshal Garth," Jared continued once the two Lords had

departed, "I want the trucks unloaded when they arrive. You will set aside forty rocket launchers and ten assault rifles with grenade launchers and ten grenades for each. I want the remaining armaments destroyed except for each man's personal arms. I am going to Quarin to have the remaining trucks unloaded and sent in to retrieve the wounded."

"What do you intend, High Lord?"

"We shall withdraw to Quarin," Jared replied. "Once the wounded have recovered we shall again press into Umbria. In the meantime, the Dread Lords are going to ensure that Erelvar does not return to attack us there. Carry out your orders."

"Yes, Lord Jared."

Steve set the torch to the pyre and ran like hell. This was going to be a funeral pyre to beat all funeral pyres. In addition to the bodies of the fallen, all of the Morvan munitions had been added to the pyre.

Well, not quite all. Steve had held out a dozen hand grenades and two rocket launchers for himself as well as an AK-47 for Arthwyr. The Umbrian was getting to be a pretty good shot. Even so, Steve had thought it best to remove the grenade launcher before giving it to him.

He leapt onto Aerilynn's saddle and she broke into a gallop the moment his feet found the stirrups. Faster than any normal horse could, she ran up the defile toward Castle Aldwyn. By the time she reached the top, Steve could hear the first sounds of exploding ammunition. Probably the bullets—they would go first.

They rounded the bend, placing the hills between them and the pyre. Aerilynn slowed to a walk as they approached Erelvar and the others.

"Is it done?" Erelvar asked. Just then a massive explosion shook the countryside.

"It is done," Steve replied unnecessarily.

"Good," Erelvar replied. "Lord Aldwyn is awaiting us in council."

Garth breathed a sigh of relief when the trucks finally arrived from Quarin. The thirty able-bodied men he had left behind with the wounded began loading the wounded onto the trucks.

Most were able to board of their own accord. There was a

good chance that those who could not would not survive the trip, but then, that was war.

"Do you have the situation under control, Marshal?" Lord Jared asked.

"Yes, Dread Lord," Garth replied.

"Then we shall be off," Jared replied. "Are we all clear on the strategy?"

"Yes," Phelandor replied. "We surround the castle and fire once into whatever openings are available. Then we immediately proceed to the Delvan position and fire once on their position."

"And then," Fanchon added, "we depart and regroup a league south of the castle before proceeding on to intercept King Dryw."

"Very good. Then let us begin."

"So," Cai Aldwyn concluded, "we are agreed. We shall await the arrival of King Dryw. Then our forces and his shall march on the camp of the wounded."

"I doubt they will be there," Steve objected again.

"If they are not, we shall march on to Quarin," Erelvar replied. "All of their troops who were able to fight were destroyed in the battle in the valley."

"Fighting is one thing," Steve replied. "Sitting on the battlements and taking potshots while we try to attack is something else. We should move to intercept them *before* they can reach Quarin."

"Steven," Erelvar said, "we all want this to be over. However . . ."

The sound of trumpets interrupted them.

"The alarm?" Cai said, rising and moving toward the door to the council room.

Erelvar and Steve had both started to rise as well when the wooden doors to the stone-walled council chamber burst apart into fiery splinters. The force of the blast knocked Steve, and presumably everybody else, to the floor. With a crash of breaking timber, the ceiling collapsed.

Steve attempted to move, but found his right leg pinned by a fallen beam. How had the Morvir gotten close enough to the castle to attack?

Steve lifted the beam slightly and pulled his leg free. He

almost blacked out from the pain. Broken. It had to be. He dragged himself under the table, which had miraculously survived to create a clear space underneath.

"Erelvar?" he called, hoarsely.

"Here . . ." a voice replied weakly. Steve pulled himself to the place where Erelvar had been sitting before the blast hit.

"Steven?" Arthwyr's voice called. It sounded stronger than Steve's.

"I'm all right," Steve replied. Like hell he was.

"I . . . could use a . . . hand, lads," Tsadhoq's voice called.

"Arthwyr," Steve called, "find Tsadhoq and Morfael."

"Yes, my lord," Arthwyr said. He, too, was underneath the table. As he crawled past he saw Steve's leg.

"All right, eh?" he said, accusingly.

"I'll keep," Steve replied. "Find the others."

"As soon as I get a tourniquet on that leg. Now be still!"

Steve winced as Arthwyr tied a strip of cloth around his leg and twisted it tight.

"*Now* you'll keep," Arthwyr noted.

Steve smelled smoke. Listening carefully, he could hear the crackling of flames.

"Not if that fire reaches us," he said. "Hurry and find the others."

"Right," Arthwyr replied. Steve returned to his task of finding Erelvar.

Steve found him. A heavy ceiling beam laid across the Morvan's chest. Bloody froth coated his lips. Not good—not good at all.

Steve reached out and began to summon the Power. Before he could extend his senses into Erelvar's body, however, Erelvar grabbed his wrist.

"No," he croaked. "Give me . . . my . . . dagger. Can . . . not reach . . . it."

"Erelvar," Steve objected. "I can save you—"

"No," Erelvar said again. "I can . . . save us . . . all. My . . . dagger . . ."

"All right," Steve said. He found the dagger on Erelvar's belt. As he drew it, he could feel the Power in the blade. It was consecrated.

"Here," he said, placing the blade in Erelvar's hand. Erelvar lifted the blade and placed the point against his own chest.

"No!" Steve shouted, grabbing Erelvar's wrist.

"I must!" Erelvar said, pulling away. "I shall . . . not die, my . . . friend. Trust . . . me."

"All right," Steve said, releasing Erelvar's wrist doubtfully. "But if you're lying to me, this is the last time I listen to you!" Erelvar chuckled.

"Indeed." He placed the dagger against his own chest.

"By . . . my . . . own . . . hand," he said, and then drove the dagger into his bosom.

Erelvar collapsed back onto the floor with a ragged sigh. Steve began to reach toward him and stopped when a bright light formed around the blade. Erelvar's eyes opened and he drew the knife, bloodless, from his chest.

Without apparent cause, the beam that was pinning Erelvar to the floor lifted and freed him. The debris filling the rest of the room shifted and moved, releasing other pinned victims.

"Let the living live," Erelvar said, his voice oddly resonant. Steve cried out in pain as the shattered bones of his leg straightened themselves. The pain passed quickly.

Steve found that he could use the leg. He crawled from beneath the table and stood. The crackling of the flames had vanished.

"Erelvar . . . ?" Steve began.

"That is *not* Erelvar," Morfael said.

"Then who is it?" Tsadhoq demanded.

"The Arm of Death," Steve replied, quietly.

"Dreamer," Erelvar/Mortos commanded, "you shall ride with my army. You have earned the right."

"Y-yes, Lord Mortos," Steve replied.

"The living shall remain here," Erelvar/Mortos continued, turning to face Morfael and Tsadhoq.

"Yes, Lord Mortos," Morfael replied, sounding less shaken than Steve.

"Follow me," Erelvar/Mortos commanded, turning to leave. For a moment, Steve thought the command was directed at him. When the body of Cai Aldwyn and the guards rose from the floor and fell into line behind him, Steve knew otherwise. Cai's body was burned beyond recognition and still had pieces of the door embedded in it.

"I think I'm gonna puke," Steve muttered as he followed them out of the council room.

Outside the castle was even worse. Hundreds of corpses waited for the Lord of the Dead to pass before falling into place behind him. The smell of bile and other body fluids were staggering.

Aerilynn and another horse were waiting for them. Steve briefly wondered who had gotten her ready for travel before deciding that he probably would rather not know. He mounted.

Without a word, Erelvar/Mortos rode out of the gate and the army of corpses followed. Outside the main wall, thousands of corpses waited. Steve fought to control his stomach at both the stench and the sight.

A hand touched his shoulder and the nausea, as well as the stench, passed.

"Thank you," Steve said quietly. Erelvar/Mortos nodded. Steve rode quietly beside him. This was *not* going to be the most pleasant trip he'd ever taken, to put it mildly.

Dryw Botewylf was in council when the attack came. Through the walls of the tent, garish red light erupted with the sound of an avalanche. Instantly the quiet night was filled with the shouts and screams of fighting men.

The king and his advisors rushed from the tent in time to see ten trails of white fire shoot down from the night sky. One trail struck less than a hundred feet from him.

It was the last thing the young king ever saw.

The walls of Quarin came into view. The army of the dead had marched without rest all night and all through the next day. Now night had fallen and the moonlight shone off the walls of the city.

Without a word, Erelvar/Mortos halted. The army of corpses surged past them, advancing on the city. As Steve watched, they began to scale the walls of the city by the simple expedient of climbing on top of each other. Steve swallowed. He may have earned the right to be here, but he wasn't certain he *wanted* to be.

"You may leave at any time," Erelvar/Mortos said.

"Uh," Steve stammered, "I . . . I think I'll stay." There was no response.

Alarms were sounding all along the wall. Steve was *very* glad that he was not one of the defenders at this point.

*   *   *

Garth was near the east wall when the alarm sounded. Most of the Special Forces were still in the makeshift infirmaries, recovering from their wounds. The rest, about forty men at this point, were on standby in case of attack.

Garth ran toward the barracks. If those men weren't on their feet and moving *long* before he got there, there was going to be hell to pay!

He need not have worried. The door to the barracks flew open. Garth adjusted his course to intercept the men before they reached the wall.

"You men, scatter yourselves along the wall!" Garth ordered once he was in earshot. "We have to reinforce the conventional troops! I want one man every—"

He was interrupted by screams from the direction of the wall. He turned in time to see over a hundred men on the battlements desert their posts. What in Mortos's hell . . . ?

"Disregard!" he ordered the men with him. "Seal that breach! Move it!" The men ran off toward the tower nearest the gap in the defenses. Garth trembled in rage. There would be some executions tomorrow for this. . . .

The enemy swarmed over the parapet. They seemed to be a mix of Umbrian and Delvan troops. Garth raised his field glasses to survey the situation.

Hackles raised down his neck and arms at the sight through the binoculars. The light of the abandoned watch lanterns fell on sightless eyes—for those of the enemy that still *had* eyes. All were severely burned. Many were missing an arm or a hand. Some few were actually headless.

Garth lowered the binoculars, fighting to control his stomach. Even from here, he could smell the stench of decay. What foul sorcery was *this*?

His men reached the battlements and opened fire on the army of the dead. Corpses fell, only to rise again a moment later.

"Fall back!" Garth shouted, doubting that the men could hear him. "Fall back!"

Whether they heard him or not, the Special Forces began to withdraw. They had little choice. The enemy's advance was not even slowed by their efforts. If they did not withdraw they would be overrun.

A shuffling, dragging sound reached his ears. Garth turned in time to see a corpse, dressed in Umbrian burial garments, emerge from an alleyway. Unlike those atop the wall, it had obviously been dead for *many* weeks.

Sounds of fighting reached him from within the city. Were all of the graveyards giving up their dead as well? Garth heard the sound of armor and turned again, glad that reinforcements were finally arriving. His hopes fell when he saw that Morvan corpses were now joining the ranks of the enemy.

Garth turned and ran toward the inn that served as Lord Jared's command center, telling himself that he was merely hurrying to report.

"Lord Jared!" Marshal Garth shouted as he stormed into the council chamber. "We are under attack! The enemy has cleared the wall!"

"What!" Jared said, rising to his feet. "By whom!"

"By Death, Dread Lord," Garth replied.

"What!" Jared, Phelandor and Kephas all exclaimed together.

"An army of the dead has attacked the city!" Garth explained. "Our forces can do nothing to them! Each man we lose rises to join the enemy. The dead are also rising from the city's graveyards!" For a moment Jared said nothing. He simply stared at Garth, hardly daring to believe what he had just heard.

"We battle the gods themselves," he finally said quietly, retaking his seat at the table.

"What shall we do?"

"Withdraw," Jared replied. "And leave the city to the dead."

"I shall give the orders . . . ," Garth began.

"No!" Jared countermanded. "*We* shall withdraw. We four. It is too late for the troops."

"We have lost," Phelandor said.

"Not exactly," Jared disagreed.

"How can you say that?"

"With certainty," Jared replied. "We have destroyed Quarin and both the Olvan and Umbrian royal families. The Veran Guard lies at the bottom of the sea and the Delvan Royal Guard has been slaughtered. We have *won*, my fellow Lords. But it is time to withdraw—for now."

Chapter
-------- Nineteen ------------

LIFE IN THE Umbrian quarter had almost returned to normal. As normal as it could, considering that the rest of the city was, for all intents and purposes, gone.

Still, the bodies had been removed and burned, and all the Morvan weapons had been carried to the sea by barge and dumped overboard. The Umbrian refugees had returned and shops were once again open for their patrons. Life went on—for the living.

Steve looked out the window of his room at the inn Erelvar had appropriated. Its proprietor had not been fortunate enough to remain alive to reopen it.

The days were cooler now. Soon, autumn would turn the leaves golden, red and brown. Then the snows would come. Erelvar had his hands full, stocking enough provisions to keep the city going through the winter. Fortunately, funds were already coming in from the temple of Mortos and from Olvanor. Tsadhoq had promised aid from the Delvir once he and what was left of the Royal Guard returned home. Quarin would be rebuilt.

The door opened behind him and Aerilynn entered the room. Steve smiled at her and turned back to the window. Mortos's last act, before withdrawing from Erelvar's body, had been to change Aerilynn's nature. She was still the horse, but only when she wished to be. Most of the time now she stayed in her Olvan form. It certainly made life easier.

"They are serving dinner, Steven," Aerilynn said.

"Good," Steve replied. "I'll be down in a minute."

"Something is troubling you," Aerilynn observed.

"Just a little homesick," Steve replied.

230

"Come," Aerilynn said, embracing him from behind. "A good meal will make you feel better."

"The docks on the bluff have almost been rebuilt," Erelvar said. "Soon we will be able to begin work on rebuilding the fortress."

Steve nodded, swallowing a mouthful of food and following it with a swallow of wine.

"That's good," he said. "How long will it take to complete?"

"Much less time than when it was first built," Erelvar replied. "Since the stone is all available, probably about three years, if all goes well."

Steve blinked. Three *years*?

"That's . . . good," Steve noted.

"It will be good to have the fortress restored," Glorien said. "Quarin is needed for the next time we have to face the Morvir."

"*If* we have to face the Morvir," Steve said. "With the Mistress gone, their social structure should fall apart pretty quickly."

"I do not believe so," Erelvar disagreed. "There are still ten Lords in Morvanor. And with their alliance to the Coasts they have shown their ability to improvise. No, Morvanor shall not vanish. Now, however, they are just another kingdom."

"Another kingdom without the Mistress," Morfael observed. "And without the *kaivir*, if the word we have received from Theron's people in the Coast can be believed."

"I believe it," Erelvar said. "The Ten could not allow such a threat to their rule to continue to exist. So that is at least one threat we shall not have to face."

"Thank God for that," Steve said.

Jared passed his hand over the bowl of quicksilver, dismissing the image of the diners.

We are not completely without the kaivir, *my friends*, he thought. His studies under Master Fallon were proceeding quite well. The other Lords were also proving adept at learning the sorcerers' arts.

As Erelvar had said, the *Kaimordir* had been forced to improvise. But in a few years the Ten would be masters in their own right. Then, in another decade or two, Morvanor would again have the *kaivir* at its disposal.

This war had bought Morvanor its survival. The next would buy it much more than that.

The work of clearing the debris from the bluff had begun. Steve picked his way through the sorted piles of snow-dusted rubble to where Erelvar was inspecting the work in progress. His Olvan cloak kept him warm against the first chill of winter.

This phase of the work would be able to proceed throughout the winter as the workers brought order to the destruction wrought by the Dragon. In the spring, they would begin setting mortar to stone, and Quarin would begin to rise from its ashes.

Also in the spring, the river traffic through this area would again bring in income from trade. Quarin would thrive. Its location was too ideal for it to do otherwise.

"Greetings, my friend," Erelvar said. "What do you think?"

"It looks like a rock pile," Steve said. "But at least it's an *orderly* rock pile."

"Much of the foundation has survived," Erelvar replied. "Not only that, but a great deal of the outermost wall is still three or four feet high."

"That's good news," Steve observed.

"Yes," Erelvar agreed. "However, you did not seek me out to discuss the rebuilding of the fortress. What troubles you, my friend?"

"Restlessness," Steve answered. "You once told me that you would not have me 'lying about your castle, growing fat and lazy at your expense,' if you'll recall."

"That was long ago," Erelvar said. "You are no longer that boy." That was certainly true.

"I've decided to do some travelling with Aerilynn," Steve said.

"To where will you travel?"

"I haven't decided," Steve replied. "Aerilynn knows the ways of the wood. We'll just see how far that takes us, for now."

"I had a barony in mind for you," Erelvar said. "Out where clan Taran's lands used to be. It would be challenging— bringing order to the Plains. . . ."

"Thank you, Erelvar," Steve said. "I'm . . . honored. Really . . . I had no idea. But I'm just not ready for that yet. And neither are you—not for a few years, anyway."

"No, not until Quarin is rebuilt," Erelvar agreed.

"I'll be back," Steve promised. "Maybe by then I'll be ready for that barony." Erelvar nodded.

"When are you leaving?" he asked.

"On the morrow," Steve replied. "I thought people might . . . want to say goodbye."

Steve cinched the saddle tight around Aerilynn's ribs. Steve smiled—the perfect knight's mount. Shotgun on one side, .30–30 on the other, rocket launchers and hand grenades in the saddlebags.

"We're loaded for bear, all right," Steve said, patting Aerilynn's neck.

"Goodbye, Steven," Morfael's voice said behind him. Steve turned to face him and found that all of his friends had gathered to see him off.

"Good-bye, Morfael," he said, embracing the Olvan warrior. "I'll miss you—all of you."

"I cannot help but think of the last time you rode away after the battles were over," Morfael said.

"Don't worry," Steve assured him. "I'm a big boy—I can take care of myself."

"Not to mention, this time he has Aerilynn with him," Erelvar noted.

"Yes," Glorien agreed. "You take good care of her, Steven."

"I shall, my lady," he said, embracing her in turn.

"Good-bye, Steven," Erelvar said.

"Good-bye, my lord," Steve replied. "I shall return some-day."

"I know you shall."

Steve turned to Arthwyr.

"Good-bye, brother," Steve said. Arthwyr said nothing, just stepped forward and embraced him.

"My place is with you," he finally said.

"No," Steve replied, stepping back. "You were there when I needed you. But now Umbria needs you. The king and his army have been killed. The kingdom is in chaos. They need you now."

"What can one clanless man do?"

"Maybe Umbria's next king should have no clan," Steve replied. "Maybe it should be a man who places his love of the kingdom above any one clan—including his own."

"Me?" Arthwyr said, his eyes widening. "King? That shall never happen!"

"No?" Steve asked. "I bet the Aldwyns would support you. And Erelvar, too, for that matter. You could do it, Arthwyr. With no clan of your own, you could bind them together like no king has before."

"You would have my support, Arthwyr," Erelvar added.

"See?" Steve said. "Now all you need is a magic sword and a round table, King Arthwyr."

"A round table?"

"Just a joke," Steve explained. "Although a good wizard probably wouldn't hurt your chances. Think about it."

"I . . . shall," Arthwyr said, doubtfully.

"Well, if I don't leave now, I never will," Steve noted. "Good-bye, everyone. I'll be back someday."

"Good-bye," they all echoed. Steve turned and mounted. Once through the gate, Steve turned back and waved before heading on.

"King Arthwyr," he chuckled, wiping a tear from the corner of his eye.

Epilogue

DAVE'S BREATH FROSTED in the morning air. First time this year. Soon, in a few weeks, the leaves would begin to turn. Then there would be one last wave of tourists before winter.

He turned on the Texaco sign and the awning lights and the neon sign that proclaimed this place as Dave's Trading Post. It was probably going to be another slow day. That was okay, though. He'd already made enough this season to last through the winter—if he stretched it.

The sound of hoofbeats on pavement reached him. He turned to find the source of the sound and froze.

The man riding toward him was completely armored. He rode a huge, white horse with blue-green eyes and led another horse, loaded with supplies, behind him. On his back he carried a sword, and Dave couldn't help but notice the rifle and shotgun he carried in saddle holsters on either side of the horse.

The rider stopped and dismounted. He didn't hitch the horse anywhere—just dropped the reins to the ground. He removed his helmet and hung both them and his shield on the saddle somehow. Now Dave noticed the .45 on his hip.

"Good morning," the man said as he walked up.

"Mornin'," Dave replied, uncertainly. The man laughed.

"Yes," he said. "I imagine I do look a little strange. Do you have a map of the local area?"

"In the station," Dave replied. "On the wall by the Coke machine."

"Thanks," the stranger replied, turning toward the station.

"Just a minute," Dave said, hurriedly. Sue and the kids were in the back.

"Yes?" the man asked.

"I'd . . . appreciate it if you left the artillery outside," Dave said.

"Oh," the man said, looking down at his hip as if the gun had suddenly appeared there. "Of course—my apologies. I didn't even think about it."

Dave watched as the stranger walked back to his horse and stowed the sword, the gun and a knife that Dave hadn't noticed on the horse. He patted her affectionately on the neck before heading back toward the station.

Dave followed him into the station. He didn't seem to be a bad sort. But he sure was a strange one. . . .